RISING TIDE

Published by Mundania Press
Also by Susan Roebuck

Perfect Score

RISING TIDE

SUSAN ROEBUCK

Edited by Kelley Heckart
Cover Art © 2015 by Niki Browning

First Mundania Edition May 2015
Trade Paperback ISBN: 978-1-60659-857-3
eBook ISBN: 978-1-60659-742-2

Published by Mundania Press
An imprint of Celeritas Unlimited LLC
6457 Glenway Ave., #109
Cincinnati, OH 45211

DEDICATION

I dedicate this book to my long-suffering but very patient husband. And I'd like to thank my invaluable editor, Kelley Heckart and cover artist Niki Browning.

The waves were white, and red the morn.
In the noisy hour when I was born;
The whale it whistled, the porpoise rolled.
And the dolphins bared their backs of gold;
And never was heard such an outcry wild,
As welcomed to life the ocean child.

The Sea by Barry Cornwall

CHAPTER ONE

March—Gulf of Alaska, USA

The swell hit the *Alaskan Star* broadside making her roll with stomach-churning dives into the troughs.

"Dude," cried a greenhorn, trying to keep his feet, "the weather *stinks.*"

"Whatcha expect?" the ghostly voice of the skipper in the wheelhouse sounded over the speaker. "Mellow fruitfulness? Net's full."

Mellow fruitfulness. Leo grinned as he watched the winch turning to bring the net in. His father would've continued the poem: *Close bosom friend of the maturing sun…* Leo set his sights on the tilting horizon to the west and wondered how his father and brother on the *Goblin* were faring. If they were reaching the standards they'd set for her, she'd be underway about twenty miles off by now, probably keeping to the same course: due south.

Leo hitched up his rubber pants that were stuck to his ass, pulled his woolen hat further over his white-blond hair and stepped up to the platform to help steady the net, keeping a careful watch on the cable. Boy, this wet-weather gear didn't live up to its name. The wet was seeping through his waistband.

The trawler rose and fell with the mountainous waves while Leo braced his legs against the jolting. He waited for the right moment to hook the net that held tons of Pollock and, hopefully, not too much by-catch, although he knew this skipper from the past—the bastard often had the escape holes in the nets sewn up.

His father said they were going to christen the nets and were heading out to the southern salmon grounds. The *Goblin* had the makings to be a great seiner. Leo couldn't wait to get off this rust-bucket of a ship and onto the *Goblin* so he could work alongside his brother and father again.

The skipper's voice echoed from the hailer over the deck. "Shine, watch what you're doin'."

Breaking out of his daydream, Leo pushed past Lofty, the other deck hand on the net, so they could both hook and drag it forward level with the hopper. Lofty had earned his name for obvious reasons, but Leo matched him in the lanky-build and height department and was forever grateful he'd stayed with his proper name, perhaps because of his yellowy-green eye color. And if anyone was even tempted to call him 'Blondie' then said person would lose an essential body-part.

"Take a look at that man starboard, Shine," the skipper ordered over the screaming sea gulls and gannets following the trawler.

For the love of God, how many hands did the guy reckon he had? Leo scanned the deck before he spotted the greenhorn who had been set to mending nets but whose only visible part now was his yellow ass while the rest of him hung overboard. Leo calculated he had half a minute before the net dumped its load so he clambered onto the hopper and jumped down on the other side. The guy was puking his guts up, his arms slack on the sides surely oblivious to the fact he could get caught on flying ropes. Goddamn skipper was a stingy asshole and nothing came cheaper—or more dangerous to the rest of the crew—than a virgin greenhorn no one had the time or the patience to train up for the job.

An immense wave surged over the side, gushed across the deck with a roar before it retreated, gathering loose gear with it. Leo grabbed a lifeline with one hand and the puking greenhorn's collar with the other, and held on.

As the last dregs drained away and the cursing deck crew found their feet, Leo freed the kid. "If you're going to puke," he told him, yelling in his face to make himself heard over the din of machinery, gulls and howling gale, "make sure it's downwind. And hold on to the lifeline."

Leo went back to the net rigging. Oh man, he was tired. Eighteen hours on deck, blasted and buffeted by cyclonic wind and breakers, and the sea was yielding less than ever. Maybe he'd get an hour's sleep later. Another torrent of sea surged over the bow and hurled itself across the deck, again sweeping the crew, and Leo, with it. Like the previous one it washed debris and tumbled fish back into the sea while Leo counted heads and checked the puking greenhorn. Everyone was still on board. This time.

No one should be out here in this weather, not in a tin can of a boat like this.

"Shine. You need to stay focused. Or do you need *more* time out?"

Goddamn ship needed time out. "Twenty foot waves, Skipper," Leo yelled back.

"You reckon I don't *know* that? And that last one was sixteen."

Like hell it was. Once stable again, Leo clambered over to the winch and stood on one side to help drag the net towards the hopper. While Lofty secured it, Leo reached up to open the side and within a moment they were ankle deep in fish. To the greenhorn it probably looked like a lot, but to Leo it was just a normal catch even if there was a fair amount of jellyfish and mackerel mixed in. They'd get fair wages from this trip if this amount of catch continued for the next four days.

Waves still pounded against the hull, the wind continued to howl, but Leo detected a shift in sound.

"Goddamn port engine's cranking," Lofty muttered. "Could this get any worse? Chrissakes, where's that green-horn?"

Last time Leo looked, the guy had been over by one of the smaller winches on the afterdeck. Leo headed there, tied himself with a winch rope and leaned over the side under what felt like a raging waterfall to make sure no one was in the sea.

A high-pitched whine caught his attention. Was it the wind? But the wind was constantly shrill; this one changed an octave and was coming from behind him. Leo straightened and followed the sound until he tracked it to a tarpaulin near the hatch on the trawl deck. Lifting a corner and peering into the dank gloom, he saw the boy, legs curled up to his chest, eyes tightly closed as he rocked his body. "We are all going to drown," he keened.

"Take him to the galley," the skipper, who'd come down to the deck told Lofty, who'd followed Leo. "And you won't drown," he said to the greenhorn, "not with Shine on board."

Leo inwardly sighed. How many times had he heard he was a mascot on a ship because he was born with a caul about his face? Maybe one day someone would say they took Leo Shine on because he was the best deck boss in Alaska. He'd rather be known for that. "It's me that won't drown," he said. "What happens to the rest of you has nothing to do with me."

"Whatever." The skipper's mind seemed to be on other things. Fact was his stare was beginning to creep Leo out. The skipper licked his lips twice before he cleared his throat. "Perhaps you should've gone out with Tom and your father. You know, you with your good luck."

Leo tried to gauge the man's face to get a better idea of what he was trying to convey. The guy wasn't himself; instead of shooting his mouth off, he was fumbling for words. And what did he mean by Leo should've gone with them? He'd wanted to go on the newly fitted *Goblin*, true enough, but his father and Tom had other ideas:

****

"Do another turn with Lofty," his father had said, patting his shoulder. "We'll need your earnings from the *Alaskan Star*—anything to help pay off the *Goblin's* loan. I want to see how she runs, then you and Tom can put the *Goblin* through her paces yourselves." He threw him a look that Leo knew so well—the one that scared the shit out of any crew member who might be thinking of answering back, but which his sons could read right down to his pussy-cat heart. "Don't you go thinkin'," his father quirked an eyebrow to add emphasis, "the *Goblin* is your boat, but…"

"Yeah, yeah," Leo finished for him, "thirty percent of the overall earnings is yours."

"Don't feel bad." Tom had playfully punched him on his bicep before they left the family home on Wharf Street. "We're only taking her out for a ride. See how she rolls."

The *Goblin* wouldn't roll, Leo knew. Not with her steady platform on that beautiful hull.

****

Now, on the *Alaskan Star*, the skipper cleared his throat to get Leo's attention. Strange, normally, he'd have yelled in Leo's ear to do that. The skipper looked down at the deck and addressed Leo in a halting voice. "I'm not turning back because the port engine is about to blow a gasket, nor because a deck-hand is freaking out on me. No." He shook his shaggy head and stared fixedly at a rope coiled to the left of Leo's shoulder, saying words that Leo would never forget. "I'm going back because a mayday signal just came over the VHF."

"Mayday?" Leo's stomach contents churned in fear. "The *Goblin?*"

CHAPTER TWO

September—North Norfolk coast, UK

Piper eyed the bucket of crabs. For the first time in her life, the idea of picking one up, turning it on its brown back to plunge the knife in, so she could dig out the spongy lungs, made her stomach churn.

What was wrong with her today? She was bloody angry, that's what was wrong. *Or are you jealous?* A tiny voice in her head asked. She picked up the sharp knife and jabbed it into the rough kitchen table-top. "One, two, three, four," she said aloud before putting the knife down. Nope. Counting hadn't made her feel any better. Bugger. OK—she was jealous. Jealous that her father had a stand-in job for a deck-hand on a trawler fishing, and she didn't.

The wormy floorboards behind her creaked as her father made his heavy way over them. Out of the corner of her eye, she watched him pause on his way to the front door, shift from foot to foot while he scratched at the front of his old blue gansey, salty stiff with sea-water, before rubbing his hand through his brillo-pad hair making it stand on end. She found herself mimicking his gesture, rubbing her hand through her own short dark hair.

"Yew'll mek your hair all fish-smelly, Pips," he said, the crags in his prematurely weathered face deepening with his smile. She knew that expression and loved it even if it was his *please don't ask too many questions* smile.

She didn't return it. "It's only the smell of the sea—briny and salty. Nothing wrong with that."

Amazing how in a short space of time she could go from feeling bubbly and excited to downright miserable. An hour ago they were doing what they did most days, something she enjoyed most, zipping along away from the shore in their little skiff. As usual, Piper had been at the outboard cutting through the pitching grey swell, zig-zagging against the stiff onshore breeze, Pop at his look-out point in the bow, heartily singing, *Oh a drop 'a Nelson's blood, a drop 'a Nelson's. Oh a drop 'a Nelson's blood won't do us any harm*, complete with dramatic gestures that rocked the boat and made Piper laugh so hard she misjudged a wave and needed to make a quick steering adjustment, so they headed into it instead of taking it broadside. They didn't want any more seawater on board; it was already at ankle height. Once they reached their pots, they whooped like a pair of kids every time they hauled in a heavy trap full to the brim with crab. "Only Pip knows where the crab hang owt," Pop quipped as he released a cage-door.

"Oi'll be orff then," Pop now said, breaking into her happy thoughts.

Although he'd often take himself off to substitute a sick deck-hand on a trawler, she always missed him.

"Wish I could come too."

"Aw, Pips. Yew know we tawked abowt this."

Yes they had. He'd explained the skippers were saying it was bad luck to employ a woman on board. Utter crap. It was Pop who was keeping her away from the only thing she did well and all because the last skipper—who had registered a significant jump in his daily haul since she and Pop had been on board—had eyed her and said, "She's strange."

She said nothing now, just like she'd said nothing to the skipper at the time, but followed her father through the door. The wind competed with the shrill cry of oyster-catchers echoing across the marshes as he strode, heavy and rolling, towards the car parked a few yards along the sandy pathway that had been, in parts, washed away by last night's high tide. It had been higher than she could ever remember, bursting over the dunes and taking her raspberry bushes on its return journey. Soon the ever-rising sea would reach the cottage and claim it too; she just hoped to God it wouldn't be tonight when she was on her own. As if the weather knew what she was thinking, a streak of lightning flashed, farther west, a storm heading off towards Norwich.

The wind caught at her feathery hair that was like her father's in length yet softer and darker. It would take a hurricane to make a strand of his stiff mop shift.

Once they were by their Ford Escort, he looked down at her, a large bear of a man to her five foot three. They were quite different; his eyes the color of a calm summer's day sea, unlike her own dark ones which he said were like the nighttime sea, flecked with fluorescent plankton. "Aww, Pips," he said, his hand on the car door. "Oi'll be back real quick."

She nodded but knew it was what she called a leaking promise. He kept so much to himself and hadn't even told her he had the fishing gig today until fifteen minutes ago.

That was nothing new, but his ability to forecast when he'd be back was on so many occasions way out. He could be back tonight, tomorrow, next week. His gigs of one full day or one full night, sometimes two when they were far out in the fishing grounds, inexplicably turned into three or four days absences. Time that he wouldn't account for. One thing was sure, she wasn't going to make his favorite crab and pea soup with plenty of chervil in it for his supper tonight because it would just go to waste.

He climbed in the dented and battered car that was covered in salt and sand, hit the ignition twice before it fired up, and then he rolled down the window. "Can yew take them old crabs to Old Todd's? He'll give me a roight rollicking if he don't get 'em today."

Without waiting for an answer, because he knew she would do just as he asked, he and the car rocked off down the muddy path, falling into the new ruts and channels with a squeal of dodgy suspension.

Just what she needed right now, she thought as she trudged back to their lopsided cottage, a visit to Old Todd the fishmonger whose duggerlugs of a son was a pain in the arse.

If the kid, who suffered from acne the size of the Milky Way and seemed to be all elbows and knees, was serving in the shop, he'd stare at her with wide eyes and an open mouth. His gawp wasn't from admiration, she was perfectly aware of that; after all, he'd hardly reached puberty and she was at the great old age of twenty-two, which would probably be ancient to him. What annoyed her was the muttered question every time he paid her for the fish she supplied: "Is tha' true what moi dad say? That yew're a might sorft? Talkin' squit an' stuff."

She so wanted to laugh about this with Pop and say that you only had to look into the lad's eyes to know which one of them wasn't quite all there, but if she did tell him what the kid said, she knew from experience Pop wouldn't find it amusing and they'd be on the road before nightfall, upping sticks to yet another ramshackle place along the coast where no one knew them. They'd done enough moving about in her time and she'd learned that it was best to stay quiet, let people talk about her all they wanted and hope they did it when Pop couldn't hear. She didn't want to move again, unless the ever rising tides had other ideas.

She sighed and stared at the grey sea where, beyond the coastal swell, fog rolled over the waves and where a sleek seal's head bobbed just beyond the surf line. A tern bombarded it, forcing the seal to dive, which was just what she fancied doing right now: disappear into the depths when life got problematic.

Thoughtfully, she entered through the cottage's cracked front door into the fug of mildewed carpet and dust. As the door closed, the bones of the cottage creaked to accommodate the load around the bare flint walls and draughts blew through the cracks, shifting plaster in a blizzard. The whole place, which thrummed with the aggressive, unpredictable weather, was out of whack.

Looking again at the crabs, she knew they had to be prepared, ready for Old Todd to sell fresh, but her heart just wasn't in it because something, apart from her father's absence, just wasn't right. A space on a shelf caught her eye. Where were her books? The ones she'd spent years collecting. Her treasures. The ones she could swear were on the shelf that morning, sitting like friends waiting for her to enjoy: Alice Walker, Michael Chabon, Dave Eggers, Bill Bryson, Terry Pratchett.

"No, no, no." She stalked towards the shelf, hoping her books would magically appear, but stopped before she reached it.

And where was the TV? True, it wasn't much of one and sat at an angle on a broken stand, but it *had* been there last night. She'd watched *The News at Ten* on it. Rubbing her brow, she stared at the clear television-sized patch in the dust that coated the top of the now empty stand, and punched a fist into the palm of her other hand. Not again. More stuff missing. The money he earned on his substitute deck-hand work never seemed to find its way home. What did he do with it?

Her glance fell on her father's mobile phone sitting on a sagging armchair. Ironic—that was one item that *should* be with him. As if on cue, it shrilled.

Tightening her jaw, she picked it up. Maybe it was another skipper needing Pop to replace a crew-member. If it was, she was going to take the job.

"Hello?" asked an elderly man, rasping like the shingle being churned up on the shore. "Is that Pines Taxi-Cabs?"

Pop had said he'd put a notice up in the local newsagents to advertise his new, barely thought-out, service. "Mebbe help with the school-run," he'd said. "Per'aps make us a tidy sum, eh, Pip?"

He'd put the ad up months ago and they'd never had a response, which didn't surprise her. Who'd want to use their old Ford Escort that kangarooed on a smooth road, guzzled petrol and was probably responsible for major melting at the polar ice-caps?

Apparently, at long last, someone did. "Uh…"

"My sister and I need to go to Heathrow Airport. Urgently."

Piper paused. Heathrow? Lummee. She'd never been farther than King's Lynn in the car. Sounded like an expedition, and one that she was more than ready for.

"Would you mind going in a van?" she asked.

CHAPTER THREE

March to September—Alaska, USA

Leo stomped and stamped the length of the plunging deck, yelling at the skipper, "You got a Mayday? Then we head that way. You got the coordinates, change course for Chrissakes."

Lofty put his arm around his shoulder. "The first response will be out, Leo. They'll get there first. They're twenty miles off, other ships are nearer."

Leo shook Lofty's arm off and stared at the grey sea, the waves boiling and seething, in as much turmoil as his mind. He was *this* much away from jumping overboard and swimming to the *Goblin*. If only.

"Change course," he yelled again at the skipper on the bridge. "All ships in the vicinity…"

"Nah. You wanna join them in the drink? Any case, we are changing course, heading back to port. Coast Guard's orders."

Did that mean Leo's father and brother were safely back on land? Maybe they were hurt, that's why they wanted Leo back. He paced again, oblivious to the wave that poured onto the deck and swept him off his feet until he crashed into the side with Lofty hanging on to one ankle.

As the *Alaskan Star* limped into harbor three tortuous hours after the news of the Mayday signal, a Coast Guard officer waited on the dock.

Leo was frantic to hear news but before the dock line was over the cleat, the officer yelled, "What do you know about this, Leo Shine?" He held up what looked like a bone.

"What is that?" Leo asked, not believing what he was looking at.

"Walrus tusk," Lofty responded from beside him on the deck.

Walrus tusk? What the hell? Why was the officer showing him that?

"It's not just one," the officer continued, seemingly content to have captured not only Leo's attention but also that of the rest of the crew, as well as most of the employees from the canning factory and everyone else on the wharf. "We got a whole stack of them. And, surprise, surprise, a few bear pelts."

"What's that got to do with me?" Leo asked as soon as he was on land and could talk without having to shout. "And where's my family."

"Bottom of the sea." The officer shook the tusk he was holding. "I'm just showing you what's left of some of the *Goblin's* cargo. 'Course you'll have seen these before since she's your boat too. *Was* your boat, rather."

Although his heart had been going at a hundred beats a minute since the skipper had mentioned a Mayday signal, Leo's world now tilted at a sickening angle. His family was where? "You are bullshitting me, right?"

"Nope. The Fish and Wildlife Service have been suspicious about illegal trafficking in this area. Tom Shine was on their list of suspects. And, how 'bout this for coincidence? On the DEA's list too."

During the next hour, Leo tried to maintain some kind of calm as he heard the story that would change his life.

"We got her EPIRB signal and had her on the radar but in the blink of an eye she was gone." In the small room they'd led him to, the Coast Guard officer who'd met him on the dock spoke the facts with the same blunt tone he would later use to report the incident at the official inquiry. "When we arrived at the scene, we traced the tail end of her long spin downwards on the sensor and sonar. There were no other reported ships in the area, so we concluded it was the *Goblin*. There was some wreckage on the surface, mostly broken crates, but we fished out enough to identify the cargo. Tusks and pelts."

Leo, sitting on the other side of the bare table, forced himself to speak without a tremor in his voice. "That shit didn't come from the *Goblin*," he insisted. "Tom's life is fishing. He doesn't do anything else, and I should know—we live together and have for twenty-six years." He intertwined his fingers, resting his hands on the table to prevent anyone seeing they were shaking. "Anyway, what would he want with tusks and pelts?" He had a pretty good idea, but it was so far beyond what could be true, it didn't make sense.

The officer supplied the unsurprising answer. "All part of the peddling ring in Alaska, that's like a fucking epidemic. As if you didn't know, Shine. What were they going to do? Offload the cargo to another boat when they were out of territorial waters and exchange it for what? The main deal is drugs and the penalty for even *knowledge* of that carries a nine year sentence."

Despite his anger and frustration, a chill ran up Leo's spine. "What you found didn't come from the *Goblin* so maybe you'd just better concentrate on finding survivors."

"You reckon the Coast Guard's not doing that? We have a search and rescue 'copter out, a lifeboat and a cutter in the area. If your brother and father got into the life raft, they'll find them. See? We don't treat traffickers different to honest folk. Not 'til they're on land."

Leo quelled, with difficulty, a desire to punch the guy's

lights out but his anguish was also growing. The chances of finding a life raft in those rough seas were low, and no one clinging to wreckage in such freezing water could last long.

Lofty was waiting for him when he stumbled down the steps into the windy street. "I saw Tom loading her up with something yesterday morning," he said as Leo joined him. "Boxes. Lots of them."

"That was just last minute stuff," Leo said, snatching off his woolen cap and squashing it between his hands. "They were going to try and get some salmon. It was ice you saw them loading." God, he didn't honestly know what they were putting on board; he'd been busy helping get the *Alaskan Star* ready. Tom would've been storing the usual supplies too, surely, for Chrissakes. What Leo did remember were their proud faces that no doubt mirrored his own as they stared at their new ship, refitted to the Shine family's specifications. And his father loudly squawking, *"Come get your duds in order for we're gonna leave today. Heave away me jollies, heave away."* To anyone who didn't know him, this sounded like he'd sunk a few shots, but Leo knew his father only hit the bottle once he was back on land. Except neither he, nor Tom were ever going to that again. And Leo already missed them both with an ache he knew would never ease.

Three days later and once the Coast Guard had called off the search, Leo cleaned out his savings accounts, liquidated stocks by paying for his own search, hiring helicopters and a private search-and-rescue plane. But that had only resulted in breaking him financially and convincing himself he hadn't done enough.

With the last of his dwindling resources, he took a boat out to the last co-ordinates the *Goblin* had given. The sea was calm, with waves no larger than Leo's arm lapping the hull, and the air crisp. Too crisp, perhaps, for the time of year. Did that mean that the Arctic ice pack was moving south?

The Coast Guard had concentrated their search going north in line with the predominant currents. Leo focused on the glittering path of sparkles on the wavelets.

Leo was seeking energy. He knew what it was, having felt it so many times—a force that he sensed and had experienced ever since he went on his first offshore trip. Tom often teased him and called him loony, although their father rarely commented except to tell Tom to leave his younger brother alone and, "See?" when Leo proved right and a storm blew up or the sea turned rough.

Out there on the shimmering water searching for his family, there were two dimensions: the surface waves and the prevailing current. But deeper, Leo could feel or sense echoes of the storm that had probably stirred up the rogue wave in this deep-water shelf. The wave would've dumped on the *Goblin* like a vicious blow of a hammer, shattering hull, stern and bow in all directions. It did not necessarily mean all the wreckage would head north on the current. For a while the sea would've been a maelstrom, and, if Leo was right about the Arctic ice pack, then there was an underlying current heading south.

So he sailed maybe ten miles before he found it: a half-submerged wooden crate which, when he fished it out, was half broken but still housed a cellophane-wrapped package that, although it had split, still contained a walrus tusk, several teeth and a sodden piece of polar bear pelt. The piece of crate was of the same blond wood as the ones Tom had been loading onto the *Goblin* the morning they set sail.

****

It rained the day of the bleak memorial service where there were no coffins to prove Leo's brother and father were dead and where only a handful of people turned up to pay their respects—a few days ago they'd have come out in the thousands. Once the service was over and Leo and Lofty were outside, most of the mourners disappeared without a word and just three of them patted Leo's shoulder with muttered words that gave him no comfort at all.

"Hard," Lofty said, standing beside him at the gate when everyone had gone. "It was hard for people to come when they know what the *Goblin* had on board."

Leo turned on him, growling like a crazed dog. "Whatever the *Goblin* was carrying was a *mistake*. Tom and Dad didn't know they had it," he yelled into his friend's face, grabbing his collar and shaking him with every word. They glared at each other for a moment before Leo looked away. He released Lofty and murmured, "Sorry."

Lofty took a pace back. "What you trying to tell me, *buddy?*" His harsh words echoed Leo's tone from a moment ago. Lofty shrugged himself back into his jacket, his face pale. "They didn't know they had illegal walrus tusks and bear pelts on board? Well, have I got news for you. That idea stinks."

"They didn't know they had them things on board when they left," Leo insisted, quieter now.

" 'Course they did," Lofty spat the words, his lips pressed against his teeth. "How can you not know what you got on-board your own boat? And they sure as hell weren't going to come back with them. Now let me think what they'd likely be bringing back." He pretended to ponder a knotty problem, scratching his head and staring at the sky. "Could it have been a few guns to send to Iraq, perhaps? Drugs to kill your kids? Might have had a few salmon in the hold though, just to *pretend* they'd been doing some honest fishing."

Leo's body tensed. But then his anger retreated and he took a step backwards. What could he say to a man whose twin brother had been killed in Iraq and whose wife was in rehab trying to get free from her cocaine habit?

"And you wanna know why you only got me to agree to crew for you on the *Goblin's* next trip and no one else?" Lofty jabbed his finger in Leo's chest, emphasizing every word.

Because you're our friend and you offered to do the job of two to help us out with the cost of wages? Leo wanted to respond, but he knew how lame it sounded since Lofty was right—no one else had applied.

"Because," Lofty said, "the Shine family's unpredictable, that's why. No one wants to work with you."

Leo stifled the urge to pull Lofty's poking finger off. Instead he acknowledged his buddy's final words, "You mean the anger issues?" He tried to keep his chin up against his mounting shame that Tom lost his cool sometimes. "The greenhorn incident?"

He referred to the time they had worked together with Tom—who had been deck boss—on a long-liner. The young greenhorn had riled Tom with his inability to master the art of knots, and Tom finally snapped when a mooring line slipped a cleat for the second time. He told the boy that he was beginning to piss him off.

Leo, who had been watching the incident, closed his eyes in silent prayer that Tom would control himself when the lad retorted: "Just how much piss are we talking about here, Tom?"

No, Leo thought. *Very wrong answer.* For a long time afterwards he wished he'd moved quicker to save the boy as Tom threw the lad across the deck where he hit his head on the capstan.

Later, Leo had paid the kid out of his own pocket twice his rightful earnings, which had hopefully compensated in some way for his concussion. But the incident added another notch to the Shines' reputation. A reputation old Judge Pearson had confirmed at the *Goblin* Inquiry. "Tom Shine, nay the Shine *brothers,* chose a wayward life and both have been consistent and thorough in carrying it out."

By the end of the Inquiry, Leo, whose soul seemed to have turned to stone, listened to the judge's final assessment that the *Goblin* had been sunk with all souls by a rogue wave with a strong suspicion that the ship had been carrying illegal cargo.

Leo could hardly control his shivering as he left the court. He hunched under a storm of flash-lights and heckles: bastard should be in prison, you knew what was on board right enough. Save the walruses and bears from this abomination. Child-killer with your drugs.

Yes, he knew what had been on board, he was sure he did—and it wasn't illegal. Of that he was certain. Tom and his father would never have trafficked anything, not knowingly. And surely this was proven after the Fish and Wildlife, along with the DEA guys, had searched the house on Wharf Street from top to bottom and hadn't even found an ivory fragment or one polar-bear hair, or a speck of cocaine. This exonerated Leo, "But," a DEA guy said, "if the name Leo Shine ever appears in the same sentence as trafficking ever again, I'm going to make sure your ass hits the jail cell floor with a crash that'll be heard from here to California."

"What you gonna do next?" someone—a stranger— yelled at him as Leo walked down the street soon after the court verdict. "Catch whales and dolphins?"

Leo didn't answer as he headed to the Halcyon Bar, a place much favored by fishermen onshore. At least here he hoped to find some kind of understanding from his colleagues and friends. But if he'd known what awaited him, he'd have told the stranger in the street he wasn't going to catch anything next. Even if he wanted to he couldn't: he was black-balled.

"If you ever think of looking for jobs, boy, ain't none for you," a harsh voice grated in his ear as he settled on the bar stool. Leo turned and found the manager of the largest processing vessels in Alaska standing behind him. If anyone ruled the waves around this harbor, it was this guy.

Leo clenched his fist around his cold beer. "Guy can come in here who's not necessarily looking for a job," he said, his words squeezing between his teeth. It was true, he wasn't looking for a job—yet—he'd just fancied some company. "And don't call me *boy*."

The guy narrowed his eyes as he let his gaze drift from Leo's yellow slicker down to his grubby jeans and boots as if his attire was alien to the community. Then they locked gazes until the manager looked away, saying, "Don't give me that clankety-clank. There ain't no jobs for you. Nor no more service in this bar neither."

Leo forced his ice-cold beer down in sips, taking his time, pretending the asshole hadn't riled him up, persuading himself he could care less that the crowd of fishermen he always drank with was keeping to the other end of the bar, their backs to him. When he tried joining them in the old way, they all migrated up the other end. His heart leapt with hope as Lofty sauntered by on his way to the restroom. He paused as he came level with Leo, leaned in without looking at him and said out the corner of his mouth, "Remember that time I said you were the best? I take it back."

When he finally drained the last drop of his beer, Leo dawdled by the pool table watching the game, ignoring that the players didn't invite him to join in as they would've done once. After taking time to read the fishing notices by the door, he wandered out with what he hoped was a care-free roll in his step.

Outside he gazed at a rain-drenched haze heading in from the horizon and a salmon seiner chugging out of the fish plant.

"I'm not wrong," he muttered, his hands deep in his

pockets as he leaned into the ever-coursing wind and headed for home. Even if his brother and father had been plotting something without telling him, Leo wouldn't have missed the signs. They never hid anything from each other. *You can't even fart without the others knowing about it*, he thought. *Couldn't*, he corrected.

He spent days and nights going over the few weeks before the sinking, searching for clues to prove the hearing's verdict wrong. His father had been so normal on their final morning together at breakfast, his weathered, leathery face scrunched as he sniggered at the cartoon in the newspaper, a steaming mug of thick syrupy coffee balanced in one hefty hand. *Had* there been a crease of worry between his brows? Maybe. Maybe not. He visualized Tom, his hair as blond as Leo's, the evening before, sitting on the porch, his chair rocked on two legs so the guitar lay flat against him, his head tipped back and his feet on the rails. Girlfriend of the day—what'sername—sitting on the gritty steps, dress hiked up around her thighs, rocking to the rhythmic plucking of some bluegrass number. The next morning Tom had said she'd been sexy in a pretty dead kind of way. Nothing out of the ordinary there, then.

One night, a week or two later, something flicked a switch in Leo's head, just as he was half-way down a vodka bottle. A thought flashed into his mind and would've flown out again if he hadn't managed to grab it and try to shape the fleeting, sleep-swamped memory:

A short while—maybe a month or so—before the accident, Leo had been under his Impala, removing the oil drain plug, when Tom had wandered by, saying, "Fuckin' *primos*."

In itself, the phrase wasn't unusual. *Fucking primos* was a standing joke; just something the three of them said out of habit whenever a Christmas card arrived from the cousins in Portugal each year at the end of January. When Tom said it that day, it wasn't January and a note of frustration in his voice made Leo roll out from under the car and say, "What's up?"

Tom looked back from the porch before he headed inside. "Idiots only want me to visit them."

"What? In that dead-horse Portuguese place? What's it called? Illuminating?"

Tom looked back at his cell phone screen. "Yeah. Luminosa. Assholes must be short of money. Want something, that's for sure. Well they ain't gonna get it."

No one had spoken about it again and Leo hadn't thought of it until now.

And now he couldn't let it go. He went through every desk and cupboard looking for letters or scribbled messages—anything that would give him a clue about what the *primos* had wanted. But he found nothing, not even old Christmas cards; his father must've thrown them away when he received them.

Tom's phone had accompanied him into the deep, so Leo had to check with the phone company, but they had no records of messages or calls from Portugal.

The *primos* were relations of his barely-remembered mother who was long gone from the family home, having left their father when Tom was ten and Leo four. He was still bruised at her abandoning them, and not even Tom saying, "Fucking *primos*" did anything to heal him.

He was often puzzled by his possible Portuguese heritage because everyone said Leo and Tom were their father's sons; they all shared fine white blond hair without a dot of pigment in it. Barbers weren't high on either Tom or Leo's priorities, so both had hair that reached their shoulders and while Tom let…used to let…his fly loose, Leo usually wore his tied back with a leather strip. The Portuguese genes—which, by the look of things, would have made the Shine boys dark, stocky and short—had lost out somewhere along the way.

When Leo had asked Tom what she was like, he'd grabbed Leo's collar so tight, he had a red ring around his neck for days afterwards. Tom had pushed his face into Leo's so that the full force of the remnants of last night's Indian curry and cheap beer had washed over him and said, "You wanna know something?"

As best he could with the strangle-hold around his throat, Leo nodded.

"You want this conversation to be over. Understood?"

Leo nodded again. "Understood," he said.

The threat of getting cold-cocked didn't exist with his father, but it was just as unnerving because, when asked, his father's face would pinch at the mention of her name and the temperature in the room would drop to zero. So Leo had taught himself not to think about her either. She could be shacked up with Jabba the Hutt for all he cared.

Now, hoping he'd never need to go and seek out his cousins, he picked up the newspaper cutting that reported the sinking, and searched it, hoping to find a different clue that would lead him down another road.

He didn't read the text, he knew it by heart. Instead he stared at his father's and brother's photographs: sterile and overexposed taken in a cheap booth when they'd renewed their permit cards; neither picture doing justice to their father's wise smile nor Tom's lopsided grin. Leo forced himself to look at the photo of the *Goblin,* bright in the sunlight after her refit, her blue hull sitting proud and high in the water. She looked just fine. *No she didn't.* Was that Tom's voice in his head? *She couldn't withstand a forty-foot wave.*

Maybe the *Goblin's* refit hadn't been up to standard. Maybe that's where the problem lay. Without thinking how unlikely that was, he stormed down to the shipyard where they showed him the sea-worthy certificate. From there he red-lined it to the regulator who'd passed the safety documents, but he met Leo's frustration with a vacant stare that pissed Leo off even more. "You got a kick-back, huh?" Leo growled, angry enough to hiss like a cat and mad that this possible avenue looked like it was heading down a dead-end. "A little beak-wetting?" The next moment he was out on his butt in the street, still spitting anger but with dirt mixed in.

One evening, just after an ex-girlfriend—who'd otherwise been on pretty good terms with him—had crossed the road to avoid talking to him, a man dressed in a voluminous slicker walked towards him. Leo didn't know him and took no notice until they drew level and the man paused. Speaking softly, he asked if Leo was interested in otter pelts.

"Enough's enough." Leo jammed his hands in his pocket as he stalked off home. He'd eliminated all other possibilities, except for one. Without removing his jacket, he found his father's tatty address book and stowed it away in a pocket. Minutes later he locked the door on the family house, leaving a pile of Chinese takeaway cartons stacked in the living room and a sink full of dirty dishes. He dropped the keys off at the real estate office that had sold the place and then headed straight for the airport and got on a plane to Lisbon.

If he found out the *fucking primos* had a hand in his family's destruction, then he'd fucking destroy them.

CHAPTER FOUR

September—Norfolk to Heathrow, UK

"These old Bedford vans usually house aging hippies. I never thought I'd have to hire one. You are sure, my dear, it will get us to Heathrow?" Mr. Fletcher spoke in a low rumble, his chapped features pulled down as if by the force of gravity. He sat board-stiff straight behind Piper as if to avoid touching the stains on the leather seats.

Piper remembered making those stains years ago when she lay full-length on the seat behind Pop at the wheel. It used to fascinate her that if you licked the leather, first it went chocolate-brown then it dried lighter with a darker rim.

"Bedford?" whispered the woman Mr. Fletcher had said was his sister and who now sat heaped next to her brother staring out the window through her huge black-rimmed glasses that made her look like an owl. "That's not abroad. Are we there already?" She spat on her finger and drew a circle on the fogged-up window as Piper pulled in at the curb.

"Won't be a tick," Piper told them before she pushed hard on the door to try to open it. "Sticks a bit." She smiled what she hoped was reassuringly at Mr. Fletcher's ruby-red nose. "I just need to deliver some crabs."

"If you are a registered taxi-driver," he intoned, "unexpected stops are reasons for an official complaint which, in turn, will affect your license. And just where is that said item? It should be on display here for the passengers to see."

"In the bag," Piper said as she kicked at the door. She'd grabbed the grubby linen bag after the phone call, knowing that Pop kept any document of importance, like her driving license, in it. Except there was no taxi-driver license. Pop said he didn't believe in them and refused to join the club.

The van door creaked on its hinges and shifted just enough to allow her to squeeze through.

"I'll remind you again: any normal taxi service never makes unexpected stops," Mr. Fletcher yelled back. "And certainly not three minutes into the journey. When I saw Pines Cabs advertised in the local paper-shop, I thought it was an authentic outfit."

"What, the paper-shop, or your jacket?" his sister asked, smoothing down her own creased pink jacket. It seemed to Piper that to some eyes Day-Glo orange tights, red shoes, a yellow skirt and the jacket might not go too well together, but Piper thought they were perfect on Miss Fletcher.

She opened the rear doors and pried off three crabs that were side-ways crawling to freedom. Stuffing them back in the box, she crammed the lid on and headed into Old Todd the fishmonger's.

The shop smelt as it always did of old kippers and bleach. As Piper placed her box on the counter, Todd was folding whiting into newspaper for a tired-looking customer. Together they eyed Piper's box with suspicion as the contents scrabbled and the lid lifted a fraction.

"Yew got them crabs for me then, Piper?" asked Todd, wiping his hands on his used-to-be white apron. A red claw poked through the top of the box, and his smile dropped right off his face. "Ah now, look here. Yew didn't prepare them owd crabs loik yew always do. Them's still alive. What's gorn wrong?"

"I got a call…" Piper thumbed at Mr. Fletcher's face scowling through the filthy van window. "They need a lift to Heathrow." Which would mean at least a hundred quid in her pocket. "And I hadn't done the crabs."

Todd peered through the window at the Fletchers. "Ah now, tha's too bad. Why didn't your dad take 'em?"

"He would've done it if he'd been here, but he's busy."

"You mean, he's gawn again. Dammit, Piper, yew need to keep your dad on a tighter lead." He peered at the scuffling box. "Them's no good. Oi can't sell them not dressed." He shook his head. "Oi'm not happy, Piper."

She bit back a curse. What was she going to do with the damn crabs? Put them in the puddle outside? They wouldn't last much longer and then they'd just sit there and smell. She glanced sideways at the woman and her staved-in eyes. Piper pushed the box towards her. "You can have them."

A crab, half-way out the box, snapped its claws at the woman who reared back for just a second. But Piper's offer must've then sunk in because she leaned forward again. "How do I dress them?"

"It's easy. Lay the crab on its back. Get that flap of skin on its underbelly. See?" She demonstrated. "Stick a screwdriver or a knife in and push."

The woman's hand flew to her mouth.

Mr. Todd sighed and closed the top of the box. "Don't yew worry, missus. Oi'll dress 'em. Come back in a coupla hours and Oi'll have done 'em and yew can have one, courtesy of young Piper here." They waited for the woman to leave before Mr. Todd continued, "Look here, Piper. Oi'll give yew ten pounds for these here crabs. Oi'd have given you twenty-five for them dressed."

"Fifteen, Mr. Todd. I can't take anything less."

The van's horn blasted outside. Mr. Fletcher was leaning on it.

"Yew drive a hard bargain, tha' yew do, Piper."

Piper pocketed the cash Old Todd handed her and

rushed out.

Once she was back in the van, they set off down the narrow cobbled high street.

"That man walking along there looks like a belly-button," Miss Fletcher said, breaking the silence.

"My dear, you're being very silly today, even by your standards."

"An outside-in belly-button."

Piper caught Miss Fletcher's image in the rear mirror. Her eyes held a hidden depth of understanding and a small tic of a smile plucked at her lower lip. Miss Fletcher wasn't all she seemed.

They were passing a field of bright yellow wheat ready for harvest when Mr. Fletcher leaned forward again. "Excuse me, my dear. When I learned to drive, the Give Way sign meant just that. Have things changed?"

Piper had been perfectly aware of the traffic but it was better to ignore him so, as she turned onto the A142 towards Newmarket, she resisted the urge to demand who was driving—her or him? A suspicious clanking coming from the engine made her uneasy, and they were only half way to Heathrow.

They followed the motorway with its endless corn and hayfields for several miles, the engine sending noisy vibrations through the car.

"Cats' eyes removed," Miss Fletcher muttered, this time reading a sign by the road, while her brother slouched beside her, fast asleep.

"You sure you don't want to go to Stansted Airport?" Piper asked as a rattle joined the clank under the hood. The van wasn't going to make it much farther. "You could probably catch a plane from there today."

Mr. Fletcher woke up. "You haven't done much with your life, have you Miss Pines?"

Piper gaped. Was that called for? Had Mr. Fletcher heard the villagers talking about her? About how she'd had little education? Pop and she had tried, but it hadn't worked out at all: she was too used to her own company and schools were too large and impersonal; she was too distracted by the direction of the mad wind blowing in the trees outside the schoolroom window to concentrate on writing a composition on what she did over the holidays. Instead, she'd be wondering whether Pop would go to the large shoal of mackerel she'd pointed out that morning to make any sense of fractions. They'd moved on too often for the school inspectors to keep track of her and, in the end, Pop had taught her with his own brand of curriculum.

So she'd seen how the winds stress the surface of the waters. She'd been thirty miles out where the sea was *black* it was so deep, but when you looked hard you saw the kind of violets and greens that you never saw on land. Pop hadn't needed to teach her to swim because she took to water, he said, "loik a blooming duck." She loved being in the sea, the deeper the better where she could hear the muted roar of the waves, the splash of their inhabitants and whispers of the drowned. She even thought she'd heard the creak of wrecks. She'd seen schools of fish in an explosion of lights, *and* she knew the names of hundreds of plants, birds and animals.

But the truth was, she admitted to herself, she was just a hair's breadth away from knowing nothing about anything at all.

She concentrated on a lone oak on the flat horizon until Miss Fletcher piped up from the back and said in a sing-song voice, "From a mere nothing springs a mighty tale."

Piper looked at her again in the rear-view mirror. The woman had a colorful luminosity—almost like an aura—compared to her dull, lusterless brother.

Mr. Fletcher leaned forward and tapped Piper on her

shoulder again. "What about your mother? Couldn't she have driven us while you sold fish or whatever it was you were doing?"

His sister continued, "Not sure if that little saying I just quoted comes from Greek or Latin but whoever said it first wasn't Portuguese. I'd know if they had."

Piper's world tilted on its axis and it took all her will-power to keep the van steady. Two main enigmas in her life had just been mentioned, almost at the same time. Portugal and her mother.

Piper didn't know about her mother. The first clear memory Piper had of talking about her with Pop was when she was six or seven or thereabouts, lying on the sofa watching "Blue Peter" on the television, recovering from chicken pox, smothered in pink calamine lotion and trying not to scratch. She dug her hands down the side of the sofa cushion she was lying on and pulled out fluff balls, a 10p coin, crumbs, a peanut and a photograph which she studied. The colors were fading but the picture was of two people, one of them a young man who was clearly a younger version of Pop, his thick wavy hair hadn't gone grey yet, sitting on a rock on a golden sandy beach, waves lapping about his bare feet, his trousers rolled up and shirtless. He looked tanned and his arm was around the shoulders of a young woman, or girl, her dark hair flicking around her eyes, so it must have been a windy day. Her mouth, wide in what must've been a roar of laughter, revealed that she had two front teeth overlapping, which made Piper glad she wasn't the only one with crooked front teeth. She didn't think she'd ever seen Pop look like that, his face free of worry and so happy.

"Where's that then, Pop?" she'd asked her father.

He'd glanced at it and then torn it from her hand. "Well tha' would be," his voice quavered, "tha' would be Per... Per...Portugal, wouldn't it?"

Her Pop never stuttered. His nervousness made her wonder. "Is that Mummy, Pop?"

He waited a moment, unable to take his gaze away from the picture, before he replied. "Yes." He hesitated, shuffled from foot to foot, still staring at the photo, before he raised his eyes to the ceiling, closed them and slowly handed the photo back to Piper. "Yew keep it," he said.

"She died, didn't she?"

His eyes were still closed, his face creased in physical pain. "Yes," he whispered.

"Before I was born, Pop?"

He opened his eyes and they softened as they regarded her. "Not before, my Pips."

****

Piper swore those giant planes in the sky were flying in figures of eight. Or maybe it was her eyes. It was all this concentration on trying to avoid collisions with people who drove on the M25 like psychotic hummingbirds that was doing her head in. Was that a sign to Heathrow terminals? Bloody miracle they'd made it this far with the Bedford on its last legs.

"Terminal two," Mr. Fletcher told Piper while digging his sister in the ribs to wake her.

The van's engine roared as they juddered through a curving tunnel. Terminal one, Terminal three. Where was Terminal two? There it was, the great concrete monstrosity.

They'd just pulled in at the curb when the steering wheel decided it had had enough at the same time as steam rose from under the van's bonnet.

Great timing but now what was she going to do? Piper wondered as she unloaded suitcases onto the pavement. Towing the van would cost a fortune and, she knew, was beyond repair.

"Perhaps you'd be kind enough to find me a trolley," Mr. Fletcher asked as he helped his sister squeeze through the door that was jammed half-open. "In there." He waved towards the terminal building where the entrances were wedged open with people.

Crowds made her head ache, so Piper grabbed the first empty trolley she saw and returned to the van to find Mr. and Miss Fletcher gone, bags and all.

"What the…?" Then she spotted them, his stooped bony shoulders and his sister's rainbow-colored ski-hat at a rakish angle, her pink, orange, yellow and red outfit un-mistakable. She was clinging to his shirt-tail as she shuffled along in his jet-stream.

They hadn't paid the fare yet, and even if crowds gave her the willies, she was buggered if she was going to let them get away. She retrieved her linen bag from the van that was slumped at the curb, avoided a policeman with a notebook coming her way, and headed with the determination of a can-non ball towards the gap in the human wall that was rapidly closing behind the old couple.

Elbowing her way through the narrowing space, she was flung into a blast of noise and the reek of caged-in human-ity. She stood on tiptoe, hoping to catch a glimpse of Miss Fletcher's rainbow hat, but what she spotted first was Mr. Fletcher's tweed jacket. She stalked over to him.

"Where have you been, my dear? One hundred and thirty pounds, I believe we agreed?"

"No. One hundred and *seventy* I *know* we agreed." She put out her hand. It was the only way she could stop her finger from heading up his nostril.

His mouth widened in what could have been a sharp yellow-toothed smile but looked more like a grouper-fish's permanent expression. A grouper with a bum-fluff moustache.

She wasn't going to give in, so she stared him down, mimicking a look she'd seen on Pop's face when a trawler skipper had once asked him if it was true Piper could tell where shoals of fish were simply from colors she saw on the surface of the sea. The look was designed to make the receiver question his place of ranking in the animal kingdom.

"Here, sweetie," a soft voice said beside her as Miss Fletcher put a bundle of notes into her hand. Miss Fletcher grabbed her brother's arm with a force Piper couldn't have imagined she had. "You old skinflint," she said as she pulled him along. "Bye, Pippy," she cried as the crowd engulfed them.

When Piper counted out the money, she saw she had two hundred pounds.

The clamor of the airport faded to nothing as she considered what she should do next because the Bedford van wouldn't get her away from the curb, let alone back to Norfolk. Spend it on getting the van towed? But then how would she get home? She rubbed her sweaty hands down the sides of her jeans before taking out her purse and searching for the familiar and only photograph she possessed of her mother and father. As she'd done so often in her life at times of stress, she spoke to the laughing woman on the beach in the picture. "What shall I do, Mum?"

She turned it over, even though she knew full well what was written on the back of it: *Praia da Luminosa.*

"Why not?" She had over a hundred and seventy quid and now might just be the time to start finding some answers to all the questions in her life.

She spotted a man in a dark uniform looking like an airport worker. "Can you tell me," she asked him, "where I can buy a ticket to Lisbon, please?"

CHAPTER FIVE

It was dark outside; the night had closed in, when Piper stood in the Arrivals Hall of Lisbon Airport. She hadn't managed to get on the first flight out of Heathrow and had to wait for a later one, so she'd bought a book and passed the time wedged into a corner out of the way of the crowds and read 'A Guide to Portugal.'

Luminosa wasn't in it.

She spotted a Tourist Information desk where a woman in a pink uniform looked like she was packing up for the night, but she gave Piper a welcoming smile.

"I need to go to this place," Piper told her, showing her the back of the photo.

"Luminosa, Luminosa. I have never heard of it. Where is it?"

"I'm not sure."

The woman sighed and, although she looked at her watch, she sat back onto her stool and booted up her computer again, her smile firmly fixed. The blue light from the screen reflected on her face, but, as each minute passed, the smile fell a little more. "I can't find it," she said. "It would help if you knew the region."

"Wait a moment," Piper said as she pulled out her mobile phone and pressed her Pop's number. Its screen was blank. "It's not working."

The woman leaned over and looked at the phone. "You

probably don't have roaming. And the phone shops are closed now. There are some phone booths over there if you need to make a call."

Piper had changed some sterling into euros at Heathrow. "I've only got notes. Maybe I'll go and buy a paper and get some change there."

The woman must've been unwilling to wait any longer, because she put a phone on the desk and said, "Oh go on, use this one. It's after nine o'clock so the calls are cheap now. But be quick."

Piper didn't hold out much hope that he'd answer but when he did, she felt dizzy. "Pop?" He'd been away for less time than she'd thought.

"Where are yew, flower?"

"Portugal."

"Blarst, Philippa," Pop shouted. "Yew gone crazy? Yew get roight home, roight now. Yew hear me? Oi never heard such nonsense..."

His voice loud and tinny, she held the phone away from her ear. She tried to smile at the woman who watched her with round eyes. "My father's going apeshit," Piper explained as she put the receiver against her ear again.

"Tell me, where are yew?"

She took a deep breath. "I'm going to Luminosa."

The only sound that came down the line was a loud gasp followed by silence.

"Pop?"

His next words were hoarse. "Yew are goin' to give me a heart attack. Philippa, yew turn around roight now. Listen, yew don't take one step in that place. Yew head to Sines. Yew hear me? Sines. Then back to Lisbon."

"Sines?" she repeated, looking at the woman who nodded and returned to her computer. Pop must think she— Piper—was in a taxi or a bus already on her way there.

"Yew don't go nowhere near Luminosa. It's dangerous, Pip." His voice softened and her heart melted to hear it. Fury she could cope with—that's when he called her Philippa. But now he seemed just plain scared for her, and fear and worry were emotions that hit him far harder than anger.

"Why Pop? Why's it dangerous?"

"Because the bastard is dangerous. Evil old git."

"Who? And why?"

His deep groan sounded like someone had hit him in the solar plexus. "Why didn't yew tawk to me, Pippy-girl? Why'd yew do this without telling me?"

She licked her lips, forcing herself to remain calm and not remember the way he'd change the subject or leave the room whenever she'd try to talk about her mother or her connection with Portugal. "Because you weren't at home to talk to, and I went to Heathrow because there was no one else to take the clients and I couldn't contact you, and I didn't know how long you'd be away. Anyway, I felt it was time to come here. I tried to ask you about my mother so many times and you never ever want to tell me anything. I want to know her, Pop, and that's why I've come."

A sniff sounded down the line. "It was so hard, Oi didn't want to scare yew and Oi didn't know what to do for the best."

Her eyes welled with tears; she'd rather hear him angry than upset. When she was sure her voice sounded normal, without any wobble, she said, "I understand that, Pop. Who's the dangerous man, and why's he out to get you?" It was almost laughable. Who could possibly want to hurt her big sweet bear of a Pop?

His voice was harsh as if he forced the words through his teeth. "It was because she…she…your ma. Aw, moi girrrl. Come on home and we'll tawk about it. Yew an' me, quiet-loik."

It was tempting; it would be so comforting to be with him and hear him tell her the whole story she'd yearned to listen to. Ah, come on. Who was she trying to kid? Leaking promises. She knew exactly what would happen: she'd go home, ask about her mother and he'd turn the waterworks on, go for a long walk by himself, probably find himself a job that would involve being away from home. Then they'd just go back to their lives with the unspoken problem hanging between them, each skirting the issue. When she was in his sphere, she thought and behaved just like he did, accepted how he wanted to live and let the world pass them by without interfering. If she went back now, she'd never be the wiser.

She straightened her back. Get real, now, she told herself. She was twenty-two years old, a long way from her father's presence; and it was time to butch up. "Pop," she said carefully, "if we'd talked this over before, I might not be here now. But now I am and all I want to do is to go and see where my mother came from. Does that make sense to you?"

There was a long silence while he digested this.

The woman at the desk sighed, looked at her watch, and coughed into her hand.

"If yew do go, promise me yew don't tell them who yew are. Can Oi ask yew to do that? Can yew just do that one thing for me? Don't ask about your ma, don't mention her name, just tek a look around, get a feel of the place and then come home."

"Yes, Pop. I will do that. Tomorrow I'll get my phone fixed and then I'll call you. As you say, I just want to take a look at the place, get an idea of who my mother was and then come home on Monday night."

She disconnected, her heart beating wildly at the despair she'd caused him, but hoping her assurances had consoled him. It was only at that moment she realized she'd forgotten to ask him where the hell her books and the TV were, and her resolution that she was doing the right thing hardened.

The pink-uniformed woman tapped at her screen. "I heard you say Sines," she said. "It's a big port in the Alentejo, a couple of hours away to the south by bus. Once you're there, they'll give you the directions to this place you want to visit."

Chapter Six

Alentejo, Portugal

Leo woke to find the sun on his face. He raised himself onto his elbow, disorientated. Had he slept too late? He'd kicked off the covers during the night and was butt naked, his body sweating in the heat. Shouldn't it be raining? It always rained in September. The crashing of waves sounded familiar enough, but where were the other usual sounds: the clanking of the dockside crane as it dipped and swung from the fishing boats' holds, the wagons rumbling towards the canning factory, the glad shouts from crews on the vessels returning home? Where was the everlasting stink of fish and gasoline? Why did it smell of freshly baked bread? He scratched his head to free it from the last clouds of sleep and forced his eyes open wider to look around the cramped room. Against the wall was his open rucksack with his few spare clothes spewing out onto the floor.

Glancing at his watch, he saw it wasn't that late and then it dawned on him the sun was in a different position, that's all, because he wasn't in his bedroom in the family home on Wharf Street; he was six thousand miles to the southeast and he'd arrived last night.

****

Leo had wondered during all those hours on the planes

if he should charge in when he arrived in the village like a storm trooper and shake the first inhabitant he saw until information rattled out of him along with his teeth. He snorted at the idea. No, he'd play with them like a fish on a line and then reel 'em in once they took a bite of his enticing bait. And if it turned out they had played any part, however small, in the *Goblin's* sinking then he, like Luke Skywalker, would be a force to be reckoned with.

But when he did arrive last night, a stocky and very hairy guy asked, stating, Leo thought, the damned obvious, "Just arrived?" He said his name was Serafim as he placed a dish of steaming fish stew in front of Leo.

This was a *primo*. The main one. Serafim was the guy who sent the Christmas cards and he hadn't been difficult to find in this one-horse town since the sign *Serafim's Bar/Café* was the first thing Leo spotted on arrival.

It felt strange, though, finally meeting a relative who wasn't his father or brother, and for a moment Leo was tempted to wonder if he could get away with introducing himself. Nah—bad idea. Hadn't he already decided the best action was to keep schtum? Anyway he was too hungry and he eyed a fragrant dish brimming with clams, white fish fillets, golden potatoes, and chorizo sausage with almost the first feeling of pleasure he'd known since March.

Leo chewed on a briny clam and eyed possibly more of his relatives: a handful of fisherman who arrived, creating a buzz of too many voices so the air was thick with sounds and a fishy odor that didn't come from his plate. They didn't look much different to the hard-lined, weathered fishermen he'd lived and worked with all his life, sitting at the scuffed bar on bar-stools that had been broken several times and patched up, their shirts stained with fish blood. Except money wasn't flowing like it would where Leo came from. In the dingy Halcyon Bar back home there would be a constant ringing of a bell when guys had had a big catch and a bunch of money to spend on buying rounds. Here they hugged their one beer, chewed what looked like flat yellow beans and spat the transparent skins out onto a saucer.

Still, their leathery faces looked cheerful enough and they'd given him a wave or two as they passed, even though they couldn't have a clue who he was. Course, they might all be dimwits. His father had once referred to the *primos* as "all inter-married and crazy as Crackerjacks. Won't change a thing in the village, it's like walking into a time slip and going back a hundred years."

When it came time for Leo to ask about renting a room, Serafim told him there was one above the café and didn't even ask his name.

****

This morning, Leo clambered down the wooden staircase and opened the door that was the inside entrance to the café. The only things he desired right now were freshly baked bread and a coffee.

The café was empty except for a plump woman holding a straw basket, her ankles so swollen they rose over her shoes and spilled down the side like beer foaming over a glass. She turned as Leo came in, saying, "Good morning," and her weathered face creased into a brown-tooth filled smile. "Welcome. I do hope you have a very pleasant stay."

His mind tumbled in confusion. Where did these people learn their English? It wasn't like everyone in the country spoke fluently. The cab driver last night had stumbled and tottered over his words several times before he'd managed to convey to Leo he'd have to drop him at the top of the hill that led down to the village because he didn't think his cab would get down the narrow street.

Unaffected by Leo's lack of response, the woman continued, "Would you like a coffee the likes of which you've never had before? Just the way Serafim knows how to make it, thick, strong and short—a bit like Serafim himself, but not so hairy." The woman gargled what could've been a chuckle. "One and a half cups and you'll be buzzing."

"Sounds good to me," Leo said as she threw a final laugh in Serafim's direction before she placed what looked like jars of honey on the counter and then clattered through the chain curtain hanging at the door.

Leo turned to his *primo* behind the counter. *Primo.* Goddammit, families were people you had feelings for and the only people he cared about had been wiped out by a rogue wave. In any case, Leo didn't think Serafim and he resembled each other in any way.

"*Bica* I presume?" Serafim asked, offering the tiny steaming cup of coffee with an elaborate bow.

In the fug of ground coffee-beans, tobacco, stale beer and wine, Leo held the tiny cup of thick brown liquid to his nose, inhaling deeply before adding three packets of sugar. The coffee began to work its magic, bringing a warm glow to his insides on a par with a gulp of brandy.

"We aim to please," Serafim said, obviously reading Leo's expression correctly.

The guy had attitude and Leo had to admit he liked it. Serafim wasn't morose, nor a meathead, and probably neither were the guys in the bar last night because after Leo had turned in, he heard a coarse-voiced chorus from downstairs which had lulled him off to sleep. "You speak good English," Leo said.

"Practice, that's all," Serafim said, handing over a warm roll with butter and jelly that, he told him was, "all homemade. If you want any ask Rosa, she's my sister and the one who just left."

So he'd just met another *primo,* had he? Rosa? Shame, he'd kinda liked her.

A tattered newspaper cutting was framed on one wall. Leo had already seen it last night but, to take his mind off these *primos,* he took another look at Serafim's photo and chewed on his sweet bread roll, soft as a cloud, as he read the cutting's small print. His smattering of Spanish helped him translate the headline: *Pescador Português Apanha Robalo de Tamanho Record   Portuguese fisherman catches record size sea-bass.*

"That's you," he said.

"I'm younger there," Serafim spoke over his shoulder, his breath tickling Leo's ear. "Just a sprat." The figure in the photo was in yellow rubber overalls and holding a huge fish while his smile matched the size of the bass.

"That was a good day," Leo said.

Serafim beamed, his bright red lips burrowing into his facial hair. "Unfortunately those days are few and far between. Now."

"Catch not so good?"

"Not like it was. The inshore catch has really fallen off this last two years. You want your other *bica?*"

"Why not?" Leo resisted the urge to grab Serafim by the neck and shake more information out of him. If he hadn't just had clue number one, then he, Leo, was Davy Jones's boyfriend: fishing had dropped off, and the village was piss poor. Trafficking could be their only source for survival. And who could help them out? Their cuzzes in Alaska, that's who.

His fists clenched, he parted the chain curtain covering the door just enough to allow in a breeze which carried the smell of ozone straight off the sea. It helped ease his rising anger and tell himself not to blow his top yet. Not until he was a hundred percent sure.

The brisk breeze ruffled his long hair and, sipping his second coffee, he watched the crests of white horses on the

Atlantic's choppy surface. The golden sandy beach was now, unlike last evening, empty of the row of colorful artisanal wooden vessels, each with an open deck and high curved sweeping bows. His welling despair now soothed by the familiar sight of the sea, he found he could speak without anger tightening his voice. "They're out now, are they?" He nodded towards the empty beach. "The fishermen. What are they after? Sardines?"

"Yes. These days they leave earlier and come back later. Mostly sardines. Some mackerel. "

"But they're not the only vessels here, are they?" Leo had already spotted a rubble breakwater to the west of the beach that formed a harbor where larger craft would be protected, and a jetty with small, well-oiled winches and tires for fenders. It didn't take a genius to know larger hauls than sardines were offloaded here.

"You're right. The scabbard fleet will be back tomorrow."

Leo stared at the glittering water. "How long do they stay out?"

"A couple of days, three maybe. More perhaps."

"More if they're not hauling much, huh?"

Serafim snorted before he said, "Exactly. You never said a truer word."

"Time's not so good then?" Leo's pulse increased at this confirmation of his suspicions. Boy, he was a good sleuth. Call him Sherlock.

"They're getting a rise in houndshark and rays farther down the coast. But the sea's not giving up its treasures so easily now. Fewer fish on the lines. Sometimes bream."

"Is that right?" Leo sucked on his lip. So they were going downhill fast. "They ever go further afield?"

"Some join the Spanish tuna seiners heading east. Not many. Most of us prefer to stay in the village."

To delve further, or mention Alaska, would make Serafim suspicious and Leo didn't want that. He'd find out, with careful questioning, what part they played in the trafficking ring.

In any case, Serafim had disappeared behind the old-fashioned counter which fascinated Leo with its carved wooden panels and grey marble top that had ashtrays strewn across it because everyone smoked in the café with the attitude of being exempt from no-smoking laws. From the clatter of bottles and crashing of metal objects, it sounded like Serafim was doing some spring-cleaning. Either that or there was a rat on mescaline in the house.

From his position, hidden from view, Serafim asked, "What are you going to do this morning?"

"Take a walk. Check stuff out." It occurred to him again as he left the café that no one had asked him his name. Nothing seemed quite normal in this village.

Chapter Seven

Leo turned left when he left Serafim's café/bar, letting the chain curtains swing behind him. He took his rucksack with him, not wanting anyone to rake through it when he wasn't in his room.

The main street of Luminosa wasn't much of one. It stretched about a quarter mile in the direction he was going with nothing more than a dusty tarmac road and a low sea wall separating the almost identical cottages from the sandy beach. The narrow cobbled sidewalk had orange trees planted along it at intervals, fruit hanging off them like Christmas baubles against the dark green foliage. Serafim's was the second or third cottage along from the start and the only one with a striped awning and metal chairs and wobbly tables set on the sidewalk, although many had a stool or small seat outside their blue doors for the occupants to sit and pass the time. The walls of fishermen's cottages shone blinding white in the bleaching sun, the doors, windows and walls trimmed in deep-sky blue while most of the terracotta roofs sprouted vegetation.

He thought the place would be empty, that everyone would be out with the fishing fleet, but he could hear the sounds of hammering from behind one of the cottages. Another had its front door open and an elderly woman, who nodded at him, sat in the cool interior weaving on a wooden loom.

A younger woman holding a wicker basket full of bread rolls to her ample bosom passed, and he stood to one side to let her go by. She patted him on the arm as if she met him every day. *"Bom dia,"* she said before clattering along the cobbles on worn-down clogs. As she passed the little junction that joined the main street with the road up the hill, she shouted a greeting toward the corner cottage at a neighbor who was hanging out clothes to dry. Her small yard was chock-a-bloc with trees laden with ripening lemons and glowing oranges, as well as fruit he had no name for. While the woman hung out the clothes, she brushed away branches of a brilliant crimson bougainvillea that cascaded over her fence, and ignored several brown chickens that chuntered and pecked around her ankles. She shouted a return greeting at the woman with the clogs before she waved at Leo.

He waited a moment, contemplating the rest of the row of fishermen's cottage along the main street, then decided to take the road up the hill, the same one he'd descended last night.

This was where the majority of the villagers lived, their cottages sandwiched in rows along mazes of alleys that wriggled off from the small road. Each cottage stood just a little bit higher than their neighbor's so each one had their own view.

As he started to climb, beside him, a blue-painted door swung open with a creak, emitting a rush of cool air from the interior and a small girl who ran straight into his legs.

"Whoa there," he said as he steadied her back onto her feet.

She beamed at him and squeaked, *"Olá,* how ya doin'?" before she staggered off after the woman on chubby legs that kicked up the dust into clouds. Jesus, even little kids spoke English.

When he'd started out from the café, his mind had been

full of his own thoughts and, if anyone had asked, he'd have said the place was as silent as a tomb, but now he listened, and he realized as he passed the small places on the hill that the village was filled with sound: clattering plates, women's voices—some cheerfully loud, others murmuring as if soothing babies. Canaries sang piping songs, while the static of radios and televisions buzzed through the fragrant air filled with the scent of fresh bread.

In the shimmering heat, he continued up until he reached the asphalt road where the cab had dropped him last night. He patted the weather-worn stone sign that announced the village of Luminosa, crossed the road and continued along a rocky trail.

Right now it would be raining in Alaska with swathes of fog following the squalls into the bay and clouding the mountain peaks. The waters would be chilling with a trace of a metallic ice smell in the air. Here, he could be on another planet: the heat burned down into the sandy earth of the track and threw up a spicy scent of herbs and dust. On either side of the track, ripening blackberries weighed down bushes that intertwined with tall bamboo canes.

A horse blew air through its nostrils right behind him. He hadn't heard its approach so the noise startled him and made him step back into the bamboos barely a second before a huge grey and white beast high-stepped past him, the rider's stance as proud as the horse's, upright, haughty and stiff.

Get a load of those pins, Tom's voice whispered in his mind. Leo took in much more: slim, long legs—clothed in skin-tight black pants—strongly gripping the animal's side, her wide-angled hips, her neat figure in its tight black riding jacket, swaying sensuously in time with the horse's motion.

She could have been a robot for all the emotion she showed. The thought was barely out of his head before her wide brown eyes swiveled sideways and the corners of her mouth turned a fraction upwards.

Still watching her neat rear swaying on the seat in time with the horse's movements, and hoping he didn't look like the family Labrador gazing at the pot-roast being carved, he followed her along the trail.

From a shady tunnel of eucalyptus and pine, he watched her turn into an open wrought-iron gate that led into the grounds of a large rambling house built of rustic dun-colored stone with high steps leading to a carved wooden door. The place looked sturdy as if it had withstood the social and natural demands of centuries. In a nearby field, horses lined up along a trough, swishing tails their only movement, and farther out, black cattle slumbered in the shade of spiky-looking trees.

Nearer the house, in a dusty corral enclosed by an open-barred wooden fence, the woman he'd followed now trotted her grey horse round the perimeter. He waited by the gate like a lame-brained teenager hoping for an invitation to go in, but knowing he wouldn't get one. The smell of combined horse and its shit and the dust thrown up by its hooves was bitter, yet a faint feminine fragrance that came out of a bottle overlaying it wasn't at all unpleasant. If he was Tom, he'd leap through the bamboo hedge, through the barrier of spiky aloes and saunter up to her with some remark like, "You're good at that." And she'd probably respond, "Good at what?" with a cute little smile and so the banter would start. Tom never had problems, the girls always orbited around him because he wasn't shy, and he was lean and strong from his work.

Leo might be lean and strong as well, but banter wasn't his *forte*—he tended to dry up too quickly and feel like he'd said something dumb.

So he didn't tear into the clump of tall bamboo. Instead, he watched her through it, trying not to look like a voyeur, yet knowing that's exactly what he was and ignoring Tom's whispered *"wuss"* in his ear.

The horsewoman nimbly dismounted and handed the reins to a waiting attendant in a cloth cap, saying something in a language of mangled consonants and tongue-defying strings of vowels.

The man in the cap led the horse out of the ring, while the woman kicked at the sand in the middle as if waiting for something to happen. She didn't have to wait long before the guy returned, opened the gate and stood aside to let a black bull flash past, heading straight for the woman.

That was when Leo did force his way through the bamboo and prickly aloes, tearing his jeans in the process, and raced to the corral. The world seemed to stand still as he grabbed the woman—one hand on her collar and the other on the material covering her ass—and flung her to one side. He'd just released her when a hard object knocked him in the back of his knees with a blow that sent him flying.

He ate grit, dust and bitter God-knew-what-else while two hard points butted at his thigh. A harsh shout and the attack stopped.

Leo lowered his arms from where they protected his head, and uncurled his body so he could take a better look at where the danger was coming from. Flies buzzed in his ears and the blue sky whirled in a dizzying spiral as he took a moment to get his senses in order. A pair of dusty boots came into his line of vision, and he followed them up until he stared into a pair of dark eyes. Her hair was so black that it seemed impossible to reflect any other color in the sunlight. But it did and shards of auburn flared as fierce as her blazing stare. Her face showed a perfect cocktail of contempt and fury as she loomed over him, her hands dusting down the front of her pants.

Pleased to see she was unhurt, he stifled a groan as he

got to his feet. It didn't look like he was going to get any thanks, though. Or, at least, if he did, he didn't understand any of the tangled words she let loose. Her meaning became clear when she jerked a pointed finger towards the broken bamboo stalks and the bent clump of aloes that doubtlessly had been his work when he'd dashed through it.

The guy in the cap stepped forward. One of his eyes was an unseeing milky white orb and a white scar carved down the side of his dark weathered face. He took a step nearer and his good eye held a glint of menace. Leo raised his hands. "Whoa," he said. "Hold your horses…"

His gesture or his words halted the man and the stream of words issuing from the woman. "American?" she asked, her stance and expression relaxing.

"Nearly an ex-one."

Like a flower unfolding, the shadows on her face shifted. The corners of her mouth turned up, as they had earlier when she passed him on the track, creating a small crease in her cheek. She slowly lifted her hand and swiped sweat off her upper lip. "What you think you was doing?"

"Saving your ass," he muttered, noting her foreign accent which didn't sound Portuguese to him. A smattering of gratitude in his direction wouldn't go amiss.

The small smile that teased her mouth grew as her gaze flickered over him, which fired up a pleasant glow inside him.

But the one-eyed guy's expression hadn't softened. He took another step towards Leo and jerked his head in the direction of the dirt track outside the property.

"Out?" Leo asked, raising an eyebrow. "Fine by me." He eyed the high mound of barbed aloes. "The same way?"

The woman put her hand on the one-eyed man's arm. "*Espere*, Gaspar." She turned to Leo and asked, "So you think you *salvar* me? I didn't need. I am in 'armony with the animal and can 'owyousay mesmerize it. You, 'ero, were not needed."

Leo hadn't been called a hero before. Fishermen didn't tend to call each other by such names; sticky bastard was more like.

She spoke again to Gaspar who shot Leo one more look that said if he had his way, he'd leave him to the bull to sort out. Instead he nodded and headed back to the pen where he'd presumably somehow stashed the animal away.

"Mesmerize," Leo said. "Like the horse whisperer, except a bull whisperer." His jeans were torn where the little bull—if it had been a little one and he thought it must have been otherwise he'd have been dead meat by now—had butted him, and his thighs hurt like hell. But there was no sticky blood and he'd have bruises in parts that didn't usually see the sun.

She eyed him with her head tilted, affording him the sight of a prominent pulsing vein in her neck. "Bull whisper. I like. Lili is my name." She held out a leather-gloved hand. Despite her recent close proximity with a bull and horse, she exuded a sweet scent, one that even over-rode the warm, natural fragrance of herbs that drifted on the breeze. She was as enticing as an overflowing crab-trap.

Ever since he'd left Anchorage International Airport, he'd been playing with names to call himself. He never came to a conclusion, deciding he'd just wing it when the time came.

But she didn't wait for him to introduce himself. "I am terrible *'owyousay* hoster, hostess. You are here for the party, yes? And I must tell you what I am doing with you."

He was here for a party? And he couldn't wait to hear what she was going to do with him. If she said he was, then, sure, he was game for a party.

Go for it brother-oh. And I'll betcha she don't wear panties under them tight pants.

Ah Tom, Leo responded silently. Will you cut it out? You're making me lose sight of my objectives. He might be getting the hots for Lili but if it turned out she had any dealings in his family's deaths then she wouldn't be exempt from his fury.

The granite path they followed out of the corral reflected the heat of the sun. It shone on Lili's hair and made him sweat. As they neared the solid walls of the house, she told him it was seventeenth century. "Very old. Much needs doing. Old and…old. But is all…this." She waved her arm in a flourish as if to say the hectares of vineyards, the land beyond with the cattle and cork trees, and the orchards on the other side all belonged to her. Was she the lord and master that Serafim had referred to?

A white marquee stood on an emerald-colored lawn to the far side of the courtyard. Sprinklers hissed their incessant spray as a line of people dodged the water, to-ing and fro-ing between the house and the large now-open wrought-iron gate at the main entrance where a large van had parked, while a bull knocked the crap out of Leo.

"All is ready by tomorrow," she told him, indicating the marquee that drooped in the middle. "You early, you know. Everyone arrive *amanhã*. Mr. Grady, *claro*, already here. He's the man of the project design. Big, big investments from Americans, British. I think you will be 'appy with investment if you pay. It is *alegria* to have so rich and influence people here in *Herdade Albatroz* this weekend."

This half-English, half-Portuguese speech wasn't easy to follow, but if he took *investment, plans and rich* then it didn't take a genius to know something big was going on. It was laughable that she thought he—Leo—rich and influential. But then maybe those kinds of people usually went about wearing woolen hats in eighty degrees, torn jeans and ancient t-shirts with *I Got Bait* printed on the front.

Herdade Albatroz. That must be the name of the place. Some kind of big farm or estate, he supposed, judging by the fields surrounding the large house.

She led him up the steps and through the heavy wooden doorway with a coat-of-arms depicting three crossed swords and a ship carved in stone over the top, into a cool dark hall with a vaulted ceiling and polished red terracotta floor tiles. They stepped into a large room with portraits of grim, constipated-looking old-timers around the walls. Glass cabinets packed with porcelain tureens, jugs and plates. Carved white marble busts of even older dudes than those in the pictures stood about the room. A small crystal chandelier with circular metal holders for real candles hung from the high ceiling.

"Cool," he said. Looking at all this stuff, it was clear that Lili wasn't short of a buck or two.

"Old," she corrected. "Need much work. I want it all red and *minimalisto*. I hate all this," she waved her hand at the furniture, "all this old, miserable dark…"

She wanted to pretty the place up. Still, it seemed a shame to destroy all this historical malarkey, especially since the stuff was probably worth a fortune.

"Oh." She'd picked up some papers from a heavy-looking desk and sounded disappointed as she shuffled through them. "My list of names no here. Wait a moment. I get it. Names of all the *investors*." She eyed him slowly, starting at his head and lingering just below his waist. "But as you first to arrive, I think you stay here and not in hotel. We have a good room for you." She grinned at him.

Hornyyyy, Tom's voice echoed through Leo's brain.

She shimmied from the room. Leo raised his eyebrows. She really did think he was an investor ready to part with some money. How would she react when she discovered he didn't have any?

He wondered how he was going to bullshit his way on to the guest-list. Unless she really was struck by his manly good-looks—he snorted—once sussed as an imposter, he'd better be prepared when the time came to get kicked out by the one-eyed muscle-man.

Come on, man, he thought. Some quick thinking was needed to bullshit his way into this with a convincing story. The laptop on the table pinged. The screen showed a small icon indicating a new message had arrived. Curious, he clicked it. The message was from a company called *3GDeveloping*, addressed to Lili Carneiro with the title *Albatrozinvest*. It was thankfully short:

Ms. Carneiro,

This is to inform you that, for personal reasons, I will not be attending the Albatrozinvest presentation this weekend.

I would be grateful if you could convey to Mr. William Grady that I no longer wish to be involved in your project but wish you every success.

Sincerely,

John Hughes

Here was Leo's ticket on to the guest-list. If John Hughes appeared, Leo would have kissed him. He read the message again before deleting it from the inbox and then from the trash box.

He returned to the desktop and spotted a folder entitled *Festa Investimento.* Leo clicked it: *password required.*

He tried Lili, Albatroz, Portugal, Sex, sex, SEX, sexy, but none of them gave him access.

Footsteps clacked along the flagstones outside giving Leo just a second to spare to click on the *close* box.

"Here we are," Lili said, coming into the room and concentrating on the paper she was holding. "Now, you must be…?" She quirked an enquiring eyebrow at him.

"John Hughes, ma'am, from 3GDeveloping." He crossed his fingers in the hope she'd never met the guy.

"*Perfeito.*" She ticked a name off the list. "So, John, I show you your room."

He followed her into the hall and to a wooden *Hello Dolly* staircase. There was enough timber in the place to reforest the Amazon basin.

She stopped on the first step and turned, a teasing smile brightening her face. "Guess what we have? I believe you cannot guess."

"Nope, guess I can't." Unless it was her nicely wrapped in glittery paper. He might not have lost sight of his objectives, but he was still a man.

"Our present. Is normal, no? To have present at these parties. This time we have very special one. Very nice."

He paused. "Great."

"You cannot wait, no?"

Control yourself, little bro. Not a good idea to have a roll on a staircase, wait 'til you get upstairs.

She stood on tiptoe and whispered, tickling his ear. "It is an iPad. One for each. One for you. *Amanhã.*" She was so close, her mouth rosy, proud and assured.

Sofa lips.

"Amazing," he murmured.

"*Sim.* Amazing." She slowly looked down his body, letting her gaze stop for a tad too long on his crotch before she turned and continued up the stairs.

The bedroom was bigger than their living room on Wharf Street but it smelled of polish, dust and mildew instead of forgotten bait and wet oilskins.

"I hope you'll be comfy," Lili said, patting the yellow-with-age white cotton comforter.

Get to it, little bro, Tom's voice whispered again.

Before he could process that thought and decide the best form of advance, she turned on her heel, brushed past him—so close he felt her left breast against his arm—and said in a voice that was all business and not at all flirty, "Dinner, John. Eight o'clock. You talk to Mr. Grady about agenda."

He didn't know if he was pleased or disappointed but it really was time to shape up. This was neither the right place nor the right time to be fooling about with a woman who was no more than a cock-teaser.

To take his mind off his uncomfortably tight jeans, he decided it was time to do a bit more exploring. Maybe the upstairs rooms first? Except that Gaspar guy stood outside one of the doors watching him. He tipped the beak of his cap in what was without doubt mock-subservience and folded his arms. Leo got the message: no poking about upstairs. He'd just have to concentrate on downstairs and hopefully get another look at that computer. But, when he reached the office, Lili was in there, her back to him, sitting at the computer and tapping her long fingernails on the table top as she read something on the screen. With an irritated sigh and what sounded like *merde,* she pushed her chair back and reached for a phone.

As happened so often after a while spent indoors, even in the freezing Alaskan winter when he wasn't at sea, he felt the dark walls closing in on him so, since there was nothing he could do here right now, he'd get some air.

At the wrought-iron entrance gate to the dusty trail, instead of turning right towards Luminosa and the sea as he'd planned, he had a notion that he should check the trail out further up, so he turned left.

CHAPTER EIGHT

How life could change in twenty-four hours. Yesterday at this time she'd been battling a bad tempered sea in a leaking skiff; today she was heading over a suspension bridge that reminded her of pictures she'd seen of one in San Francisco. This one, though, spanned the wide Tagus River and was so high the geometric roofs of Lisbon lay below her like a bright tapestry unfolding. The river itself looked polluted but there was life in it; Piper could identify mussels for a start—that copper red shimmer was vast, great seed beds which the fishermen knew about judging by the little boats bobbing in the area with piles of shellfish in their bows. Some flounders in that glimmer of moss-green in the curlicues, grey mullet too. And, in the distance, the Atlantic Ocean in a mighty good mood today gleamed with a strong, eye-watering blue. A great day for fishing.

Once over the bridge, the land flattened out and they left the river behind. She shuffled in her cushioned seat, comfortable at last.

From the airport she'd taken two underground trains rather than taking a taxi which would've dug into her already much diminished funds, having used most of it for the plane fare, and arrived at the bus station in the early hours. A policeman had asked her in broken English if she was well. When she told him she was fine, just waiting for a bus, he'd shown her a quieter spot behind a pillar where she could stretch out on several benches and doze. So she'd spent several hours listening to the elephants trumping and tigers roaring from the nearby zoo. The noise of the animals, mixed with the creaking cicadas in the heat of the night, made her wonder, while she drowsed on the bum-numbing hard seats, whether she'd arrived in Africa.

Now she gazed through the coach window at the land-scape—as flat as the North Norfolk coast but sandy brown and dry, dotted with dusty squat trees. Once the land became miles of vineyards and lines of stalking electricity pylons, Piper closed her eyes and slept.

She opened them when she sensed movement from the other passengers who had started to get up, and many swayed with the movement of the bus as they lugged their bags from the overhead racks.

They passed an oil refinery chimney and she asked a fellow passenger, "Sines?"

"Sines," he confirmed.

The port was in a natural basin that created a harbor for container ships and petrol tankers, although her eyes were more drawn to the fishing wharf loaded with gear, and the long sandy beach stretching for miles to the south. Pity she had no time for exploring because first she had to find out where Luminosa was. The bus station ticket office sorted that one out; the place was a mere ten kilometers to the south. The phone shop was the next stop where they got her mobile working again. It was late afternoon when she was back on the road heading for Luminosa on a bus quite different to the air-conditioned coach she'd left Lisbon in but, of the two, she preferred this one. It trundled along the narrow coast road that was only wide enough for one vehicle, so every time a car came in the other direction the bus had to tilter on the edge of a precipice. One crumbling stone and they'd fall to their deaths on the glorious sea-washed beaches below. The windows were all open to let the cooler afternoon air blow in, so different from the wave of blazing heat that had greeted her like a slap in the face when she'd got off the air-conditioned coach in Sines.

When Piper boarded the bus all the window seats were occupied, so she sat next to a woman with shiny dark hair, streaked with grey, tied back in an untidy bun. She smiled at Piper, revealing such white teeth that Piper wondered if she was a dental hygienist. The woman wasn't fat but full and broad, and her pink t-shirt sporting the logo, *When gran's mad, we're all mad,* was a couple of sizes too small for her.

"That is so sweet," Piper said, mouthing the logo's words.

The woman gave a wry smile and said, "Etta bought it for me. I don't even have grandchildren."

"It's cute though," Piper replied, giving the woman a second glance and wondering if she was English or Portuguese.

They slogged along past groves of fruit and spiky olive trees, and thick forests of pine, the bus engine sounding like it had the same trouble Piper's van had at Heathrow Airport. She'd forgotten to tell Pop about that.

She'd pulled her phone out of her linen bag to call him when the woman beside her asked, "You going far?"

Piper put the phone back in the bag again. "Luminosa. What about you?"

"Me too. I'm going home—I've been doing some shopping in Sines. My husband, Serafim, dropped me as he does on a Friday but I always come home by bus. You must be going to work at the party, because we don't usually get any visitors." The woman observed Piper's t-shirt with bright eyes that looked like plump raisins had been pressed into her face. Piper wondered if she was looking at it because it gave off a pungent two-day old whiff of crab, but the woman didn't wait for Piper's response and carried on, "I hear it's good money for just two days' work. And they want people who speak good English."

Two days' work, huh? A party would mean lots of people she could mingle with and talk to. Some of them would be bound to know her mother. There was a problem, though. "I didn't register for the work or anything so they're not expecting me."

"Shouldn't worry about that, they're desperate for English-speaking people."

"If you live there and you speak such good English, which you do, why don't you work there for the weekend?" The woman was surely bi-lingual, Piper thought. She hadn't yet met anyone in Portugal with such perfect English and, from her dark features the woman could easily be Portuguese.

"They want people from outside, not from the village."

"Seems a waste of money. Does everyone in the village speak such good English?"

"Most. See, we spend so much time with Victor and Etta who used to own the Main House. Then, they'd throw the doors open to all the villagers and so we all grew up speaking English. Even now, although they're in their little cottage, they're very much part of village life and the children just adore Etta."

An elderly man behind them tapped Piper on the shoulder and, with a cracked, dirt-encrusted brown hand, offered them each a piece of soft yeasty bread.

Piper looked at the woman beside her with raised eyebrows, wondering if she should take it or not.

"It's all right. It's good. Thanks Henrique." The woman took hers so Piper took the other one with a smile for Henrique and an "*Obrigada*" which made his weathered face crease into a broken-tooth smile before he responded with the same ease of English, "You're welcome." Roughly pulled-apart slices of cheese came next. "Goat's. From our own herd."

"Lovely." Piper munched on the bread that was crunchy outside and moist in the middle. The cheese melted on her tongue with a satisfying salty taste.

From the row across the aisle, a woman dressed in black handed Piper two plastic cups full of rough red wine.

"Thank you." Piper beamed as she passed one cup to the woman next to her; she was getting a real feast here. "I don't have anything to give you back."

"I have *sonhos*—dreams, to you, my dear—and you have to try them," the woman next to her said and took out a plastic box full of what looked like small doughnuts, but when she bit into one, Piper found it much lighter, soft as dreams. *Sonhos.* "There're almonds in this. And applesauce. It's lovely. Did you make them?"

"I did. Just like Henrique's wife made the bread and cheese, and Elsa over there made the wine with her husband and son. I'm Prazeres, by the way."

"I'm…" Piper hesitated. She'd promised Pop she wouldn't say who she was but this motherly-looking woman surely couldn't harm her. "Piper."

With the contented feeling she was with friendly people and that Pop had exaggerated, and combined with the wine that made her drowsy, she settled back comfortably in her seat, her belly nicely full.

She must have drowsed because it seemed like only a few minutes later when she opened her eyes to find that the afternoon had turned to twilight outside. Prazeres dug her in the side and said. "We're here."

CHAPTER NINE

Jesus wants me for a sunbeam, to shine for him all day.

The singer with a wavering voice came into Leo's view: an elderly woman whose glittering silver hair escaped from a wooly cap, not unlike his own, except hers was rainbow-colored and his was grey. Her eyes shone like sapphires behind huge black-rimmed glasses and a beatific smile lit up her face. She was a beautiful lady, perhaps in her sixties, who smiled at him like her heart burst with pleasure at the sight of him. Maybe she knew him, although he had no clue who she might be.

Once he'd left the main gate, he'd followed the rutted trail past groves of twisted olive and gnarled cork trees. The olives were easy to tell from their fruit-laden branches, but he'd assumed the others were cork when he'd pressed the nude-pink colored bark of one and his finger had sunk into what felt like spongy cork.

Sheep and brown cattle grazed in dun-colored meadows strewn with boulders. He paused for a moment in the shadow of a tall water-tower where a stork had built its huge nest on top.

"Gosh, you're a long drink of water, aren't you? Here." The woman held out a furry peach. "Have one."

Wasn't there something illegal about wearing skinny yellow pants, a long turquoise jacket, shoes that looked like she'd grape-trodden in a variety of paint-cans and an assortment of chunky beads and scarves?

"Thanks, ma'am, appreciate that."

"You're foreign."

Leo smiled, tempted to say, 'No, ma'am, *you're* foreign.'

"I'm good at foreign," she told him. "I once had to tell my brother, who was grumbling about a gentleman, that the said gentleman wasn't drunk, just Canadian."

"Well, ma'am, I'm American. So that's OK."

"Oh yes, that makes you more than OK."

"Thank you, ma'am."

She shivered. "I love that ma'am doo-dah. Usually I'm just called an old fart. But I'm really Etta—short for Marianetta Fletcher."

"That's a cute name, ma…Etta. I'm…" he hesitated.

"You have cat's eyes, yellow specks that look like a lion. But don't go to England. They remove them there. Cat's eyes. I read it on the road."

"Are you from England?"

"I'm from here. But I was recently in the UK on holiday where my brother spent a lot of time looking at birds with feathers in the Norfolk bogs. We had a wonderful journey to the airport with a loose crab that crawled right over my brother's foot and he didn't notice. A girl called Pippy."

"A girl crab called Pippy crawled…?"

"My brother grumbled because she went down the M25 on two wheels, but I enjoyed it. Like being at the funfair on the dodgems. D'you know," she said, leaning on his arm as she led him up the trail. "All Americans remind me of film stars."

"That right, Etta?" He slapped at a gnat biting his ear.

"You look like Steve McQueen."

"Ah."

"Except you have really blond long hair with the sun shining in it."

His cap had fallen off when the bull hit him, and he still held it in his hand. "Salt, probably, ma'am. The salt makes it lighter." That was a lie. He could spend a year indoors and it'd still be white blond.

Dust from the crumbling earth beneath their feet caught in his nose and his shirt was wet when they reached the top of the hill, but Etta wasn't even out of breath.

"Best spot to watch for enemies," she said, looking backwards.

"There are enemies?"

The sky was hazy with heat, cicadas sang around them and the land stretched out, some of it covered with fields of drying sunflowers while the rest just rolled into the blue distance broken only by the occasional white farmhouse or lone cork tree.

"I liked Pippy," Etta said, guiding him into the shade of a rustling dusty tree. "She's just peaceful and you don't find many of those, do you? She's a lovely girl, got hair a bit like yours, all feathery, except it's light brown and short, cut like a pixie's. Actually you've got the girl's hair and she's got the boy's. She's tiny. Doesn't smile much, but it's lovely when she does. She does it slowly. Smile, that is." Her glasses glinted as she looked at the sky where a raptor circled. Then she looked down the hill towards the endless russet-tiled roof of *Herdade Albatroz.* "Do you like my house?"

"It's yours?"

She considered, her head tilted on one side like a bird eyeing a worm. "Not since Nelson oozed his way in, it's not. He's the enemy. Would you like to hear the story?"

"Indeed I would, ma'am, Etta."

"Then let us sit upon this big old boulder here and tell sad tales…you see, once upon a time, there was a man called Salazar who ruled the country and he loved us all very, very much. Which was a pity really, because we could've done with a bit less loving. And when he became older than dirt, he fell off a chair and died and everyone was in a fearful temper, including God. My brother said to me, 'Etta, are you prepared for what's to come?' and I replied, 'I'm ready for anything as long as it's muscular and in a thong.' I was younger then, of course."

"So what happened?"

"The opposite of muscular happened. Nelson came along and we lost the house. *Cave*! Enemy at six o'clock." She pointed at the Main House to the side of the corral where a person, a man Leo thought, was being pushed in a wheelchair past the corral towards the emerald lawn where the marquee stood. Leo would bet it was one-eyed Gaspar who was doing the pushing.

"What's he doing?"

"Probably giving the staff their daily share of indifference."

"Why's he the enemy, Etta?"

"He's Nelson," she said, making it obvious that Nelson and the enemy amounted to the same thing. "Look at him glaring up at us. He thinks I'm plotting to get my house back."

"And are you?"

"Not now, although Victor, that's my brother, never gives up—he's always hoping. It was going to return to the Portuguese in the year two thousand so the place is not ours now anyway. Look at him." She hauled herself up from the boulder, nodded down at the figure in the wheelchair and stood with her hands on her hips. "He heard I'm back. I sang the news loud enough from the front door this morning. I thought he'd hear. *I'm baaack, all the way from London town,*" she warbled. "Did you like that?"

"Lovely. Ma'am, Etta, if you don't live in your house down there, where do you live?"

"Here." She turned and pointed just a little farther up the

track to what looked like an oasis in the sunburned landscape. From a dense green clump of trees, tall bushes and shrubs, a bright white chimney protruded.

"So," he said carefully, hoping he'd glean some information that might be helpful to him, "why were you kicked out of your big house down there? And why does Nelson own it now?"

"Shall I start at the very beginning? It's a very good place to start."

"I guess that might be best."

"In the eighteen hundreds…"

This tale sounded like it was going to take a helluva long time, so he helped her back down and then settled himself on the boulder, his back as comfortable as it could be against the bark of the tree.

"…In the early 1820s, once he'd come out from hiding behind a nut called Brazil, the King of Portugal was so pleased with some of the British who'd fought during the Peninsular War, he ordered that they be rewarded. One of them was the Duke of Wellington's fellow-fighter and friend, the courageous Colonel Fergus Fletcher."

"Your relative?"

"Indeed. Actually, our family tree goes back to a conker but it wasn't until Fergus came along that the Fletchers became great. He was such a pal that Wellington called him Fungus and he was my great, great, very grand grandfather. No, wait," she put one finger to her lip, "my great, great, great, great grandfather. Anyhow, the King gave him a nice medal, the house down there and all this land for his delight and pleasure," she waved vaguely around her, "and he, as only a Fletcher can do with alacrity, grabbed the whole kit and caboodle with both hands and didn't look back. And the Portuguese didn't mind because he'd been living in Portugal since the end of the war anyway, and had battled against

Napoleon's lot like a fat, middle-aged nineteenth century version of Spiderman.

"Even so, the authorities here knew the British were a little careless because they'd lost the United States a few years before. So, just in case this Englishman carried the same lax gene and lost the *Herdade* to, Heaven forbid, a Spaniard, there was a weeny condition in the decree to say the *Herdade* would return to the Portuguese in the year two thousand which to everyone at that time, probably meant the end of the world would've come and gone anyway by then so it wouldn't really matter."

"And it stayed in your family all that time."

"Exactly. And so the *Herdade* passed down the generations." She made a spiral with her hand. "All the way down the line, past granddad Herman, Amos, Aunt Julia and so on until it was just my brother and I.

"But, as I told you, Salazar kicked the bucket and there was a revolution, and a lot of old blighters sat in parliament and tried to rule. In 1974 Nelson Carneiro went to these new authorities and said, 'I really want to live at *Herdade Albatroz* so much, but those grasping foreigners hog the whole caboodle.' And they said to him, 'You poor, poor thing. Here you are.' And, lo! They said, 'We wish we could give you two *Herdades*, but there's only one we can ransack right now. Take it and bugger the capitalist foreigners who still have sixteen years to run on their ill-gotten lease, but who cares about that? However, to show we are good chappies at heart, let them live in that run-down shepherd's cottage up the hill, suit 'em down to the ground and then they can't say we made them homeless.' "

"You mean they kicked you out, just like that? Didn't you fight it?"

Etta frowned, looking thoughtful. "Victor tried his best but only ended up getting thrown out of Parliament on his bum for calling a bigwig communist 'worm scum.' That's what clinched their decision, in my considered opinion, that since Nelson was from the village it meant he was one of the down-trodden people and would continue the traditions and therefore the employment of the villagers."

"But wasn't he a fisherman?"

"Oh yes."

"So how could…and *can*…he afford to live in that place?"

"He got rich quick. Something to do with coal."

Leo picked up a small stick of bamboo and stabbed the dusty ground with it. "Coal?"

Etta pondered before she said, "I don't think it really is coal but it's called something like that. White stuff, powder that people stick in an orifice and it makes them feel good."

It took Leo a moment, but he thought he'd have a stab at it. "Cocaine?"

"Don't they give you that when you have a toothache? Whatever it was it got him rich quick. One minute he was a fisherman and the next, *bingo,* he was richer than Croesus but bankrupt in the taste department."

Leo's mind whirled. Could she really be talking about cocaine?

"There was a popular saying that I think came originally from one of your countrymen, perhaps you knew him? Oh no, you'd be too young, but you'll know the one saying I mean: a rising tide lifts all boats. Made such sense because at first everyone, including my brother and me, thought that Nelson's new-found wealth may well benefit the village but they soon discovered he only wanted the rising tide to lift his own boat. We kept hoping and applying to get our property back but the year two thousand passed and nothing had happened in officialdom, so our time was over. Nelson and I do try to get on, and I should be more charitable. I mean, even if he does have the disposition totally unknown to science, we all have our faults. I personally have a drink problem."

"I'm sorry about that, Etta."

"Perhaps a bib would do the trick." She held out the end of her lime green blouse to show him a dried stain on it. "Orange juice. I do dribble. Terrible problem." Her glasses reflected a sunbeam or there was a definite twinkle in her eye, he wasn't sure which, but one thing for sure, this lady wasn't as wacky as she made out, there was a lot going on under that kaleidoscope of color.

He paused for barely a second before he asked, "Etta, do you know if there is any connection between Alaska and Nelson?"

"Well," she began but got no further because a voice from the cottage in the green oasis called, "*Senhora? Dona* Etta? Serafim's taking me to Sines in a minute. It's Friday. Would you like to come in and I'll show you what I made for lunch?"

Etta smiled at Leo. "Prazeres wants me. Time for a tinkle," she said, turned her back on him and walked towards her house. "Toodleloo ...*to shine for him all day.*"

CHAPTER TEN

Leo mulled over events as he leaned on a wooden five-bar fence.

A white van drew up beside him, and Serafim leaned across the passenger seat to talk to him through the open window. "Having a nice walk?"

"Yes. Awesome."

"You looking at the vineyards?"

"Right. Fabulous grapes you got there." Heavy crimson bunches strained on the vines like overweight children.

"Time for harvest soon. The villagers make quite a party of it—perhaps you'll stay for it. Quite different to the shebang they're preparing for this weekend at the Big House. Have you met *Dona* Etta yet? You have? I hoped you would. Quite an experience, eh? But she's a wise old bird, and not as batty as she makes out."

"I got that. She's no loony-tunes. Serafim?" Leo leaned down to look at the bearded face that peered through the window like a friendly werewolf. "You know anyone with a computer?"

"I have one, but I never use it and the battery's probably dead. Or maybe one of the kids in the village is using it right now. I don't know. Hate those things. Tell you what, Victor has one. Why not ask him, or Etta? Ah, here comes Prazeres, that's my wife. Gotta go, I'm taking her into Sines for her shopping. Be back in an hour or so."

A dark-haired woman with a round, pleasant face emerged from Etta's one-story cottage nestled in its green oasis of plants. She waved at him. "Hello," she called as she climbed into the van beside Serafim. "Didn't get a chance to talk last night. Hope Serafim fed you well."

"Thanks, ma'am." God, these people were just too damned amiable. But, then, they didn't know who he was, did they? Or why he was here.

Serafim's van disappeared down the track in a cloud of dust just as Leo's cell phone finally pinged to life, showing that at last it had a signal. He checked it but no one had called him or left a message since he'd left Anchorage. No surprises there then.

The signal, though, was so weak the Internet would take hours to connect. If he was going to be convincing that he belonged at the party Lili invited him to, he needed all the information he could get about John Hughes and this 3G whatever.

"Coo-eee."

He was still outside Etta's cottage, its dun-colored roof tiles and beige stone walls blending with the thick wood of pine trees behind the house. She was sitting in a wicker chair on a white, stucco porch. "I've lost Prazeres," she called. "Come and keep me company."

Her front path was checkered with uneven flagstones. "Ma'am, Etta. Do you have an internet connection I could use for a moment? My phone's not picking up much of a signal."

"Do the Portuguese like coffee? Of course we have one. A big one. Victor's always playing with it."

"I don't want to disturb him if he's using it."

"He's not on it now; he's up on the cliffs twitching. He's a twitcher."

"I'm sorry to hear that, Etta."

"Always after birds."

Etta seemed to be expert at talking about stuff totally off his horizon, but this time he reckoned he got what she meant—birds of a feathered kind.

Inside her cottage, Etta's notion of decoration must be to have Christmas every day, the more sparkles the better. In a room full of rainbows from sunlight shining through a variety of crystal lamps and decorations at the window, he picked his way around a leafless, dried up tree covered in blinking fairy lights, past what looked like a stuffed hairy brown dog, standing on its back feet with tinsel around its neck and a busboy's cap between its Bakelite ears and holding a plate of candies.

"It's through there." She pointed to a closed door he could only reach by negotiating three sofas covered in psychedelic-colored cushions. It was like being in a prism.

The Internet connection was fast, and he found John Hughes's 3GDeveloping on his first Google search. The company was a tiny real estate developer in Idaho and only seemed to have one person working there: John Hughes. Leo now had more bars on his cell and within a minute, he was talking to the man.

Leo told Hughes he was at the *Herdade Albatroz*, was sorry Hughes couldn't make it and hoped he wasn't sick.

Hughes hesitated a moment before he agreed it was a shame he couldn't get to the party.

"I'll be truthful with you, Mr. Hughes." Leo took a jump off the deep end and half-lied. "I'm here this weekend and I'm having serious doubts about whether I was wise to come."

A long pause followed while Hughes pondered. Leo hoped he wouldn't put the phone down.

"Who did you say you are?"

Leo looked around to make sure Etta wasn't listening. "Shine, Mr. Hughes."

"Mr. Shine. You're there representing which organization?"

That was a stinger. "I'm here as an investor, Mr. Hughes."

For someone who's obsessed with always telling the complete truth, bro, you're doing a humdinger of a lousy job here. Proud a ya.

"Individual investor?"

"Uh-huh. I don't have much to invest, but I also can't afford to lose it. I heard you weren't coming this weekend and just wondered if you'd heard anything contrary or negative about the investment propositions they're putting forward here."

"Look, Mr. Shine. I'm not here to make statements that might not be true or are just rumors. Suffice to say we've decided to pull out of the investment project Mr. Grady's presenting this weekend. Since you're an individual investor, I suggest you visit these sites." He reeled off three website addresses. "And make your own mind up. Mr. Shine, I wish you luck and a very good day."

The first site was a news item about a building project in East Asia in which rules and regulations had been flouted by authorities along with accusations of bribery, corruption and the use of influences. Investments had been made but because of the irregularities and accusations of money laundering, refunds had never been made. Several names of foreigners were involved, people the FBI and Interpol were still seeking, but none of them were familiar to Leo.

The second site was another snippet of news about a man called George Westerham who had fleeced several millionaires on an exclusive Caribbean island. He was still on Scotland Yard's wanted list.

Finally the third site was about officials in a European country being corrupted and bribed to invest in a US-Indian project selling military helicopters. Wesley Gibb from the US-Indian project, who was allegedly the one being charged, was still at large.

Leo looked back at the first story of the East Asian project and wrote down the names of those thought to be responsible, listing them on a piece of paper. One of them was a Gerald Walsh.

Sitting back in the chair, Leo tapped his fingers on the table as he studied the list of names: George Westerham, Wesley Gibb, Gerald Walsh. They all had their initials in common, even if they weren't always the same way round. Would someone be such a jackass to use the same initial? Someone, perhaps who's so full of himself, he thinks he can flip the cops off?

And what was the name of the guy currently at *Herdade Albatroz?* William Grady.

Bingo!

It was another lead. He was still puzzled about the story of Nelson and cocaine, and getting rich quickly. It would take a dimwit not to realize times were hard for the village. Nelson was part of the village and that house down in the valley must cost a fortune to keep going. This William Grady may well be the link between Luminosa and the *Goblin* disaster.

A man's voice wafted through the closed door, disturbing Leo's thoughts. "Really Etta, how do you know who he is? You do not invite strange people in."

"He's not strange," Etta replied.

"He's on my bloody computer."

Etta murmured something Leo couldn't catch.

"Is he?" Victor replied. "Oh."

The door opened and a man in his sixties came in wearing what Leo had seen in pictures of golfers a hundred years ago: knee length woolen pants, long socks and brogues. His only nod to the heat was a crisp white open-necked button-down shirt. A pair of binoculars hung from his neck.

"Well good afternoon," the man said, his hand stretched

out. "I'm Victor Fletcher."

"Afternoon." Leo shook his hand and nodded at the computer. "Your sister said it was OK to use it."

"No problem, my boy. Did you find what you wanted?"

Leo wondered how far to trust him. He was foxy-looking, red-faced and sweaty, with a regimental-straight haircut which Etta may have, no definitely, had a hand in cutting. Could Leo exclude him as a drug trafficker? He didn't look like one. But then Etta's Bakelite dog with the cap could be packed to the brim with heroin for all Leo knew.

Etta's jingling bracelets announced her arrival. "Victor, isn't it wonderful to have a guest?"

From Victor's immobile expression, it was obvious he wasn't as enchanted as his sister, although his thin lips did lift a tad in what could've been a smile. "Indeed it is. Now, tell me, what do you think of all this kerfuffle going on at the *Herdade* this weekend?" His voice made Leo think of rancid butter. "Or is it a big secret to you too, Tom?"

Tom!

Leo stared, unable to form a response.

His silence provoked a "Hmmm?" from Victor. Quick thinking now. Quick decision. Wouldn't it be a helluva relief to talk his heart out and unload? But how could he be sure of people he'd just met?

Etta saved him from the knotty problem, stamping her feet and putting her hands on her hips as she faced her brother. "Oh Victor. You're short of an inkling or two. The boy wanted to keep it quiet. Didn't I tell you that after Prazeres said Tom had arrived but was obviously trying to hide the fact that he was Tom?" She licked her bottom lip. "Does that make sense?" She looked at Leo. "You're a bit shy, aren't you, Tom?"

"Ah." The space between his ribcage expanded and the room seemed too bright.

"See?" She leaned forward, stood on tiptoe and planted a kiss on his forehead. "But it's all right, we can keep a secret, except I'll tell you an itsy-bitsy secret: problem is, everyone knows who you are. Well, everyone in the village, that is. And us. Don't suppose they know in the *Herdade* because they don't talk to anyone."

"How did you know?" Leo managed to stammer.

"Because we've been expecting you for *months*. Your uncle Serafim has been talking about nothing else non-stop: *Tom's coming. My nephew I never met. Look, here's a photo…*"

A jolt ran down Leo's sternum. "You had a photo?"

Etta raised her eyes at the ceiling. "Your dad sent one, *so we knew how to recognize you.*" She separated each word as if speaking to a moron. "Took you a while."

They had a photo. His father had sent one? When? Why?

But if they thought Tom still alive, then they didn't know about the *Goblin* going down—no one told them, which if they'd been involved, didn't make sense.

And, another fact filtered through his whirling mind, Serafim was his uncle! That would mean, his mother's brother. Leo's world shifted before he mentally shook himself. *Come on, get over yourself. So you have an uncle but nothing's clear yet, nothing's solved.*

Nevertheless, he felt a lightness in his spirit with the realization that it was unlikely Serafim was involved in the *Goblin's* demise, nor this odd couple. But that man down in the Big House, or the *Herdade*? That was a whole 'nuther thing. And just what was Lili's part in it all?

Victor clapped him on his back, yanking him from his thoughts. "Well, my boy, it's very nice to meet you and all that, but I think it's down to business, don't you?"

If he'd been playing cards, Leo would've pushed all in. "Yeah."

"So Tom. What have you been doing on my computer?"

Leo would carry on letting them think he was Tom. That was the right decision, he was sure—he wasn't denying anything and that's how it should be at the moment. After all, how could he trust a guy like Victor who smiled like a skull and who spent so much time on the cliffs with binoculars. How many goddamn birds were up there anyway?

"I've been up on the hilltop trying to see through to the property but, apart from a lot of activity backwards and forwards of people I don't know, I couldn't discover anything. Most annoying."

So Victor didn't only watch birds.

"I'm not sure what's going on, sir."

Etta dug her elbow into her brother's side. "Sir. Did you hear that? He called you *Sir.*"

"My dear, the young man is polite." Victor turned from his sister back to Leo. "Well, Tom. Since you belong to the village, so to speak…"

Leo gulped. He did? Well, yes, he supposed he did.

"…I think it behooves us all to see if that clown occupying my place at the *Herdade Albatroz* is trying to destroy us all. What have you found out?"

"Not much. Except I figure it's some kind of information exchange or presentation on development and investment incentives here."

Victor's eyebrows shot into his hairline. "*Here?*" he repeated. "Has Nelson gone off his rocker? What's he got to offer investors?"

"Codswallop?" Etta suggested.

"Let me show you what I found so far on your computer. You're right, there is a presentation going on this weekend down at the Main House and one of the organizers is William Grady. I don't like the sound of the guy at all." He showed Victor the sites Hughes had told him to read.

After studying the screen for several minutes and listening to Leo's theory about the suspects all having the same initials, Victor pinched the loose skin on his neck. Finally he cleared his throat and asked, "What do you think this man, this Grady fellow—I won't give him the courtesy of calling him gentleman—is going to present as an investment?"

"I believe it has something to do with the land around here. I could be wrong."

"They cannot be considering developing or selling the *Herdade*. The land does not belong to individuals. It's royal land, shall we say, and always has been even when it was gifted to the Fletchers, my family, for two hundred years. It's protected by the State and those that inhabit it pay to do so. Speaking of which, I do hear Nelson is hard-pressed to pay his way nowadays."

"How does he afford to stay there?"

"Lord knows. The maintenance must be very high now, although I do hear he's letting the place go downhill fast. The other costs, such as paying the lease is a very small amount, last updated in the early nineteen hundreds. Even the fields are rented out to the villagers for just a small amount, so he gets very little income. "

"Maybe there's some kind of illegal trafficking involved."

"There used to be. But now?"

"He really was involved in drugs? But not now?"

"Unlikely," Victor said. "Although not impossible. It's true Nelson made his initial money from being the middle-man in a Caribbean to Ireland drug run, but that was in the seventies. He's too old for all that now. The fortune he amassed at that time enabled him to take over the *Herdade* in the first place. He kept it ticking over until he married Lili five years ago. The problem of money then arose because Lili's always wanted to build up her ridiculous bullfighting dreams—horses and bulls, in that order, being all *she* thinks about—and she's using up his capital. She must've gone through most of it by buying those horses and state of the art stables in the first two or three years alone."

Leo's mind reeled. Lili was married to Nelson? And she'd been prick-teasing him like that?

Tough noogies, little bro.

Oh, Tom's voice never gave up. Leo took a deep breath to steady himself. "So what's he, this Nelson, been living on since then?"

"Good question. Especially as Lili is a very demanding, ambitious lady. But drug trafficking? I find it hard to believe."

"Maybe Lili's been involved."

Victor blew his nose, trumpeting like an elephant into a snow-white handkerchief before he replied, emphasizing every word, "She's not bright enough to set up something like that by herself. And she gets seasick, so she'd never take out a boat like Nelson did when he used to go out to pick up and deliver goods when the ships anchored in the bay."

"What about Gaspar?"

Victor blew his nose again and wiped it for nearly a minute before he said, "Gaspar hates anything to do with drugs. He might have helped Nelson in the seventies deals, but then he lost someone very dear to him because of them. He might be a cranky piece of work and thinks the world of Nelson and Lili, but I'd doubt he'd get involved in something like drugs. But," he picked at the gap in his front teeth with his pinky before he said, "this investment scam could be a cover-up that only Grady knows about. Or maybe they all do, they're so desperate for money."

Etta shuffled beside them. "It sounds like an American film where evil sweeps the planet and James Dean comes in and leads everyone to a new solar system."

"My dear, don't be a dope. This is serious."

"Not so dumb," Leo said. "Evil may well be in the village."

"And you're James Dean," Etta cried, clapping her hands.

"Believe you told me I was Steve McQueen earlier. In any case, I don't know any other universes."

"Forgive her, Tom. My sister lives in the seventies. Before you were born."

"Do not."

"Yes you do. You live somewhere completely off my radar. Now, Tom. Could you and I work together and uncover this dreadful plan to ruin my beloved village?"

Leo sucked on his upper lip, just long enough for Etta to say, "What're you going to do? Walk up to these charlatans and ask if they're involved in a fiendish plot? Oh good idea! What could possibly go wrong? Can I watch?"

Victor sighed. "We must think of a way. I do miss the old place, and if they think they can destroy it, they have another think coming because I'm going to fight it tooth and nail."

"Won't work," Etta said. "You bite your nails and you haven't got any teeth."

Leo's mind had been working hard. "Mr. Fletcher, sir. Do you mind if I write an email?"

Victor and Etta breathed over his shoulder as he typed.

"So you're going to pretend to be John Hughes, are you?"

Leo paused, his fingers over the keyboard. "Think it'll work?"

"We can but try."

"Will you back me up?"

"You can count on me, Tom."

"And me," Etta piped.

Well, fuck-me, Mr. Honest-to-Goodness. You got three sides to ya—Leo Shine, Tom Shine and this John Hughes. You ain't gonna manage to pull all that off, little bro.

CHAPTER ELEVEN

It was mid-afternoon when Leo left the Fletcher's cottage with a lighter heart than when he'd entered. He and the Fletchers had decided he should go ahead with the John Hughes plan so Leo could find out exactly what was going on. He now had a few hours to kill before arriving to meet Grady at the Main House for dinner at eight and where better to spend that time? Somewhere wild where the roaring of the sea would help him straighten his thoughts.

When he arrived down the hill to the glittering ocean, striped blue and white boats were entering the bay. The sardine fleet was returning and, with luck, the crews wouldn't say no to him giving them a hand to unload. As he made his way down to the wharf, he realized just how much he missed the smell of diesel and fresh fish.

Fishermen wouldn't be fishermen if they turned down any offers of help and these were more than happy to let him join them unloading the sardines in their plastic crates, weighing them and packing them in ice. And just like fishermen everywhere, they concentrated on their heavy work, grunting and swearing at the winches while pretending to smart-mouth the others—all in English, probably for Leo's benefit.

From what Etta had said, Leo had no doubt they all thought he was Tom, but no one said a word about it, nor even asked his name as they introduced themselves with typical fishermen's nicknames: Squidlips Gil, Flattie Fred, Gaffer Paulo, even Slippery Dick ("I prefer Ricardo") and Reeling Rui. Rui gave him a toothy smile. He was the youngest of the group, tall and lanky like Leo but with dark hair. He worked quietly, ignoring the chit-chat, although Leo noticed that he did frequently shoot glances in his direction.

Leo unhooked a crate from the winch onto the jetty and noticed a zebra-striped fish in amongst the silver sardines. He'd heard of those things, but had never seen one. "Holy hell, where'd this come from?"

"You know what that is?" Squidlips Gil asked.

Leo held it up by its dorsal fin and examined it. "It's a lionfish. It's not native to these waters. They have them in Florida, I heard, where they're also not native and they've become a pest. You know it's venomous?"

"Too right," Flattie Fred said. "First time we ever saw one I picked it up. Hurt like buggery."

Gaffer Paulo laughed. "He swore enough to raise the devil when it stung him."

"You want to be careful with these bastards. It's the spines here." Leo stretched one out at its base, avoiding its tip. "Dorsal and pelvic spines. That's where the venom is. It doesn't kill you but it's poisonous to other fish."

"Can something like that eat fish too? Because something is eating our sardine stocks and it isn't us."

"No idea," Leo said. "Not this fella, he's too small, he'll be feeding on your shrimps and mussels, though. But these things grow, at least big enough to eat young sardines."

"How about this one?" Gaffer Paulo waved off a group of gulls that were swirling and screaming round the wharf. He pulled a fish from a net. It was a sardine but had been partially eaten away.

Leo examined the mutilated fish. "Lionfish eat what they can fit in their mouths, they suck them in. They'll manage to ingest part of a sardine and that'll be it. I hear your sardine stock's declining and I guess this stripy sucker will be the reason for that."

"Grouper's down too."

"Yeah. They might be too big for lionfish to eat, but they'll chase 'em off, out of the area right enough. How long you noticed these lionfish about?"

"Started maybe a year ago. Perhaps less. We get them in the nets now and again and don't throw them back. We thought they were responsible for the sardines but if they eat mussels then that's a good thing, especially if they eat these little beggars." Ricardo went into the storehouse and came out with a box full of stinking shellfish.

Leo picked one up and examined it. "That's a green Asia mussel. See? It's green with a touch of brown. How did these get here?"

"God alone knows. Like these stripy devils, they're multiplying like crazy but the mussels clog up the hulls. We're having to scrape every few weeks"

"You'll probably have to scrape the hulls more often than that if you don't want them to spread. Jeez, these things give out toxins, I hear. No wonder the fish stocks are down, specially inland. You need experts here to get rid of them like a Marine Conservation organization. You got one of those?"

The one they called Squidlips Gil—and with reason, since it looked like he'd been at the lip-filler—said with a proud air, "We don't need to call on outside help. The bounty of the seas is our responsibility. It's how we live here. If we've got problems then we must deal with it ourselves."

"Fair enough," Leo replied. "But you got yourselves a helluva problem preventing these pests from spreading. The lionfish and mussels will cause a heap of damage to the local ecosystem."

"Show him the weed," Rui said, speaking for almost

the first time.

This time a box stinking to high-heaven came out of the warehouse. Leo tried to untangle a never-ending brown frond. "Looks like kelp," he said. "But I never saw it as big as this."

"We have kelp, but not this kind, whatever it is, and it's growing taller by the minute. There's a veritable forest of the stuff down there and is obliterating the bladderwrack and eggwrack which grow in neat rows, but this stuff is chaotic and just tangles everything, including our propellers and rudders."

Leo had never seen such a giant frond. "What do you do with it?"

"Rosa and Elsa from the village make pasties from the bladderwrack to help immune systems, they say. I say it tastes God-awful. Eggwrack goes to the cows. We tried this new stuff as fertilizer and the crop died which means it's toxic too."

"My God," Leo said. "You're under siege from toxins and pests. You getting any ships in the bay? Any that could be cleaning their ballasts out. Or are any of you visiting the Pacific or Asia and bringing the stuff back as pets?"

Was it Leo's imagination, or was the silence that greeted his question just a tad too long before someone—Flattie Fred—mumbled a reply? "Sometimes. They come in. Don't stay long."

"Recently?"

"A while back, year maybe."

Leo looked around him at the faces, worn and leathery with living and working hard, but all concentrating on anything other than him. "You never report them to the Coast Guard?"

The fishermen's faces hardened. "Like I said, we take care of our own," Paulo repeated Gil's words and turned away to weigh a crate of fish.

They then worked in silence without the earlier banter, clearing the hauls, hosing down the boats.

Finally, Paulo said, "Prazeres tried cooking them—those stripy fish. Zebra fish?"

"Lionfish," Leo told him.

"She pan-fries them in lemon butter. They were good and didn't kill us. She cuts off the spines and tentacles and we eat just the body meat. We tried it out on Flattie first—he didn't know what he was eating."

Flattie Fred jabbed his elbow at Paulo who dodged it. "You could've killed me!"

"We didn't though, did we?"

"Yeah, they're not poisonous to eat," Leo confirmed. "As long as you cut off the spines. Best thing to do to deplete them, catch 'em and eat them. But not the mussels, they're pure poison. You'll have to find some way of killing them."

Gaffie Paulo, who was probably the oldest of the group, said, "We need someone like Felipa Carneiro. She knew exactly which fish was where in the ocean."

"She did?" Leo was skeptical. How the hell could you do that without sonars and radar?

"I'm not lying," Paulo said, obviously hearing the doubt in Leo's voice. "All the girls in her family could. Right back through the generations. Felipa would say, *'you go out two and a half miles, three o'clock and you'll find a lovely shoal of bass, adult too.'* And, by damn, she'd be right. She'd see where all this weed was and the zebra or lionfish rubbish for us."

Must be folklore, Leo thought. "So what happened to her?"

"Dead and that was the end of the line."

There was another silence before Squidlips Gill asked with a smirk, "Do those lionfish eat squid?"

"Yep. If the squid's near enough land, and if they can

get a bit of the squid in their mouths. These things go about ten miles maximum offshore," Leo replied.

"Then, we'd best make the most of the squid we have left. Rosa, my cousin, she's got a squid stew, potatoes, tomatoes and clams waiting, and you're more than welcome to join us."

****

For the first time in nearly three months, Leo found himself whistling. He had no reason that he knew of to be happy, except the warmth of the sultry evening and the strange herby fragrances were sending his senses into overload.

It was dark when he crossed the main road to the trail that led to the *Herdade Albatroz*. A bus stopped at the top of the hill behind him and several people alighted, including two teenagers who followed him, giggling.

Two shagables on your tail, little bro.

Leo turned and checked out the two girls.

Tad thin, Tom's voice whispered in his mind, echoing Leo's thoughts. They'd better stay away from gratings, else they'll slip through.

But you still reckon they're shagable? he mentally asked his brother.

You bet your sweet…

Then you shag them.

Sweet Jesus, how he wished Tom was here to really have that old familiar banter.

He turned into the open gate where he found Lili staring at a clipboard. When she looked up and saw him, she said, "Dinner at eight o'clock. Anxious for it."

She is panting for it, bro.

Leo ran his hand through his hair, wondered about telling her he'd hold on to that thought, but before a word could pass his lips she'd landed, full-body, smack slam-bang on his chest. She must've tripped.

As he steadied her, he became aware of a girl with dark eyes observing him. She wasn't one of the teenagers that had been following him, she was slightly older and shorter with fine feathery light brown hair, and she looked at him with a small frown creasing the bridge of her freckled nose.

He set Lili back on her feet and glanced at the solemn-looking girl who still studied him with an intensity that made him feel like liquid gold had been poured through him. The sensation made him shiver, and he wasn't sure if he liked it or whether it creeped him out; he just didn't understand it. So he turned his attention to Lili and said, "Eight o'clock. I'll be there." It was only when he was halfway across the lawn that he realized the impression the girl had had on him wasn't unlike the first time he'd felt energy from sea-currents.

Chapter Twelve

It was night as the bus trundled off in a cloud of exhaust. Piper disembarked and watched Henrique and Elsa waddle down a dark lane into what seemed like a black chasm. Two girls who'd also been on the bus crossed the road to a path, not more than a trail, that went in the opposite direction.

"I'll walk up with you." Prazeres took Piper's elbow and led her across the road behind the girls. "I need to check on *Dona* Etta to see if she needs anything so I'm going your way."

The girls, who were giggling and pushing at each other, weren't much more than teenagers, their youthful figures in tight jeans and vests. The target of their barely stifled enthusiasm was a figure walking ahead of them: a man, whiplash lean, whose hair almost reached his shoulders and gleamed in the moonlight. He sauntered along, his hands in his pockets, with that sort of sailor's roll to his walk, the kind needed to balance on a bucking ship and not on the land. The girls giggled again, louder, and Piper had to admit his rear view, even in worn denims with a tear between the knee and his, well, bottom, was worth ogling. The man looked round at the sound of the girls, but said nothing and just continued on his way, his boots stirring up dust. He hadn't come off the bus, Piper was sure.

It wasn't long before lights shone through the tall rustling plants on either side of the rough path, and a wrought iron gate came into view.

"Here you are," Prazeres announced, "*Herdade Albatroz.*"

The man, closely followed by the two young giggling girls, turned into the open gate where a woman with a clipboard waited.

"That's Lili," Prazeres told Piper, nodding towards the woman. "The one who looks like she bought her trousers when she was three sizes smaller, that's who you need to talk to. Good luck, dear. Hope to see you again." With a pat on Piper's arm, she carried on up the trail.

Lili was a lovely-looking woman. Piper never usually bothered to think about what people looked like. They could be ugly, non-descript or disfigured; it was all the same to her as long as they didn't give her funny looks or whisper about her behind her back. But this woman caught her eye with her midnight black hair, huge dark eyes fringed with sweeping eyelashes and that type of bow-like mouth Piper thought only existed in characters of romance novels. But when the woman looked at her, something Tolstoy wrote sprang into Piper's mind: *it is amazing how complete the delusion that beauty is.*

Lili's eyes narrowed in what seemed like annoyance as she surveyed the two girls and Piper, creating frown lines that deepened those already there; the woman wasn't as young as she first appeared. She fired off a machine gun of tongue-defying Portuguese and the two girls stared at their shuffling feet, mumbling something sounding like an affirmative. Whatever they'd said seemed to go some way to appease Lili, because she turned to Piper with a stretched rictus of a smile that showed off her gums while she tapped her pen impatiently on her clipboard.

Perhaps reacting to Piper's blank stare, Lili sighed and turned to the young man, her cheeks dimpling. She lowered her eyelids. "Eight o'clock dinner, John," she said in strongly accented English, her voice full of suppressed emotion, and giving him a knowing glance as she added, "anxious for it."

Piper took a better look at him. His hair was amazing, not white and dry like some old geezer's but white-blond and sparkling with life, disheveled and windblown, although not a breeze stirred the air. The color went well with his beach-bum tan.

His eyes assessed Lili, and he pushed his hair back from his brow. Piper just bet he was about to come back with an equally cringe-worthy response but before he could utter it, Lili stumbled as if her high heels had caught in a grass divot. It took all of Piper's effort not to roll her eyes at the sky. What a dork: Lili hadn't tripped on anything in the flat manicured grass. She'd done it on purpose, any fool could see that and if it had been Piper standing next to her, she'd have let her fall flat on her face. But the man reached out to steady her and when she plastered herself against him, his eyebrows rose in what could've been surprise or pleasure, but probably the latter.

"Eight o'clock. That's fine," he responded in a warm, chocolate brown voice—an American—as he set her gently back on her feet.

"That's five minutes," Lili called as the guy she had named John sauntered off. "Do not be late."

What was the deal with those two? Faulty knicker elastic more than likely.

Lili said something to the girls who headed off towards the marquee, while Piper sucked her lip and wondered whether she should go with them or stay where she was.

She stayed put. "I actually didn't quite get," she said when Lili turned to her, "…well, didn't get anything really of what you just said. I'm here on the off-chance. I heard there was work this weekend. You see, I don't speak Portuguese. I'm English."

"English. May be useful." Lili tapped her teeth with her pencil and then nodded. "OK. What I tell the two girls was others peoples arrive to work much earlier today." She waved a hand at a group of people who were gathered near the marquee. "And they already work preparing for tomorrow. So I think it *justo* you work now and they rest. Is OK?" Her accent was heavy as if she was chewing every word, unlike Prazeres's and the others on the bus.

"OK. Does that mean I'm hired? You know, *accepted?*"

"Is OK. Kitchen now, serve tomorrow, be nice to guests in English. Now write your name." Lili handed her the clipboard and pencil.

When Piper finished squiggling a name, she handed the board back to Lili who squinted at it. "Pippa?"

"Piper." She'd decided that keeping to Piper was safe. After all, her real name was Philippa, and she was worried that if she called herself something else she might not answer to it.

"Smit?"

"Smith." It was only half a lie, wasn't it?

"Smit. What I said."

"How much will the salary be?"

Lili frowned. "Not good with numbers in English." She scratched her neck. "Seven euros per hour. Depend how much hours you work. Cash. No checks. Pay at end."

Cash was cash. "OK."

"Kitchen now."

Piper followed the woman who stalked off, now perfectly balanced on her high heels.

The heat she'd experienced in Sines at the height of the day was nothing compared to the swelter given off by the kitchen's iron range that took up the width of one wall. Their footsteps clicked over giant flag-stones, grubby with footprints and spilled food that had been trodden in, probably from the staff using it during the day. Otherwise, the place spoke of sturdiness and tradition.

Lili turned to Piper. "Your first little thing to do is give kitchen good clean," she said.

Right now, the kitchen looked like a dozen people had sloshed food around to see how much they could get on the floor. The sink was full of dirty crockery, grime and gunge clung to the taps, and the range was splattered in grease.

Lili was looking at the ceiling where a spider had built its web from the rafters to one of the copper saucepans hanging on the wall. "If we feed public people," she said, perhaps talking to the spider, "maybe inspector come tomorrow to verify hygiene. Please, thank you, sorry, pardon." Lili laughed, her mouth stretching so that her gloss lipstick looked like she was dribbling. "Is what you English say all the time. Yes?"

No, Piper silently replied. And when you're looking in the mirror, have a go at practicing to make your smile reach your eyes.

"Dinner time now," Lili went on, sparkling like the stones in her necklace. It was a no-brainer that she was excited over something. Could that something be someone called John? "Food is already in place. Later maybe you come to take plates? Yes? Sorry? In dining room. Thank you, pardon." Her appreciation of her own wit trailed with her out the room.

Piper was about to wash a pan that held burnt-on remains when her stomach rumbled with hunger. A half-eaten fish pie that sat on the now-scrubbed table smelled off to her, so she balanced on a chair and used a sharp knife to hack at one of the hams hanging from the ceiling. The remains of a corn-meal loaf provided the perfect sandwich. She filled a chunk with thin slices of the salty ham.

Voices sounded just outside the kitchen door while she was taking a gulp of red wine from a brown clay jug. Piper heard doors opening and closing in the half hour she'd been scrubbing the floor, but this was the first real activity that intrigued her. She placed her ear to the door.

"It's not him," a man said with an American accent. His voice sounded gravelly, not like the white-blond guy's smooth way of speaking.

"You certain?" Lili asked. "But you never meet him, you say. How you know?"

"I've been told John Hughes is near retirement age."

"Maybe you confused."

"No, darling." The man's voice sounded tight as if he was talking through his teeth. "My memory's perfect. When I heard that he was older, I thought it very positive because it would mean, well...it would be good."

"Why?"

The man sighed. "Because, honey, older people can't hear too well. They make mistakes like the difference between seventy and seventeen. As in returns and percentages."

"That make no sense to me."

Piper peeked through the small gap in the kitchen door. None of it made much sense to her either except John Hughes was apparently an imposter. Wasn't the bloke she saw earlier called John? She squinted through the gap. Crikey, there was another six-foot hunk of totty out there. This one had hair as black and glossy as Lili's and swept back from his face in a wave, Dracula-style. Piper pressed her ear to the crack in the door to hear properly.

The dark-haired man continued. "Shall we just say you'll have a better income from your investment if he makes a mistake. But, back to what is important right now. That man is not John Hughes so how in the fucking name of glory did he slip in? You assured me your security was tight."

"My security," Lili piped, "is one to second."

"Second to none, I hope. In any case, it's not good enough. Didn't you ask him for identification?"

Heavy breathing filled the ensuing pause during which Piper assumed Lili was thinking. Finally, Lili said, "I think I saw him take his bag to his room."

"So what's in it?"

"I don't know. I don't look…"

The man sighed heavily. "OK, I get the message. The thing could contain anything from a bomb to a tape recorder. Get your second to one security to check this man out and I suggest now. Then come straight back into the dining room, otherwise he'll start getting suspicious at your absence."

"Gaspar is with Nelson at the moment, William."

"Gaspar? He's all the security you got? Jesus Christ."

"We save money this way *mas* now idiot Nelson say he need him."

"I demand you have better security."

"Darling William, *querido*. Security very expensive. I don't have money with all I spend already."

"It's a false saving. Didn't I promise that by the end of the weekend your money problems will be solved and then some? And you assured me there would be security. Lili, do you realize that allowing anyone to come in can jeopardize the whole project?"

"*Calma.* I have idea. You go in dining room. I will organize it to find out who this man John really is. I get his bag, OK?"

Uh-oh, Piper thought. Sounded like the white-haired hunk was busted.

CHAPTER THIRTEEN

Having changed his t-shirt in his room, Leo went to the dining room where he was the first to arrive. He examined the dark wood panels and the worn tapestries of hunting scenes on the walls, the crystal chandelier, and the ceiling decorated with a painting of a dome. Was that what they called *trompe l'oeil* in the art world?

That's right, bro. You always did know what a kick up the art was.

Then Lili waltzed in wearing pretty much half of nothing, accompanied by a tall dark-haired man around Leo's age, perhaps a year or two older.

"*Querido*," Lili said.

The little Spanish Leo had picked up from Hispanic crew members was enough for him to know that meant *darling*.

She wasn't talking to Leo, though, because she then turned to him and said, "John, here is Mr. William Grady from our company Albatrozinvest." She let out a nervous laugh. It wasn't the first time he'd heard her do that; it must be nerves.

The man regarded him with a searching stare and nodded.

Lili fluttered around the sideboard where dishes of steaming food had been placed on hotplates. "Please eat, sirs. I do not eat anything with a face. This food for you."

Whatever it was, it didn't smell as appetizing as Rosa's squid stew. In any case, Leo wasn't hungry and, it seemed, neither was William Grady who regarded the food as if it might rise up and bite him.

"So exciting this party," Lili exclaimed. "John, to remember you the agenda: Tomorrow after lunch I give opening ceremony. Second, *Senhor* Grady gives his presentation to other guests who arrive in the morning. Then my husband, Nelson, sign contract. Cannot wait. William, *querido*, you want talk to John all about it?"

So Nelson really was her husband; just a tiny part of him had wondered if he'd got the wrong idea when Victor mentioned it, but here was confirmation. What in hell was this woman doing calling Grady darling and giving Leo a *come-on* every time she set eyes on him?

"Lili," Grady said, his voice sharper than a razor. "A quick word if I may just outside." His slightly pointed eye-teeth gave him the look of a feral animal.

"Excuse, excuse," Lili apologized to Leo, giving him a wave with her fingers as Grady guided her outside.

With his ear to the door, Leo listened to them whispering outside the door and heard the name *John Hughes* who, Grady said, was older.

Leo was *mucho* in the shit, then. Not much else to do but play it cool. He stood with his hands behind his back and pretended to examine one of the worn tapestries on the wall, hoping Victor's email had come in.

When William Grady returned, his face wasn't red with anger, as Leo expected, but rather it had fallen in on itself as if with tiredness. He also looked rather yellow about the gills. "So, John Hughes," he said. "Tell me about yourself."

Try not to gabble like a duck's clacker, little bro. And I'll ask God to stop you from being a doofus.

But before Leo could come up with anything plausible, Grady grimaced, clutching his stomach. Leo managed to jump backwards as Mr. William Grady gave a huge belch and threw up on his highly polished brogues.

Chapter Fourteen

"Now listen careful," Lili whispered to Piper in the kitchen.

I vill only say zis vunce. Piper stifled a snort as the well-known phrase from a telly program came to her.

"You go up the stairs and into Mr. Hughes's room, number two door."

"Number two door," Piper repeated, and sniggered.

"Right. You take his bag to me. OK? You understand?"

Just about keeping up, Piper thought as she climbed the spiral staircase, pausing on every other step to stare at the faces gazing out of the paintings lining the wall. She was sure that all of the eyes followed her progress up the stairs and into the second room on the right.

For someone supposed to be invited to a posh party, this bloke, John thingy, hadn't tried very hard because his stuff was far from impressive: just a scuffed hold-all that looked as if it had been kicked half way across the world. He hadn't even unpacked it except to put on another t-shirt. The one he had on a little earlier was balled up on the floor under the chair. When she unrolled it, the musky smell of a male who'd been in close contact with fish filled her nostrils. She held it up to get a better look at the slogan on the front: *I Got Bait.*

She folded it up and packed it inside the bag, taking two pieces of folded paper out so they wouldn't get crumpled. OK, so she was nosy, but who wouldn't be about a guy who was over six feet of hard muscle and whose eyes had crinkled at the edges in an intriguing way when he looked at her earlier and who was pretending to be someone he wasn't.

She unfolded the first paper. Interesting. It was a print-out of the tides and water levels around the Portuguese south-western coast covering the area from Lisbon to Sagres in the south. Only a sailor would be interested in that kind of information. Or a fisherman. Wasn't there a saying that fishermen always recognize other fishermen?

She tucked it away and took the other paper out.

This one was a newspaper cutting with the headline: *Inquiry into Fishing Boat Sinking.*

The photo was a little grainy but it showed two men, George and Tom Shine, according to the title. Next to them was a picture of a seiner of some kind called *Goblin.*

"Piper!" Lili called from downstairs.

Whoops. She had to hurry. Except that photo intrigued her… She looked closer at the younger man's photo and her heart leapt. She recognized that suggestive smile that could only mean trouble. Tom Shine was the man downstairs who was calling himself John Hughes.

"Piper!"

OK, OK. She scanned down the first paragraph. Coast Guard Investigation concluded the *Goblin* had been hit by a rogue wave.

"Piper!"

Wait a sec. What was this? The *Goblin's* cargo included walrus tusks? Bear belts? Jesus H. Her eyes caught the word *trafficking.* Both men missing. But they weren't—at least one of them was here. She knew exactly what that kind of traf-ficking meant: trading in the animal corpses for drugs to sell. That man downstairs was the biggest bastard ever to walk into her sphere.

"Piper! Pelo amor de Deus!"

"Coming, coming." Piper stuffed the paper back in the bag.

"Piper! Leave the bag. Come *now.*"

Piper threw the bag, half-closed back on the floor and headed for the door. Then she turned back—she should take the bag down and reveal the bloke for the dirty fraud he was.

"Piper!" Lili sounded panicky, her voice shriller than ever and Piper hesitated. It sounded like someone was being murdered, so she'd better go; she'd deal with the bag later, perhaps present it to the police who'd know how to handle it better than dizzy Lili.

As Piper hurried down the stairs, she imagined a beach somewhere in north USA where dozens of innocent brown headless walrus carcasses and pink-skinned bears without their fur were rotting and being pecked at by the gulls.

Tom Shine was no better than a primordial germ at the bottom of a stagnant pond. She could just imagine his long-boned body standing proud at the prow of his new seiner, its hold full of bloody tusks and packs of cocaine or heroin or whatever he was going to sell to kids when they got out of school. Didn't they put it in their ice-creams? Double-bastard. Why, she'd bet he and his dad had sonar on board that could trace the shoals, so when the drugs ran out they'd go fishing by dropping a stick of dynamite overboard to slaughter fish by the thousands and bugger the dolphins and species at risk.

So their boat had sunk, had it? Good. She'd bet anything that they'd got in a life raft after the wave hit—or maybe they scuttled the beautiful ship, the kind Piper dreamed of owning, on purpose—and then made a run for it. Tom had ended up here and maybe his great wazzock of a father was on some nefarious mission somewhere else. Did Lili know what kind of person was in their midst? Actually, she didn't care too much about Lili, but did kind, motherly Prazeres who was so proud of her village know?

As Pop would say, "Oi'd trust tha' boy as much as a charleypig in me strawberries."

Lili stood at the open dining room door, swaying from one foot to the other as if desperate for the loo, her large eyes round like saucers. "Quick! *Rapido.* This not good. Not good."

At first Piper thought John or Tom Shine or whatever-the-hell his name was had murdered someone, but the stink of vomit in the dining room made Piper take a step backwards right into Lili who pushed her back inside.

There, the dark-haired man, Grady, was bent over an ever-growing pool of yellow slime, retching and groaning, while the white-blond bastard, Tom, bent over him.

What had the drug-trafficking, bear-killing *warthog* done to the poor guy? The imposter looked up at her as she approached, and she gave him her number one scary-look and felt an itch of pleasure when he looked surprised. *Yew gonna gi' 'im a clout round the lug, Pips?*

Not yet, she mentally replied to her Pop's voice. But it wouldn't be long…

Grady's face was pallid and haggard, and to Piper he looked to be at death's door.

"You need to call a doctor," Piper told Lili who was still hanging on to the side of the door, her face pale.

"No." Grady lifted a weary hand. "No doctor. Just bed. I'll be fine."

"Gaspar!" Lili yelled up the stairs in a voice so raucous the pictures on the wall shook. Then she addressed Piper. "Go," she said, shushing with her hand that held a paper as if Piper was a pesky fly, "go get *something* to clean. Cannot have this *porcaria* for tomorrow. And smell." Her pert nose crinkled. *"Go."* Pushing Piper out of the door, Lili then headed for a different room and shut the door behind her.

Coward, Piper thought.

It was, Piper admitted as she returned to the kitchen in

search of a mop, disinfectant and a bucket, quite a relief to get away from the rank stench, but the bugger of it was that she had to go back and clean it up. When she returned to the hall, the walrus killer, whose eyes she decided now looked shrewd and avid like a cat's, and another man who must be Gaspar, were hauling Grady up the spiral staircase, while Lili brought up the rear waving a piece of paper and gabbling.

"Is good, no?" she said, seemingly aiming her words at Grady's green face. "I check email now and I receive email from 3GDeveloping. I sorry I didn't see it before. Come hours ago. Says, *John Hughes Senior will not be coming but will be sending son John Hughes Junior instead.* See? All is well. John," she said to the bear-pelt trafficker, "why you not say you the son?"

"I did," the fraudster said, puffing with the effort of climbing the stairs backwards and supporting Grady under his arms.

"Oh. Then I not understand. Sorry. My English. How funny."

Funny? Every ounce in Piper's body wanted to yell. It's downright *wrong* you plonker of a Lili. John Hughes—he's Tom Shine! But the moment she took a look at the dining room floor and the malodorous drips that led to the stairs, every thought fled from her mind except that she needed to clean up the filthy mess before it ruined the beautiful carpet.

By the time she'd finished, she felt too nauseous to do any more work and the thought of washing up the dinner dishes made her heave. It was time for bed. But one thing was sure, at the first opportunity she was going to *out* that guy Tom Shine—perhaps to Prazeres. Yes, she'd be the best person.

Piper found the staff dormitory housed in a small chapel near the stables. It was impossible to see if it was single-sex, because the dozen or so sleeping people were covered up with sheets and only their hair poked out. There weren't any mattresses free, so Piper would have to sleep on the stone floor, and, anyway, the tombs around the walls spooked her out.

She'd find somewhere more private.

As she passed the stables block, a horse, looking over his doorway, snorted at her. She jumped at the sudden sound and stopped. It thrust its grey head up and down. "Hello," she said. The horse stamped and its ears went back when she approached.

She held out her hand until the horse finally stilled and studied her with shiny dark eyes. "It's OK," she whispered, tentatively holding out her hand and was surprised when it snuffled its soft nose in her palm, probably seeking sugar or an apple. An empty stall next to the horse's was full of fresh straw. "Can I sleep there?" She was rewarded with a toss of the horse's head. "I'll take that as a yes, then, shall I?"

She drew back the catch on the stall and stepped in. It was hot inside, the air thick with the smell of horse, straw and shit but a million times better than that mausoleum of a dormitory.

Flattening the straw, she lay down and wondered if the dark-haired man, Grady, was feeling better and if he had anything catching, in which case Tom Shine would be wonderfully incapacitated tomorrow. And she'd be damned if she was going to clean it if he vomited on the floor.

Something furry skittered in the darkness and a small lizard with sucker-like toes watched her from the wall. With a tired smile, she wished them a good night, closed her eyes and went to sleep.

CHAPTER FIFTEEN

Thank God Victor Fletcher helped him create the false email address on his computer and even copy 3GDevelopment's logo. They'd even temporarily changed Victor's name to John Hughes to make the message look even more authentic. If there was anything unusual on the email, Lili didn't notice.

Grady was now flat out on the bed, a bucket on hand to catch whatever he still had to bring up. Gaspar stood with his hands on his hips and his nose screwed up against the smell that permeated the room, while Leo glanced around and spotted what seemed to be a roll of plans on the dresser. While Gaspar and Lili's attention was on Grady, Leo sidled closer to the dresser, grabbed the plans, backed out into the hall and headed to his room where he could study them spread out on the bed.

They were building plans as far as he could make out and a detailed map of the area, showing Luminosa fishing village, the beach, the land just north of the *Herdade* and the main house clearly marked in pink.

Leo sat back on his heels. According to these papers, if completed, the *Herdade*, its land and the whole village would be turned into housing plots, a hotel, a couple of golf courses, a leisure center, and a large shopping mall, or, "retail outlet park" as it said on the map, complete with a huge parking lot.

"Piper!" Lili's voice echoed through the walls and Leo's closed door.

The very mention of that girl, Piper, left Leo scramble-brained. She'd looked so ticked-off at him in the dining room earlier, as if he'd been the one to vomit all over the floor and on purpose at that. Although he felt he didn't deserve that look, Lili shouting at her like she was some kind of slave made him uncomfortable, and he wanted to defend her.

"Any problem?" he asked, sticking his head out of his door.

Lili was leaning over the bannisters, her rear end, which had attracted him earlier, well to the fore. "I need that girl to stay in William's room."

"I reckon he needs a medic, you ask me."

"He doesn't want. If girl sleep in the room, then she can…help if he vomit…" She waved her hand in front of her face as if to bat off smells before she set off down the stairs at a run.

Leo followed her. "You can't do that to someone, subjecting them to a night of that."

Lili made no reply and headed straight to the disinfectant-smelling kitchen, but Piper wasn't there, thank God.

"I find her," Lili said. She kicked off her high heels and sprinted at the speed of a thoroughbred across the lawn in the direction of the marquee.

Having picked up an apple from a bowl, Leo took a large bite and stepped down the broken steps from the kitchen into the warm night. He'd wait around here to make sure Lili didn't bring the girl back in; if she did, there might be a tug-of-war with each pulling on one of Piper's arms and then he'd definitely call a medic.

The sky was a wonder. It was rare to see the constellations with such clarity even while at sea. Nothing could beat the Alaskan aurora borealis but this overhead mantle of glitter was also spectacular in its own way and proved there couldn't be air pollution here, which made the idea of the polluted sea down in the bay all the harder to bear. If, with any luck, he found what he was seeking and his vengeance lay outside the village, then he wouldn't mind staying on a while here and helping the villagers destroy those pests.

Hitch your wagon to a star, son.

I'll do my best, Dad, Leo mentally replied to his father's much remembered advice. Which one would he choose? The moon's rugged cratered surface seemed closer than he'd ever seen it and Jupiter, the Ursa Major and Minor, Cassiopeia, the Milky Way, they were all so clear. He wondered if anyone in the village had a sextant. Tom and his dad took the piss out of him for preferring to calculate celestial navigation the old way instead of using GPS. He liked figures—and not the ones Tom was fond of.

He wandered farther from the kitchen, and a horse snorted at him from the stables. "Hi big guy," he whispered, holding out the apple. "You still awake?"

As the horse crunched down on the fruit, a movement to one side caught Leo's eye. He'd always had good night vision and could see in the dark like a cat, his father always said, probably some other crazy notion about being born with a caul. He squinted into the dark. If he wasn't mistaken, someone was lying in the straw in the next stall and it wasn't a horse.

It was her: Piper, the person Lili was at this moment searching for, curled up asleep around her fists.

What was it about this girl? Every time he saw her he felt like he was floating in a pocket of warm air. He sat on a bale of hay and leaned back against the stable wall. Even when he closed his eyes, he could visualize her slender figure, dark honey-colored hair and he could swear, although they were closed and there was no light, she had hazel eyes.

****

She knew he was there, watching her. Any decent fisherman could tell what was going on at any given time within a three-mile radius twenty-four hours a day.

If he touched her, she'd dock him one from here to kingdom come, and he'd be singing falsetto for the rest of whatever life he had left to him.

He might think he was quick, but she bet she was quicker. Once, when she and Pop were crewing on a long-liner, a guy had copped a feel of her arse as she leaned over the gunwale to help the hydraulic hauler, and she'd had him strung up ready for fish bait before he'd had time to remove his paw from her rear. Word had got round and she'd never been bothered by anyone again, but that might have been because she and Pop had moved soon after.

Jesus, anyone who could hear her thoughts would label her a frigid old virgin. Part of that was right: she might be twenty-two years old and never had a boyfriend or sex, but that was because she had no idea how to go about flirting, even if she wanted to. Maybe she was antisocial, or maybe guys just thought she was weird and gave her a wide berth. It didn't help, she knew, that if anyone did find their way to the Pines's well-hidden doorway, then they'd have to get by the great bear-figure of her Pop who eyed them as a scientist eyes a deadly virus on the loose.

Lili's voice trickled in from outside as she passed the stables talking to someone in Portuguese. The guy, the blond drug trafficker who encouraged animal torture, moved away from the stable door as silently as a cat without displacing any air, probably sniffing after Lili, who was welcome to him. Good riddance.

Remembering she hadn't called Pop to tell him she'd

arrived safely, she reached into her linen bag and pulled out her mobile. Bum! The battery was dead. Nothing she could do until morning, so she settled back down in the fragrant straw, while the horse in the next stall crunched like an old man grinding his teeth in his sleep.

CHAPTER SIXTEEN

A distant cock crowing and a dog barking in response woke her. For a moment she wondered where she was, but the smell of straw reminded her and she sat up, scratching her scalp. A blanket dropped to her waist. What the…? And a pillow? Had he done that? Why hadn't she woken?

Oh boy, she was losing her touch. If he'd touched her in any way… Wait, why did she assume it was the blond git? It might have been…well, it hadn't been Lili that was for sure.

Swearing under her breath, she checked her linen bag—it was in the same place she'd left it—to make sure nothing was missing from it. Nope. Even the dead mobile phone was still on top of the documents where she'd left it. She got to her feet and kicked at the flattened straw in the corner where he'd sat. The noise made the horse in the next stall snort.

"Did you see him?" she asked.

The horse nodded.

"Then why didn't you tell me?"

The horse nodded again.

The lawn outside was drenched in dawn-cool dew that glittered on the grass like diamonds. A light mist bathed the eaves and dormer windows on the roof of the Main House as the sky began to turn from lavender to pink.

She caught a whiff of herself, went back into the stable stall and asked the horse, "You got any water?" It ignored her. "You're no good. Oh there's some." A hose attached to a tap. It was bloody cold but the water refreshed her and went just a little way to make her feel cleaner. She changed in to the clothes she'd bought in Sines yesterday, new underwear, t-shirt and jeans, stuffed her feet into her old sneakers and then headed back outside towards the marquee, hoping she might find some breakfast. On the way she passed trees loaded with pink flowers, another with what looked like red peppercorns dangling from its branches, and a wall covered with a cascading brilliant pink bougainvillea as bright as Lili's lipstick.

"*Bom dia,*" said a voice. It was one of the teenage girls she'd followed from the bus last evening.

"Hello. You on your own?"

"*Sim.* Everyone…" The girl made a vomiting noise.

"Sick?"

"*Sim.* Not me."

"What about your friend? The girl you came with yesterday?"

The girl looked at Piper sideways and spoke from behind her hand. "She go sleep with man in house."

"She did what?" She went to bed with Tom Shine? The girl only looked about sixteen. That bastard knew no limits. Bunching her fists, Piper had a good mind to go into his room and knock him out, stone cold sober. Why was she so angry? What did it matter if he was in bed with a girl? She hoped he was sleeping in the wet spots, yes she did. The guy was a devious prick, yet—she wiped her hands on the sides of her jeans—she'd felt the energy in him, the force of his wanting her and a flame of pleasure blinded her for a moment.

"Piper!" cried a shrill voice.

Oh God, just what she needed before breakfast. Lili.

"Kitchen. Go!"

"I haven't had breakfast yet."

"Eat there. Kitchen."

"Haven't you ever heard of the word *please?*" Piper said in an undertone as she made her way across the wet lawn. Still, kitchen meant food.

A bulky woman with glossy, silver-streaked long dark hair leaned on the kitchen table, talking rapidly to a one-eyed man with a crabby face and nicotine-stained eyebrows. Piper recognized her as the pleasant lady, Prazeres, from the bus yesterday, and she remembered him as the man who'd helped the sick man up the stairs last night. What was his name? Gaspar? He stared at her, somewhat too blatantly, she thought. Where in hell did he get such an awful scar that ran from his blind eye to his mouth? Without a word he turned and left the room.

"Prazeres!" she cried. How lovely it was to see her friend again.

Prazeres turned and gave Piper a wide smile, showing her strong white teeth and emphasizing her apple-cheeks. "How's it going, sweetie?"

Well, if you didn't count cleaning up vomit, sleeping in a stable and getting yelled at by a banshee every five minutes, it was going swimmingly. But she hated whiners so all she said aloud was, "I haven't had breakfast yet."

"I'll fix that." Prazeres cracked two eggs into an already hot frying pan.

"I thought you weren't going to be here this weekend."

"I was summoned, Piper. Lili's good at that if she wants something." Prazeres buttered toast and covered it with creamy scrambled eggs before placing it in front of Piper.

"Thank you."

Once Piper had wolfed down her breakfast and complimented Prazeres on her excellent cooking, she peered at her mobile phone. "You don't know where I can recharge this, do you? I really need to make a call."

"Lili will probably say we're using her electricity if we

try doing it here. Tell you what, we can recharge it at home and if your call's urgent, use the phone in the office." She glanced through the open door. "Go on. You've probably got five minutes before Lili appears; she's out there running in ever-widening circles like a chicken without a head."

****

"Pop?"

"Where are yew, Pip?"

"In Luminosa."

"Oh moi sweet Jesus, Oi prayed yew would change your moind and wouldn't woind up there. Come on home, girl. Are yew OK? Where exactly are yew in tha' owd place?"

"I'm fine. I'm actually earning some money and then I'll come home on Monday. I've met Prazeres."

"She's a good woman, but yew don't tell no one who yew are. We agreed."

"We did, Pop. Relax, I'm fine."

"Why don't yew come home roight now?"

"It's not so easy, Pop. My ticket's for Monday and I do need money."

"Oi'll pay whatever it is."

"And just how you going to do that, Pop? What you going to sell this time? Is there anything left?"

The pause this time was filled with his heavy breathing, and talking to him in that harsh way made regret stab her heart. "I'm sorry, Pop. Listen, I'll take care. I promise. And I won't tell anyone who I am." It wasn't his fault she'd ended up here with hardly any money left.

"Piper!" Lili's voice pierced the air.

"Oh sorry, Pop, I've got to go. I'll talk soon, promise. And don't worry."

"Take care, my Pips."

The softness in his voice made tears well and her determination was shaken for a second. Maybe she should just leave, but then, she reasoned, maybe by staying she could make things right for Pop, for her and for whoever wouldn't be happy to know she was in the village. And she did so want to know about her mother.

"Piper!"

Oh that woman. What did she want, now?

Wiping her eyes, she went back into the kitchen to find Lili and Prazeres glaring at each other. Prazeres issued a stream of what sounded like angry words.

Lili screwed her fists into her eyes and when she looked up, more lines creased her face, her mouth was downturned and her shoulders drooped. She seemed to have aged ten years.

"What's wrong?" Piper asked Prazeres.

"All her special catering workers are vomiting in the marquee."

"Sick," Lili spoke through her teeth and gave a scoffing laugh.

"They need a doctor," Prazeres said, her mouth a firm straight line.

"They go home. I not pay for doctors. They call taxis to take them home if necessary, but they pay. I don't pay more money. All the time, money, money. Grady want money, workers want money. So now, you work." She glared at Piper. "And Prazeres."

Prazeres shook her head in resignation. When she looked at Piper, her eyes softened. "What did you eat last night?" she asked.

"Me? I had a sandwich last night. I made it with some nice ham."

"I'm glad you're all right. And so are the other two girls who came on the bus." She turned to Lili and said, "It must have been something the staff ate during the day. What did they have? Not anything I cooked—because, as you informed me, you wanted special catering food that they brought with them."

"Eu não sei."

"You don't know what they ate? What did you have?"

"Nada."

"Nothing? All day?"

"Is OK."

"I forgot you don't eat anything with a face so it must limit your choice. Why not try a lettuce and ignore the fact it's got a heart?" Prazeres shot a wink at Piper who snickered.

"They go home," Lili said to Piper as if it was all her fault.

"But if they have food poisoning, that'll be a horribly uncomfortable journey back to Lisbon," Piper replied. "Let me at least find something to give them to help them with the trip. If I could find some goldenseal root or at least some natural yogurt. Or stewed apple? What about some ginger tea?"

Lili snorted like her horse. "No time. They go now. I do not want them vomiting on guests. Piper and Prazeres, you make lunch."

Prazeres tapped her foot on the stone floor. "So now you *do* want my cooking. For *how many?*"

Lili shrugged. "Numbers not sure. Thirty?"

She wasn't *sure?* This was getting stranger by the moment. A huge marquee for only thirty people?

Prazeres rolled her eyes. "What do we cook?" she asked, wiping her hands on her apron. "We can't serve the food your special catering staff brought yesterday because my instincts tell me it gave everyone food poisoning. And since you don't know exactly what they ate, we'll have to throw everything away."

Lili stared at her wide-eyed. "*Everything?* No good? What about beef Wellington? I pay much for that."

"Throw it away too. We don't know what caused the outbreak. Maybe someone yesterday with dirty hands was preparing the food…"

Lili held her head, grimacing.

"I know," Prazeres said, holding up a finger. "The fishing fleet is due back by now. I don't know what they've caught, but we can buy enough fresh fish and bring it back to cook."

"*Fish,*" Lili cried, bitterness clear in her voice. "Always *fish*. We give meat for the guests."

Prazeres glared at her until Lili sighed, her shoulders drooping. "OK, OK. Prazeres fix it. Piper you help her cook this *fish*." She hurried to the door and clattered through it, bouncing off the jamb, all grace and elegance forgotten.

"Bossy, isn't she?" Piper said once Lili was out of sight.

"Prazeres fix it. For goodness sakes." Prazeres looked at her watch. "We'll have to move fast. Piper, can you go down to the village while I start preparing here? Bring whatever the boats bring in. Go to the café that's called *Serafim* near the beach. Tell my husband—that's Serafim—what's happened. He'll bring the grill for sardines and maybe we can also make a *caldeirada.*"

"*Sardines?*" Lili's enraged voice entered before she did. She stomped back into the room. "We can't serve our guests *sardines* and a *caldeirada*. That is for *saloios*."

"She thinks a *caldeirada*—which is a delicious fish stew, Piper—is for peasants. Well, thanks very much," Prazeres said as she crashed a pot down on the table Piper scrubbed last night. "If it's good enough for us peasants, it's good enough for your guests. That happens to be one of our staples."

There followed another torrent of Portuguese, which seemed to be Prazeres's language of choice when she was angry.

Lili stalked out again. The woman dithered backwards and forwards as if she had no clear direction. "Why is she different to the rest of you?" Piper said, hoping, this time, Lili was out of earshot. "I mean, she just kind of acts and looks different to everyone I've met so far."

"She's not Portuguese for a start. She's a neurotic mix of something, but it's not Portuguese—she has a Spanish accent, but she's not Spanish either. I think she's from South America. Someone did tell me but I've forgotten."

"You know what? I like the way you stand up to her. Her being your employer and all."

"She's not my employer. Etta's the one who employs me. I just come along here on occasion when Lili can't find anyone cheaper, and perhaps I come because I'm fond of the old place and enjoy being back in it. It's the only time I can come back here. I adored it when Etta's family was here and we were allowed to come and go as we pleased. So, let's get started." She clapped her hands together and wiped them down her white apron. "You head off for the village, just turn right at the gate, cross the road where the bus dropped us last night, and keep going down. And I'll get to work seeing what there is that hasn't been touched by contaminated hands."

****

It wasn't until Piper was half way down the track towards the main road that she remembered she hadn't told anyone John Hughes was a fake. But then, she decided, there hadn't really been a right moment. If she told Lili then the mad woman would probably go screaming it from the rooftop and that would only give Tom Shine a chance to escape. When she got back from getting the fish, she'd tell calm, sweet Prazeres and get her advice.

Chapter Seventeen

The sea. How could she ever not be entranced by its moods, its voices and its life translated into radiant dusky or faint colors? The waves churned as they retreated on the ebb tide, hurling golden sand at the shore. Piper got a full view of it as she descended the steep hill. Was this the view her mother had every day? Had she lived in one of these blindingly white little houses, each outlined in turquoise? Had she smelled the fragrance of herbs and sweet baking cakes? But, most important, had she enjoyed the sight of the sea every day too?

It never ceased to amaze her that people said the sea was blue, green, turquoise, sapphire—marine colors. Was she the only one to see the earthy browns, mustard yellows, meaty pinks? The bramble color showed a huge shoal of mackerel, beige was whiting. A few patches of woodland green, not so many crabs here then. Towards the sparkling horizon, a kaleidoscope of hues and tones danced, most of which she couldn't identify—although the extended patch of grapefruit yellowy tinge was probably sardine, but she had no idea what the saffron yellow was that spiraled into the air and fizzled out in a puff.

The sea's new colors meant new species to Piper. Her heart raced with excitement and yearning to learn its secrets. But she had to fight with the reminder that she was here on a mission.

No lack of fish far offshore, then, but nearer land the surface was coated by a roasted coffee bean-colored stain. That was another novelty, except it made her shiver and not with pleasure. Probably weed of some kind, although in her experience that usually showed up in tones of green or cinnamon. And algae normally grew in nice orderly forests—this one seemed more random even though extensive—and whereas algae were home to so many species, this brown stain was dense with only a few small sparks of other life dotted sparsely in it.

As Prazeres had predicted, the fishing fleet was in; a jumble of boats jostled for position along the small jetty, their decks a tangle of hawser ropes and fishing line, purse seine and barnacle crusted floats. These must be the longshore fishing boats with wheelhouses and winches that went out deep-sea fishing for days on end.

Smaller craft, sardine boats she thought, were anchored in the bay and one or two had been hauled up by a tractor onto the sandy beach where the fishermen were now offloading their catch onto huge nets laid out beside them.

Eager to see what the offshore boats had caught, her heart lifted with excitement. She couldn't wait to see the familiar bustle of unloading a fresh catch, seagulls yelling fit to burst as they swooped for scraps, fishermen calling—probably swearing at each other, piles of ice slipping from decks, waves nudging at hulls and the squeak of rubber fenders.

The whole village must be down there, surging round the winches, hauling up crates. A handful of children of different sizes chased each other, their laughter filling the air like cracking fireworks, down the ramp and along the beach, dodging fishing skiffs, nets, driftwood and flotsam, and playing catch-me-if-you-can with the waves.

Piper stood on the narrow gritty path that separated the beach from the village aware she had a wide grin but unable to wipe it off. This was where she wanted to be, this place with its stinging tang of fish and sea, and a village of blindingly white-walled cottages edged with robin's egg-blue rims. This was where her mother had grown up.

An elderly man perched on a rickety chair in the sun outside one of the cottages, a pot of brilliant scarlet flowers to one side of him. A trilby hat that looked like he'd sat on it—and probably slept in it too—shaded his eyes that gleamed in Piper's direction.

"*Bom dia,*" she greeted him.

He took his pipe out of his mouth. "Hello. You looking for someone?"

How in hell did an old bloke like that get to speak English so well? Surprise made her speechless before she managed to utter, "Serafim?"

"Take four steps in a westerly direction and you're there."

How stupid she was. A sign above a faded yellow awning announced *Café do Serafim* just next door. It was a slightly larger building than its neighbors.

Serafim looked like a wise beaver—buckteeth and all—and he caught on quickly as Piper stuttered Prazeres's message. Barely pausing when she reached the end, he took her arm and they hurried out through the chain curtain that chinked in the breeze at the café doorway. He spoke in rapid-fire Portuguese at the old man still sitting by his red flowers, who nodded and creaked to his feet. "I told him," Serafim said to Piper as they hurried along the cobbled pavement, "to take care of the café. We need the van."

By now, Piper was no longer surprised at the villagers' English fluency.

In a narrow alley, he unveiled a vehicle by pulling off a tarpaulin. It was a small white van, the kind Pop described as the "scourge of the road," although he was a fine one to talk. Serafim fired it up after several tries and the van shuddered to life. "It's the only vehicle in the village," he told her as they swung out the alley. "It's mine, but everyone uses it for everything. This is what we use to take the fish to market, so sorry about the smell."

"I love it."

By the jetty, Serafim spouted words at the fishermen. Piper heard the name *Lili* and one of the men turned to Piper.

"You want how much fish for the party?" he asked.

"Enough for thirty, perhaps forty to be on the safe side."

"So what do we have to offer them?" Serafim surveyed the plastic boxes packed with fish and ice.

"Plenty of sardine."

"That'll do. Grilled sardine. Nothing better."

"And anything for a fish stew?" Piper asked.

"There's not so much scabbard. We have some squid, though, and grouper. And bass."

Piper shaded her eyes and stared at the sparkling water. "Can you tell me what's out there, and there?" She pointed at the coffee-bean brown stains she'd seen earlier. "There's plenty of it, near the coast. Kind of brown in color. I don't think it's a fish, it's too static."

As if attracted by a magnet, everyone's gaze fell on her at exactly the same second. Oh hell, she'd done it again. *One thing yew must not dew—ever—Pips, is tell people aboot the colors.* Trouble was, it seemed as natural as commenting on the weather to her and it just came out. Sorry Pop, she silently conveyed. Open mouth, insert foot.

"Sorry," she said aloud to the fishermen, giving what she hoped was an ignorant land-girly smile. "Probably pollution."

"So you're English, are you?" Serafim asked as they rumbled up the steep hill in the van.

"Yes. From…from…" *Don't yew tell no one aboot where yew come from, Pips. Keep your little mouth well closed, now.* "From north of London." That wasn't a lie. Two hundred miles north-east of London was definitely north.

Serafim drove with one hand and fiddled with the radio with the other until it blasted to life.

Over the hissing static, she could make out a tune she recognized. *"Cheira bem,* something something. *Ela é boa,"* she sang along to it.

"You know that song?" he asked, taking his eyes off the road and staring at her.

Whoops. Was it bad to know that song? Apparently not, judging by his reaction. "I think I heard it at the airport. That's it. Definitely. Heard it there."

Serafim threw back his head with a laugh. *"Cheira bem, cheira Lisboa.* It's a very well-known *fado* song; they sing it for all the tourists. It means Lisbon smells nice."

Saved, she thought. By a lie.

"Sing it again," he urged as the words of the refrain came round again on the radio.

"Um…*Cheira*…something, something…um…*ela* something *boa."* Piper purposely stumbled, hoping she'd thrown him off track.

The gates of the *Herdade* came into view and Serafim slowed down. "We hold *fado* nights in the village. Some of them have good voices but a long while ago one of our girls in particular, only about seventeen she was at the time and that was twenty-odd years ago, she had a lovely voice and that particular song was one of her favorites. Everyone said she sounded just like the young Amália—the famous *fado* singer." He got out to open the gates.

"Did she go on to fame and fortune?" Piper asked when he got back in.

"No. Did you say you heard it at the airport?"

"Yes. Definitely. That's where I heard it."

Actually, she heard the bloody thing every day. Pop sang it when he was in the bathroom.

****

"Prazeres," Piper asked when the two of them were in the kitchen, surrounded by fish. "What does *ela é boa* mean?"

"It means, it's nice, or she's nice. Or good. Why?"

"Just wondered." She sprinkled sea-salt over the sardines as Prazeres had shown her. "Wasn't sure it meant anything special."

Lili appeared, or rather, barged through the door. "*Que manhã terrível.*" She waited, as if expecting someone to sympathize or ask why the morning was terrible but, when no one ventured anything, she continued. "Piper, clean fish. Clean very clean. Then wash all the potatoes, very well clean. Wash them two times. I want not vomiting. Then," she mimicked sweeping with an invisible brush, "the floor." She drifted into the pantry that was bigger than Pop and Piper's cottage.

"Did she think we'd serve up fish with the guts still in? Let's not clean the potatoes," Prazeres said in a low voice, out of Lili's hearing. "We might have done if she hadn't told us to."

"A little bit of good clean earth doesn't hurt anyone," Piper said and giggled.

"Lili," Prazeres called loudly. "Who is serving the guests?"

"*Vocês,*" Lili answered from within the pantry. "Because all others go home. Now only you and Piper here. Piper must speak very good English to the guests and be very nice." She peered at the fish they were preparing and turned her nose up at the innards lying to one side of Piper's board. "No pretty zebra fish today?"

Piper paused. Zebra fish? She raised her eyebrows at Prazeres to see if she could shed light on Lili's comment.

"You mean stripy fish?" Prazeres said, and then said

something else in Portuguese, probably translating it.

"Very pretty," Lili said, nodding.

"When did you see them?"

"Ontem."

"Yesterday? Where? Down in the village? Did the sardine fishermen have some?"

"Yes. They say we go *deitar fora.*" Lili mimed, throwing something away. "So I take. For employees *almoço.*"

"You gave them that fish for their lunch, Lili? How?"

Lili replied in Portuguese.

"Silly ass," Prazeres said, once Lili had left the kitchen again. "She poisoned the caterers by making them eat a fish pie—which they had to make themselves with no idea how to prepare it—using those fish that have poisonous spines. She's lucky she didn't kill anyone. I do cook them, but I cut the spines off first and then they're fine. But Lili and the caterers didn't know they had to do that. So we've thrown away food that was probably perfectly all right and she had to pay for it all, plus the fish we've brought now. Serves her right for being stingy and making the caterers eat food that was going for free."

"I saw the fish pie last night. I thought it smelled funny," Piper said, pausing at cutting open a bass and shaking her head in disbelief. "She must be nuts. She's throwing money away. She has a whole village-full of English-speakers..."

"...who'd work for free just for the opportunity to be in the Main House again," Prazeres continued. "But Lili is a law unto herself."

Piper eyed the ingredients set out on the table before her. "For the *caldeirada* did you say onions first, then tomatoes? Or onions then potatoes?"

"Onions, potatoes, tomatoes. Fry them in the olive oil, that's our own locally made oil. Paulo's got a press in his garden," Prazeres said, cutting along the sardines with a filleting knife. "Lili's difficult at times like this. But some of the time she's fine, but distracted because she's thinking about horses and bullfighting." She watched Piper layering the vegetables. "Now put the peppers on with a sprinkling of the chili—that's nicely chopped—sage and cloves."

"We could put some parsley in."

"Yes, good idea." She poured a measure of fish stock over the contents of the clay pan. "And coriander. I'll just salt the sardines if you do the squid. That's it," she said, watching Piper cut into the white flesh, "that's the quill out. Oh good, you got some clams too."

Piper laid her knife down. Now was the time to out Tom Shine. "Prazeres…"

"*Sobremesa*," Lili wailed as she appeared like a phantom at the kitchen door. "We have none. Maybe the gateaux they bring yesterday is poison too."

"Probably, by the disgusting look of them. The guests can eat fruit, can't they?" Prazeres peered into the fridge over Piper's shoulder, giving her a light nudge which made Piper snort. "Figs, oranges and raspberries are ripe in the village. There's melon too. I'll call Henrique or Elsa to bring some. And maybe Rosa can make us some *sericaia*—that's a very eggy torte, Piper. Rosa has some Elvas plums she'll put on top which'll make it so sweet their mouths will pucker like cats' bums."

Lili pressed her hands to her temples. "Sugar, sugar, always sugar. Make fat people. I need pay for fruit?"

"Yes. And the rest."

"But fruit grow on trees!" Lili brushed non-existent loose hair off her forehead. "I not believe I have all this problems. *Não consigo lidar...*"

"Course you can cope. Anyway you should've thought of the expense before you started all this…all this, whatever it is," Prazeres said.

Piper gave her an admiring look. The woman had balls all right.

Lili still rubbed her forehead. "Lunch I pay for two times, my show I organize. Then the signing—champagne with that and canapés. Dinner. Now, you, Piper, work."

"We have to do canapés and dinner as well, Prazeres?" Piper asked after Lili made yet another exit; she'd be back any moment brimming with even more angst.

"She can sing for that. I wonder why she's so antagonistic towards you, Piper. What did you do to her?" Prazeres placed three huge clay pots full of fish stew on the range.

"Feeling's mutual."

"Probably because you're pretty, have clever eyes and that naughty look as if you're up to no good."

Piper felt breathless and not because someone took a dislike to her. That was nothing new and Piper could always find a reason to make Lili's aversion worse, such as by tipping some champagne accidently down the back of her neck later on. No, what made her cheeks burning hot was that no one ever told her what she looked like, at least not in a nice way. *Yew're a roight titty-toddy mawther, Pip girl* was about the best she got.

Prazeres's attention was drawn to the door to the garden. "Hello," she greeted Serafim who stood there with a smile winking through his beard. Without a word, he gestured to Prazeres with his finger to join him.

Piper, left to herself, stirred the stews and wondered how she was going to inform on Tom Shine. But, even more important, when would she have an opportunity to find out about her mother? Right now she was in a dead-end street.

After several minutes Prazeres returned and they worked side by side, concentrating on their tasks, while bird-song filled the world outside.

"Pass me the olive oil, will you, dear?" Prazeres asked.

Piper handed her the jug, tightened her grip on the spoon she was using to stir the *caldeirada* and asked, "Prazeres, does anyone, you know, like a young woman, ever leave the village? You know, to get married for example. Like, go to England?" There. It was out. Pretty badly put, but out in the open.

Prazeres stopped mixing her dressing, her whisk stilled as she contemplated the table in front of her for several seconds. Then her dark eyes looked at Piper as if assessing her.

"Piper, is your name Felipa?"

"Philippa," Piper corrected, emphasizing the first syllable instead of the second as Prazeres had done.

Prazeres nodded and tapped her fingers on the table. "Is your father Jack Pepper?" she asked.

"No. It's not." Pop was Norman Pines.

But Prazeres's expression didn't soften back to its normal cheerfulness: the worry lines that had been deepening remained in place. "Why, Piper, do you want to know about people, young women, going to England to get married? Maybe to have a baby too?"

Serafim poked his spiky head around the door. He stepped into the kitchen and looked at Piper as if waiting for an answer too. Had he been listening at the door?

When she didn't reply, he put his arm around Prazeres and said, "You want to know if we remember Felipa Carneiro, don't you Piper?"

Felipa Carneiro—was that what her mother's name was? She knew she'd been named after her mother, Pop had told her, but she'd assumed it had been Philippa like herself and never imagined there was a Portuguese version. Now she had a surname too. "Carneiro," she murmured to herself.

"Carneiros, Piper, go well roasted with potatoes and rosemary." Serafim smiled as he said this. "Carneiro means sheep and there are plenty around here."

Prazeres dug her elbow into his ribs. "Stop it."

Serafim rubbed his side as he concentrated on Piper, and he became serious. "You can see colors on the water, can't you? You can tell which fish are where."

I'm sorry, Pop, Piper mentally apologized. *You knew I'd let the cat out of the bag even though I promised to be careful.* She was such a lummox. "It's pure guesswork," she gushed, her mind a confusion of whether she could still get away with remaining incognito. "Doesn't really work, it's just colors, you know…just guessing…I don't know where the fish are. Like everyone normal."

"Piper," he said. "You remember me talking about a girl who could sing the *fado* sweeter than any of the famous singers in Lisbon or Coimbra?"

"Yes."

"Do you know what her name was?"

"No," she whispered, although she was expecting it.

"Felipa Carneiro."

"She died," Piper murmured.

"We know, darling," Prazeres said, placing her arm around Piper's shoulders and hugging her. "But we thought her baby died too, least that's what we were told."

"I didn't die." It felt so good to be in a woman's soft, sympathetic arms, warm and safe. "Are you related to me?" she mumbled against Prazeres's neck, hope making her voice rise.

Prazeres released her. "No, my duck. My parents came to the village from Ourique to the west. I was born here, but we're not all intermarried you know." She looked at her husband. "Although you, you might be related."

Serafim considered the copper pots hanging from the ceiling and counted on his fingers. "Well. Yes. I'm probably your third cousin. Or is it fourth? I'll work it out later." He held out his hand. "Nice to meet you, cuz." When she took his hand, he pulled her into a warm, sardine-smelling hug. Releasing her, he said, "I knew, as soon as I saw you, that you were related to Felipa, you're just like her, the little pixie. One thing's for sure though. You can't stay here. You're in the worst possible place."

"Why?"

"Because, Piper, it's best not to," Prazeres said obscurely. "Now what I want you to do," she spoke slowly and clearly as if trying to hammer home a message, "is to leave here quietly. When you reach the gates, turn left, not right towards the village, but left until you come to a small cottage on the right. That's Etta's place. And Victor's. They'll keep you there until we can pick you up later."

"But why?" Piper asked, bewildered.

"Because it's better that way."

"You mean Lili? I can handle bullies like her. In any case I need to earn…"

"No, it's not Lili, Piper. The villagers heard you talking about colors and news runs fast here, so let's just say you'll be best with Etta for the moment, otherwise you'll be bombarded with questions you're not ready for."

"But I want to find out where my mother lived and… and my other relatives…"

"I know. Can you wait to do that with us being present, though? We'll finish up here and then we'll all sit down in the café together and have a good talk."

Piper considered. "OK. But are you angry at me?"

"Why should we be angry?"

"My father told me that people in this village were upset with us."

"Not everyone. And we're delighted you're here. Sweetheart, when you say it's not normal to see colors in the sea, you're wrong. It's perfectly normal and right. Don't let anyone tell you otherwise."

Chapter Eighteen

Leo hadn't had much sleep last night. He'd watched the girl sleep and felt uncomfortably like a voyeur even though he'd laid a blanket over her and put a pillow under her soft nest of hair.

"Not so tough now," he'd whispered.

There was something about her that helped relieve the hollowness he felt inside, the misery he now knew he was experiencing from having nothing. She looked like a grey-eyed elf who was mad at the world for losing her invisibility spell. At that moment she shuddered in her sleep as if she was trying to come to the surface but unable to. He longed to take her in his arms and comfort her.

Like that will ever happen. She can't stand the sight of you.

Agreeing with Tom's voice, he took a final look at her before returning to his bedroom in the Main House and slept for a couple of hours until the door in the next room opened and woke him. The heavy footsteps next door sounded like Grady's and, because Leo hadn't returned the building plans to him, he slipped out of bed and padded next door.

As he replaced the roll of papers on the dresser, he glimpsed the dark head of a girl who must have been coerced into spending the night in the smelly room in place of Piper. She was lying on a blown up air-mattress—on the other side to the vomit bucket—fast asleep but her face was pale with perhaps nausea or exhaustion.

"Help you, buddy?" Grady came back just two seconds too soon.

"Nope. Just came to see how you are."

"Better, thanks. Find what you wanted in the plans?"

Leo knew his eyes narrowed as his body grew hot. He'd had enough practice dealing with ornery crewmembers, and could recognize budding animosity and false smiles at thirty paces. For someone who'd dealt with crewmembers who got shithouse drunk while working on a rolling deck, this lip-curled dude in his silk pajamas posed no threat to Leo.

"Fact is, I did." He unrolled the plans, held them upside down which hurt his navigator's heart, and said, "Trying to get a better look at what we—3GDeveloping—are interested in, that's all. But it's difficult to get a handle on these plans."

The helpless plea changed the guy's aggressive attitude. His body seemed to relax, and he leaned in to look over Leo's shoulders at the plans. The smell he emitted was enough to knock a warthog over, but Leo had smelled worse and forced himself not to flinch.

"So these are…?" Leo traced his finger over the drawing.

"First of all, man, you've got them upside down." With a small laugh that told Leo just what a dipshit he was, Grady turned the paper until it was the right way up. "Wish you'd a told me you were Hughes's son. Would've prevented a whole lot of confusion. Never mind. These are what have been marked for you." He pointed at a row of squares in the field behind the *Herdade*.

"Right," Leo said, tapping his lips with his finger as if pondering. "We were wondering about investing more and changing to something bigger nearer the marina."

"No problem," Grady's voice lightened even further. He spread the map out on the foot of his bed and leaned over it. "Some of these," he outlined some larger boxes farther west, "haven't been reserved yet. But you'll have to be quick, bud, because I'm hoping by the end of this weekend they'll all be taken. We have some real high-loaders coming: Walter Bloomton, you know of the Bloomton casinos business, for one. And some real-estate guys with deep pockets."

What a load of crock. Leo outlined part of the map with his finger. "So, these here, where you're pointing, would be where the village currently stands? Right?"

"Indeed. High-end luxury housing instead of run-down fishermen's cottages."

"And all this pink area," he traced over the area that extended right across the *Herdade* and down to the sea, "will be constructed on."

"Indeed."

"Any problems with the conservationists, that type of thing?"

"The problem's been sorted out, or shall we say sweetened? It was mostly to do with the removal of the cork-oak trees because they're a protected tree—God knows why, the place is infested with them. But the mayor came through and deemed the project to be *in the public interest*." Grady gave a stained-tooth grin. "So we've been guaranteed no loony-left environmentalist bother, which is always such a nuisance. And, thanks to the mayor we've been granted planning permission for just over three hundred hectares—that's eight hundred acres."

"Fuck me. Sorry…Christ."

"Of course 50 hectares will be taken up by a golf course."

"The entire fishing village will go?"

"I'm sure I went over all this with your father. Didn't you talk to him?"

"Of course I did. Just confirming, that's all. After all, it's our money at stake."

Grady patted him on the back, and Leo tried not to flinch at the touch. "Of course, of course," Grady said. "Once Nelson Carneiro signs the contract this afternoon, the land will be available for development. He has full authority since he's the owner of the village and all the land you see here. As you'll hear at my presentation, the current inhabitants will have more employment opportunities—there is the golf course, the hotel, the retail park. No end of possibilities."

Leo, who couldn't think of anything better than a full net and the spray of the sea on the windows of a wheelhouse, thought the villagers he'd seen might not adapt too well at watering fairways, cleaning hotel rooms or working in boutiques, not forgetting that they'd need somewhere else to live.

"So," Grady said, his dark hair flopping over his eyes as he circled a block on the map with his finger. "You're thinking about reserving this area here."

"If the price is right, Mr. Grady. We're wondering whether it's bad timing. Portugal's ratings have been downgraded yet again, there's social and union unrest. It's not the time to be planning a luxury development." That article he'd read in *Time* magazine on the plane was becoming useful. He sounded like a real pro.

"The name's William, buddy. Yep. Except the projections clearly state Northern Europeans will be the main purchasers, not the Portuguese."

"To spend winter here? What will happen the other six months? The place dies?"

"The marina will attract visitors all year round. This coast will be the new Algarve, and I've been reliably informed from the investment guys that it's almost time in the recession for the housing market to give a quick jump. So we need to get in now before it does that. You reserve those plots now and I can guarantee you a quick two hundred percent return on your investment in the short term."

The girl on the mattress stirred and muttered something. Leo and Grady looked at each other. "What did she say?"

"I go home," the girl groaned from the mattress. "I no like. And I take my sister with me."

Grady turned to Leo and said, "Mr. Hughes, or can I call you John? Like I do your father? Great. Well, I guess the young lady here needs some privacy while she gets up, and I need to take another visit—urgently—to the bathroom. I'm sure we'll work out a great deal together, and I'll outline more details and answer any questions in my presentation later. But you'll have to be quick with your decision because I have dozens of investors interested, specially in that area you pointed out."

****

So, Leo thought as he sat on his own bed, the guy was aiming his scam at investors who were willing to take very high risks. Surely any fool knew that after a leap there's always a fall. And it didn't take an idiot to know that, even if William Grady's plans were honest, John Hughes's company would be stuck with an investment that was worth next to nothing, probably this time next week. But in truth, the investors would lose their money anyway because Grady would run off with it.

Time to report to the Fletchers.

As he crossed the lawn, he spotted Serafim's hairy head near the kitchen door. It looked like he'd fired a barbeque up nearby, and he now chatted to his wife. What was her name? Prazeres? She'd looked like a nice enough lady, and he hoped the girl was with her in the kitchen because Prazeres would certainly shield the girl from Lili's vicious demands.

If the scam did get as far as demolishing the village, what would Serafim do? Work in the hotel as a barman? Would they make him shave?

It occurred to him, as he left the tall entrance gate and turned left that he might be fired up about saving the village, but he hadn't smelled even a whiff of evidence that the scam might involve illegal trafficking. There must be a link somewhere. There had to be.

CHAPTER NINETEEN

"I'm not going anywhere," Piper told Serafim, her voice at maximum determination. "Prazeres and I are doing the lunch. That's what I've agreed to, so that's what I'm doing. I'm not leaving Prazeres to cope on her own either, so don't try and dissuade me. Danger," she almost spat on the word, "that's all I ever hear but no one offers an explanation or spells out exactly what the danger really is. If someone doesn't tell me about it soon, I'll…I'll explode! And take the whole place with me."

Prazeres laughed. "A spitfire, just like…"

"My mother? Why not come out and say it?"

Serafim patted her arm. "Take it easy, now. OK. It's kind of you to help us out and," he turned to his wife, "if she stays close to us, we'll make sure she's safe."

"Did you really know my mother?" Piper thought the bird-song outside sounded louder. "Really?"

"She was a little younger than us but of course we knew her," Prazeres said. "And you're very…very much like her." She busied herself by taking a heavy pot off the range, keeping her back to Piper. "But I promise we'll talk about it all later, that's what we agreed on."

"OK. Now let's get this bloody lunch out the way and then I'll come down to the village with you. Or go to this other place that you mentioned: Etta, was it?" Piper felt like punching the air with a *yes!* and looked at her new-found relations, albeit distant ones, with fresh eyes. But, of course, Lili had to come in at that moment, looking nearer to coming apart at the seams than ever.

She was sweating, her make-up melting in streaks so that the skin on her face showed red underneath. But her frustration this time wasn't aimed at Piper.

"*Doze pessoas!*" she shouted, her voice shaking. Leaning against the table, she looked at the clock on the wall and clapped her hand to her forehead.

"Twelve people? I thought you said there were thirty," Prazeres said, her hands on her hips.

Lili collapsed into a chair, her thick dark hair covering her haggard face. "Last week *cinquenta*. Today *doze*. William say it my fault. But I email. All the time I email. All on the list."

"Didn't they reply? You know, the RSVP thing. They didn't? Oh dear. Well, we certainly do have enough food, and a lot left over." Prazeres studied the table that creaked under the weight of steaming clay pots and plates.

"I will still perform. That I do not *falta*." Lili jumped to her feet, her chest out, her head held dramatically high. "You," she pointed at Piper who felt Prazeres's hand on her arm, "you serve and speak English. Good, Queen's English. Impress. Maybe twelve people buy all." She marched out, forced optimism perhaps powering her steps.

"Drama queen," Piper muttered and then asked, "Buy what?"

Prazeres raised her eyebrows at Serafim who shook his head and said, "No idea. I wondered if they're selling a field, but they can't do that since none of the fields is theirs to sell. Maybe Lili is selling her wardrobe. It can't be her horse. She's only got one left."

The sound of a coach pulling up outside floated into the kitchen.

"Serve!" came Lili's imperious tones from outside. "They

here. Only English girl serve. Prazeres stay in kitchen."

Prazeres ignored Lili's final order by helping Piper serve in the marquee.

"Twelve people in that great big tent," Piper exclaimed as they brought back plates with left-over figs and *presunto* ham. "They could have removed all the empty tables then it wouldn't look like most of the guests hadn't turned up."

"It's so hot in there too," Prazeres said, dishing up the *caldeirada*, "and the twelve of them are polishing off enough *caipirinho* to fill a swimming pool. They think it's lemonade. I tell you that stuff's so potent that after the wine they'll have with the meal, they'll happily buy a three-legged elephant if Lili offers it. I don't know if it's just a field for sale to tell you the truth. I heard one guy saying he was expecting a two hundred percent return within just a month."

"Did you see the presents on the table? What were they? iPads?"

"I did hear someone say they were cheap tablets that break within a month. He wasn't impressed."

"I'd take whatever I was given. Perhaps we'll get one that's not claimed. Who paid for them do you think, Prazeres?"

"Three guesses."

****

As soon as the last person had staggered out of the tent to scarf down his final sardine, the barbeque had been extinguished and the last melon had been eaten, Piper, Serafim and Prazeres sat on a stone wall in the shade, sipping their coffee. The sun was at its highest and the thermometer topped forty degrees. Piper downed a full glass of water in one gulp and took another look at the guests milling about. She'd been on the look-out for Tom Shine but hadn't seen him at all, which was a disappointment. Only because, she told herself, she wanted to confront him and accuse him in front of everyone, not because she wouldn't mind taking another look at him. Oh no.

"Serafim? You know that chap with whitish-blond…"

But Serafim wasn't looking at her, he was watching the one-eyed man—Gaspar—who'd stared at her this morning—as he appeared through the kitchen doorway, dressed in short-cut tight fawn-colored trousers, a waist-length embroidered jacket, a bright red sash around his middle and what looked like a long-tailed green pixie hat.

Serafim said, "Hello Gaspar."

Gaspar's one eye glared at them. "The mistress says you can go home now." He emphasized the word *home*. "You leave the washing up and cleaning for later. Return in two hours to start dinner. But you have to go now. Maybe not you," he said to Piper. "You can start cleaning." His gaze remained on Piper, his weathered brow lined in thought.

"She'll come with us," Serafim said. "She needs a break. Labor laws and all that, don't you know."

"Why's he dressed like that?" Piper asked as Gaspar stalked off.

"I have a horrible feeling Lili's about to perform."

CHAPTER TWENTY

"This is preposterous!" Victor's spittle hit Leo in the eye. "The land is not theirs to sell! Are you saying that they've been given permission for this?"

"He mentioned the mayor," Leo said.

"To be a politician," Etta interrupted, "you must study at the University of Make Me a Special Offer."

"There're also plans for a marina," Leo said. "Maybe I'm wrong, because it *is* sheltered, but the waves come in from the right and during rough weather, judging by the way the trees bend, the wind blows from the north-west. Those are conditions for heavy seas. Bet they haven't included in the plans reinforcing the construction, because one Atlantic storm and a normal marina would be washed away."

"They do have very heavy swells in winter," Victor agreed. "It's why most of the village is set back from the beach. Bah. It's all poppycock. From what you tell us this Grady man's a trickster."

"It's my guess Grady will get Nelson Carneiro to sign some phony contract, get the money up-front from his investors—he's already told me the investment will have to be quick to catch the real estate jump—and then disappear. So nothing will get built anyway."

Victor reached for the phone. "I'm calling the police."

"Police," Etta said, "go to the University of Take a Lot of Time To Think Before Action."

Victor nodded, put the receiver down, and donned his tweed coat that made Leo sweat just looking at it. "You're right. It'll take them days to arrive. Into the fray, men," Victor cried. "It's time to save the day. Together!"

Etta got to her feet and adjusted her black-framed glasses firmly on her nose. "Let's go tell Monsieur Grady he wants a word with us, shall we?"

They entered the *Herdade* through the hole in the clump of prickly aloes broken down by Leo's rapid entry yesterday.

"Not many people about, are there?" Leo shaded his eyes against the harsh sunshine as he looked towards the large marquee that he'd estimated would hold at least a hundred. A few men and women, the average age he guessed to be around sixty, milled about on the lawn clutching wine glasses, looking awkward.

"Is that Pippy?" Etta cried beside him. He followed her stare and saw Piper sitting between Serafim and Prazeres on a wall near the kitchen.

"I'm sure it is," Etta said, adjusting her glasses on her nose.

"You mean the girl who drove you to the airport?" Leo asked. "She's called Piper."

"Good grief," Victor said, squinting at Piper. "What's she doing here?"

Piper had put down her coffee cup and walked swiftly towards a small group of people by the marquee. She took their plates, piled them on her arm and headed back to the kitchen.

"Looks like she's waitressing," Victor said, wiping his sweating forehead with a crisp white hanky. "I wouldn't have expected less of her. Definitely a foot up the career ladder from being a driver of a beaten up, broken down van to a waitress."

Leo's jaw tightened. Victor sounded like he could give

Grady a run for his money in the sarcasm department, but it didn't sit well with Leo when it was aimed at Piper.

A trumpet blared. "Ah," Victor said. "Who wants to see a bullfight?"

"Who wants to drink cyanide?" Etta responded.

Everyone, including those by the marquee, turned towards the corral where Gaspar, described by Etta as looking like an oversized, morose, Christmas elf, pointed the shining instrument in the air. He lowered it and gestured for the floundering guests, who were guzzling drinks, to gather around the corral. When they were grouped to his satisfaction, he gave another toot before he opened a gate, and Lili burst into the ring on her grey horse.

She did look amazing, Leo had to admit. A long, fitted, cream-colored jacket with embroidered roses encased her slim body. Her gleaming hair had been pulled back and fastened with a blood-red ribbon and froths of lacy cotton spilled from her jacket cuffs and over a matching embroidered waistcoat. Beige-colored pants were skin-tight and tucked firmly into tall highly polished leather boots. Waving one hand above her head and the other gripping the reins, she appeared to be at one with the horse as it cantered around the ring, tossing its head at the applause.

There was no doubting Lili's prowess at horsemanship, and Leo wasn't surprised to see many of the audience taking pictures with their cell phones. The horse was as highly decorated as the rider with matching red and yellow ribbons plaited into its mane and tail.

After Lili completed one circuit, still waving regally at the guests, Gaspar opened the gate once more. A huge, very adult, black and white bull barreled into the ring, its head butting the sand on the ground. The crowd let out a collective gasp. Once it reached the middle, it skidded to a halt breathing so hard its flanks pulsed and a pink tongue hung from its mouth. It scoped its surroundings, looking, Leo thought, zonked out of its mind.

"Bugger me," Etta said. "She's really going for it."

Gaspar, who'd been behind the gate, now appeared with a red cape in his hands. He flicked it at the bull. The animal charged him, but Gaspar leaped over the gate with less than a second to spare, otherwise he'd have been gored. As it was, he left the bull to thrust its horns into the fence. Now Lili was in position in the middle of the ring. "*Touro*," she called, her voice smooth and unwavering. She gave another tour of the ring while the bull followed, catching her up fast, its thick neck lowered so that although the horse accelerated, the vicious horns touched the horse's tail.

Leo closed his eyes. Please don't let it gore the horse. But weak cheering made him half-open one eye. The horse was safe, and Lili once again cantered around the middle of the corral circling her regal wave above her head, while the bull panted to one side, its flanks heaving, looking even more bewildered.

"Oh Jesus, save me," Victor groaned, his hands pressed to head. "She's going for it again."

This time Lili rode straight towards the bull much slower than before. When she was but a few yards away, her horse pranced in front of the bull that seemed to be having trouble focusing.

"She's good," Etta admitted. "With the horse, I mean. The bull probably wouldn't agree…"

The bull's head was down again and its front hoof scraped the ground. As it charged, Lili's horse leaped as nimble as a cat to one side, and she rode towards Gaspar, her back now to the bull.

"It's behind you!" Etta cried.

But Leo was speechless as he saw what Gaspar handed up to Lili: two spears decorated with ribbons.

The crowd grew silent, probably at the sight of the spears that were obviously meant for the bull. If Lili was aware of the silence, then she didn't show it. She accelerated towards the large animal which barely had time to lower its head and charge, before she'd lifted in her seat until she stood upright in the stirrups and with a spear in her hand.

Lili lunged. Leo was sure every person, as one, gasped. Before the horse collided with the bull, she'd veered away and left a spear sticking out of the bull's back. As she made a tight turn, a banner unfurled on the spear with the words *Welcome all!*

Leo's insides twisted.

"Holy moly," Etta muttered.

If she was aware of the lack of applause, Lili didn't show it. To complete silence, she honed in with a second spear she plunged in the bull's back, next to the first one. As she rode away, she slapped the bull's rump, and the second banner unfurled. This one read, *Successful Business together.*

Enough. Leo wasn't sure if there were going to be any more spears to torment the poor animal but, if there were, then he was going to put a stop to it.

"Hey," he shouted, vaulting the bullring fence. "I think that's…"

But his sentence remained unfinished as someone grabbed the back of his shirt. Gaspar's grip was strong and Leo felt the material give. "Buddy, you just unhand me now or you'll be spitting out gravel for the next few days. No one wants to see this, it's gruesome."

Gaspar stared at Leo through his one eye. After several seconds, he released Leo and gestured with his head that Leo leave the ring. "It's over," Gaspar said. "See? Go play with your dollies now."

Leo wanted to grab the man and rub his face in the bloody gravel. Lili still galloped round, her hand waving at the single person half-heartedly clapping. If she'd seen Leo's attempt at bravado, she ignored it, but he did notice that Piper's white face was turned in his direction. At least he'd managed to get her attention and, he hoped, her approval.

Gaspar waited for Leo to climb back over the fence before he returned into the ring where he herded the stricken bull whose flanks were covered with flowing blood back out through the gate. The majority of the audience had now turned their backs on the corral, several of them being comforted or embraced by others.

Leo, now back with Victor and Etta, surveyed the rear end of the spectacle in the corral. "What was the point of that?" he asked. "Not like she's going to eat it, is she? The bull, I mean. She doesn't eat…"

"…anything with a face," Etta ended for him. "Woman against beast, that's how she sees it. And she enjoyed herself, you have to give her that."

"So did Gaspar, so that made two of them. I'm not sure about the horse… But I still don't get it."

"Leo," Victor said. "It's the one thing she does do well. She's showing off—how else can she impress these people? I'd bet my grandfather's life…"

"He's already dead," Etta said.

"…on his grave…"

"That makes a lot of sense."

"Do be quiet, my dear. As I was saying, I'd bet anything her knowledge of finance is less than…less than…"

"The bull's?" Etta supplied.

"Less than his, definitely."

"But can't she make money at bullfighting?" Leo asked.

"She needs finance to be the best. Enough said?"

Leo nodded and turned his attention to Piper, Prazeres and Serafim, who were standing like petrified statues by the kitchen door. They jumped as Grady hurried past them, dapper now in a pin-striped suit, a blue shirt and paisley tie. If he had seen Lili's show, he gave no sign of it as he waved at the guests, bellowing a repetition of the gruesome spear message, "Welcome all."

Removing his uber-cool shades, carefully not disturbing his gelled-back hair, Grady ushered the group towards the tent, his arms wide, not unlike the way Gaspar had herded the distressed bull away.

"Let's go meet our Waterloo," Victor said, his jaw set in determination. Head down, reminding Leo again of the bull, he led Leo and his sister towards the marquee.

The sun had been shining on the tent all day and the temperature inside was so high, sweat ran down Leo's body as soon as he stepped over the threshold. Flies, perhaps straight off the piles of horse and bull shit from the corral, had formed a dancing, drifting cloud that swarmed around Grady's hair-gel like a black halo.

"Welcome, welcome," he said, flapping his hand at the flies, his tombstone teeth shining white in his still-green face as he grinned at the people who'd somewhat reluctantly, Leo thought, wandered back in. The mic gave a high-pitched whistle, causing most in the audience to clap their hands over their ears. As he adjusted the mic, Lili made her entrance, pausing on the threshold, still in her bullfighter togs, to take a small bow which no one acknowledged. With a straight back, she minced up the steps to stand next to Grady on the stage. Leo noticed she had smears of blood on her beige pants.

"I have met most of you before," Grady continued. "Others I haven't." He glanced for some reason at Leo. "But I believe you all should have chosen your plots by now. Let me just outline the basics first. As you already know, our objective for this development is quality. A sea-front home will, within just a few months, be worth over a million dollars. So those of you who are here for investment purposes can expect a nearly fifty percent profit in the very short term. For those of you planning to live here and not rent your property, you are obviously folk who are hungry for experiences, yet require a sense of well-being. This development will be a by-word for ultra-service and security."

"Do you have the necessary guarantees that the whole thing won't end up down the plughole?" someone asked.

"Of course. I have the necessary paperwork drawn up by international lawyers." Grady waved a wodge of papers. "The owners here," he nodded at Lili, "have obtained planning permission from the local council. It's all systems go."

"Remind me again about the financing," another man asked.

"Indeed," Grady said, flashing his rubbery smile. "Forty percent of the value now when you sign the initial contract today, then at least ten percent within twenty days or sooner. And, of course, the rest when the building starts."

"The forty percent's a bit steep."

"I'd rather pay the rest when the building is finished."

Grady waved away their protests. "Normal financing, I assure you. And the sooner you complete, the sooner you'll have your lovely home. As you know from the papers I sent you, I run a hedge-fund in Switzerland where any of your monies that are not immediately needed will be invested by my team of global macroeconomics managers. You will, of course, receive any interest that accrues."

"What a bunch of crap," Etta said. Her high voice went unheard among the rumble of conversation from the guests, but Lili looked her way, frowned, and opened her mouth to speak, although Grady beat her to it.

He clapped his hands for attention. "So, without further ado, I will ask *Senhor* Nelson to sign the contracts that will give us all the legal right over the land." He turned to Lili and spoke through the side of his mouth. Leo was just close enough to hear him. "Where the hell is he? He should be here ready and waiting."

"He here. Any minute. *Calma*. Old man *estupido*."

Etta was right, this was all a bunch of crap, Leo thought as the crowd of elderly people, with trust written over their faces, stared at the stage. Should he make a grand announcement and draw attention to himself? What if he was wrong about Grady and Leo's true identity came out during the ensuing confusion? The last thing he wanted was for the villagers to clam up on him if they knew who he was. Alternatively, what if Grady and Lili were caught up in the drug trafficking as well as the financial scam. Victor said Lili was desperate for cash.

Best let this thing run its course. Leo would observe carefully before leaping in. But, on the other hand, he didn't want to leave it too late.

He nudged a wall-eyed guy in front of him. "Don't sign anything," he told him.

"If you do, you'll go to hell in a handbag," Etta added. She turned to Leo. "Shall I go and spit on them all?"

"Etta, dear," Victor said with a sigh. "This is a desperate situation. Please try to take it seriously."

"They're all fat liars," she said, louder this time, to those around her. "Specially him with the greasy hair."

Grady must've heard her because he nudged Lili and gestured towards Etta. With a frown, she looked around and whispered something to Grady who smiled at the audience. "The gentleman, Nelson, is already on his way, I'm told. He's rather elderly and, I believe, needed a comfort stop…you know how it is." He rubbed the back of his neck and ran a finger between his shirt collar and neck. "Well, it's a lovely day, isn't it?" he added conversationally. "I'll be flying from here tomorrow to New York where I have a private plane to take me to Richard Branson's Nekker Island. I'd like to go with a clear conscience that we've made good business together."

"Shall I wade in?" Victor asked Leo who nodded.

"No one must sign any paper!" Victor cried, his face scarlet with heat. "Ladies and gentlemen, that man up there has initials which are W.G. for William Grady. Now this is interesting because there is an international racket going on which the police are investigating. You may be interested that these swindles are headed by a person whose initials are always W.G. or G.W. I'll give you examples: George Westerham, Wesley Gibb, Gerald Walsh."

"Is that a coincidence or what?" Etta piped up.

"Thank you, my dear. Each of those men is guilty of fraudulent activities and Interpol is after them, or him, as well as the FBI. He is a confidence trickster of the worst kind. And I can also tell you the land you think you are buying is not anyone's but the State's to sell."

"But the State, I understand, has agreed..." someone said.

"When I say the State," Victor said, holding his tweed lapels, "it means the Royal Estates. It does not mean the local mayor, who, by the way is believed to have opened an offshore bank account in his niece's name in the Cayman Islands—the newspapers will hold that story tomorrow. Have any of you been in touch with the true owner of this land, the Royal Estates?"

Shocked silence met the announcement, broken only by the buzzing of flies. A general rumble of voices began as Grady's lips thinned and his face became greener.

To Leo's surprise, Piper stepped forward. "And that man there," she said, pointing at Leo who looked behind him, thinking she meant someone else. "Isn't John Hughes. His name's Tom Shine."

Serafim's voice joined the general growing buzz as he took Piper's elbow. "Piper..." he started but got no further because Victor continued in a loud voice.

"I have called the police, and called an investigative journalist I know in Lisbon." He looked at his watch. "They should be here any moment."

"Get away from my land, Fletcher," Lili growled. "You illegal here. *Onde está Nelson?*"

"You decided not to call the cops, Victor," Leo whispered, his mind awhirl with what was happening all at once. Did Piper just say what he thought she did?

"No, but they don't know that," Victor whispered back and then raised his voice. "Ladies and gentlemen, I am a descendent of Fergus Fletcher who fought and was decorated under General Wellesley at the decisive battle of Vimeiro in the Peninsular War. This land was granted to my family and was taken by force by the old man you are expecting to see on the stage, but who has been delayed apparently. The land is *not*. I repeat, *not* available for sale."

"Pippy!" Etta waved. She nudged aside a group of people so she could get nearer the stage where Grady, who was sweating hard, held up his hands to silence the growing rumble of questioning voices.

"Ladies and gentlemen. I do apologize for this small disturbance. It's of no consequence and is complete tripe. You can take my word on that. Now, I suggest you make a line at the table set up to the right so that we can sign our mutual contracts which have been drawn up in your names along with the invoices for the relevant payments due now." He then added to Lili between clenched teeth, "Where the *fuck* is Nelson?"

Etta had, by now, reached the stage. She stood with her feet apart and pointed at Grady. "You, sir, are a cad. A man on the make." She turned to the audience and put a hand to her ear. "Hark! Are those sirens I hear? If they're not, something outside is singing fraud in a high voice."

"You." Grady pointed back at her. "Are not normal."

"Cheek! I'll have you for defecation of character."

Lili let loose a flood of angry words in a voice that sounded like she'd swallowed wasps when one-eyed Gaspar entered the marquee. He handed a paper over to Lili, although Grady snatched it.

After exchanging a few quiet words with Gaspar and studying the paper, Grady's smarm-radar kicked in and he pasted on a deprecating smile as he held up his hands, palms out. "Ladies and gentlemen, Mister Nelson has signed the paper and this gentleman…what's your name? Gaspar. He witnessed it. Oh, you didn't. Well never mind." He waved his hand as if that meant nothing and then smiled at Piper. "Young lady, perhaps you'd go back to your job now, waitressing, and take this…er…elderly lady with you." He indicated Etta.

But Piper remained exactly where she was just inside the main entrance, her hands on her hips and giving Grady a look that, to Leo, said she'd like to pound the guy into damp pulp. "Thatagirl," he murmured.

Grady wiped his hand over his sweaty face and announced, "To prove to you that all is above board, I'm going to call on the Municipality Mayor and ask him to come along and talk to you. He'll confirm Mister Nelson has every right to sell his land and property." He punched a number on his smart-phone and covered his mouth as he spoke for a moment. When he'd finished his call, he looked at the audience. "The gentleman has asked I take Mister Nelson's contract to the municipality offices right now and that he'll personally stamp his approval and accompany me on the way back. So if you'll bear with me…" He made to step off the stage.

"But it's Sunday," someone pointed out.

Grady hesitated but only for a moment. "He has promised to receive me at his private home. Shows how eager he is.

I will be no more than half an hour, so please just enjoy the wonderful hospitality here for a while longer and I'll be back."

"By the way," someone called from the audience. "My tablet-that-isn't-an-iPad doesn't work."

"And if you can receive a signal on your mobile phone from here," Etta said, looking at Grady who'd just tucked his back in his pocket. "Then you have a hot-line to God."

As Grady jumped from the stage, he knocked against Etta and dashed out the door in a flash of blue pinstripe.

"Try and catch him," Victor cried to Leo. "He didn't speak to anyone on that phone. He's making a get-away, and he's got the paper Nelson signed. God knows what's on it. Maybe it could be considered a legally binding document and he may be able to use it to his benefit."

Leo was already outside the tent when he heard Piper shout, "Don't let that bastard go! He's Tom Shine, not John whateveritis."

Leo's stomach dropped. She'd called him a bastard? He dithered at the entrance, unsure whether to go back and explain or whether to go after Grady.

"And it's my belief," Piper continued, alternating between glaring at him and glancing down at Etta who was sitting on the floor, "that he's in cahoots with that Grady man. You want to get him too." She pointed at Leo. "That's Tom Shine."

As she repeated his name, Prazeres, who was kneeling down beside Etta, looked up and said, "We know who he is, dear."

Piper seemed undecided whether to rush at Leo or kneel down beside Etta who was shaking her head in a daze. "And Batman's expected later for tea," she said.

Poor Etta, Leo thought. She was on the point of losing everything. He could explain things later. Right now he had to get Grady who was half-running towards the gate. He looked back, saw Leo and gave a jaunty wave and a thumbs-up, "I'll be back," he called as he rushed through the gate. "I'll be back with the mayor within the hour."

Leo took to his heels, dodging between trees so if Grady looked back again, he wouldn't spot Leo following. But what Leo hadn't counted on was Serafim's van that was parked just outside the main gate. *Please don't let these people be the kind who left the keys in their ignitions just like they didn't lock their doors when they went out.*

They were that kind. The van door opened and Grady climbed in.

"Fuck's sake," Leo cried, running towards the van.

He didn't make it in time. The engine didn't sound too healthy as the vehicle kangarooed away down the dusty track making stomach-churning grinding noises. By the sound of it, Grady wasn't used to a gear-shift.

Leo sprinted after the van, despair at catching the man gnawing at his stomach, his lungs at bursting point and sweat dripping into his eyes.

Then the sound of the engine changed and stopped. The van came into view, near the junction, with smoke pouring out of its tailpipe. Leo dredged up energy to put on a spurt and ducked through the bamboo canes. When he reached the tarmac, Grady had left the van and was no more than a hundred yards ahead, hesitating about which direction to take before opting for the slope that led to Luminosa village.

They both slipped and stumbled on the dusty, pitted cobbles, but Grady made it to the jetty just ahead of Leo. A small fishing boat was moored there, its engine still ticking over; Leo could hear someone—probably the boat's owner—moving about in the small transit shed where the newly-caught fish were kept on ice.

Grady untied the boat from the bollard and jumped in. The movement made the boat drift free from the wharf. He was no more than a yard away when Leo took a running leap and landed beside him, making the vessel sway violently and forcing Grady to cling to the sides.

CHAPTER TWENTY-ONE

Poor Miss Fletcher had been brutally knocked flying by that Grady man who was in such a hurry to leave with that imposter, Tom Shine.

Piper knelt down to help Miss Fletcher sit up, supporting her back as she wiped her forehead and straightened her thick-rimmed glasses. Piper looked around at the lingering elderly people in the tent. They looked lost, which wasn't surprising considering how much alcohol they'd consumed as well as the trauma they'd experienced in the last hour or so.

She'd seen horror and cruelty during her stints on trawlers: illegal gillnets that had dragged every living creature from the sea bottom; bloated drowned people fished from the water; deformed unidentifiable fish near the nuclear station at Sizewell on the east coast; a man's expression as he was accidentally caught up in a descending anchor rope. But the ugliness of the spears Lili had plunged into the bull's back was just downright sickening and cruel, as was keeping the horse's tail so close to the bull's horns, putting the horse in danger of being gored. She'd heard one of the guests utter that he'd rather stick rods up his nose than watch that performance again, and she agreed with him.

It had been surprising that Tom Shine should try and put a stop to the dreadful performance. Fancy him leaping over the bullring rail like that. He could have been attacked by the bull. But maybe he had an ulterior motive, such as getting people to pay him attention. Or didn't he enjoy seeing the animal tortured either?

Right now she wasn't going to think about Tom Shine. The old lady was more important. "Are you feeling OK, Miss Fletcher?" she asked.

"Oh yes. I say, couldn't have had more excitement, could we? Please call me Etta. Or Old Boot if you like. But not Miss Fletcher. How lovely to see you again, Piper. Can I call you Pippy? I can? Lovely. What is your surname, by the way?"

"Pines. Don't you remember Pines's Taxis?"

"An experience never to be forgotten but very happy to repeat. Now help me up, there's a dear." Etta's forehead had stopped bleeding and she looked perky enough, so Piper helped her to her feet.

"Did someone say the police were coming?" Piper asked.

"Maybe sometime in the next month, dear. Where has Prazeres gone?"

She was patting the shoulder of a woman who was sobbing. "But who's going to settle our hotel bills? That awful Lili said Grady would pay."

"Then Lili will have to pay them, won't she?" Prazeres soothed.

And there was Serafim, tugging on his beard, his eyes almost invisible under his thick frowning eyebrows.

"Come on." Piper grabbed his arm. "Let's go after those two crooks. We need that paper he kept, the one Nelson signed. Victor, take care of your sister."

"She's a tough old bird," Victor said, hurrying after them. "Prazeres will look after her. I'm coming with you."

Piper arrived at the main gate first, followed by Serafim who was puffing hard. Victor hadn't made it quite half-way yet.

"The van's gone," Serafim gasped between breaths. "I bet Grady's stolen it."

"No, it's down there. Look." Piper pointed down the track where a cloud of smoke hung over the vehicle. "Come on, they can't be far. Look, I think I can see the top of Shine's head."

"Piper…about Tom Shine…" Serafim puffed.

But she ran on ahead. Whatever it was Serafim wanted to say, they could talk about it later.

Shine and Grady had a good start on her but if there'd been one thing she'd excelled in during the little time she'd spent at school, it was sprinting. She cut through the bamboo canes and dashed through the tall grasses in the field, sending up clouds of midges and leaving Serafim far behind. It was easier going than running on the shingle of Norfolk beaches, and she managed to keep the shining white-blond hair in her sights. When she reached the main road, the evil pair weren't that far away, racing together down the hill towards Luminosa.

She reached the jetty just as Grady released the rope of a fishing boat, and Shine jumped in after him. The phrase *so near and yet so far* zipped through her frustrated mind.

Serafim arrived beside her, his breath coming out in painful-sounding wheezes, and he had to bend over with his hands on his knees to recover.

Against the strong sunlight and sparkling water, the boat was a black shadow drifting on the current. Footsteps sounded behind her.

"What the hell…?"

"They've taken your boat, Rui," Serafim said, standing upright.

Piper recognized Rui as one of the fishermen she'd seen on the jetty that morning. He looked about the same age as she was, tall and peaceful-looking, and he'd just come out of the storage shed with an empty plastic crate in his hands. Now he stared at the boat drifting farther out.

"Your boat?" she asked, and he nodded. "Is there another one we could use to catch them?"

Rui shook his head, still speechless.

"They've all gone out again," Serafim gasped.

"I came back early," Rui whispered, unable to take his gaze off his boat, which wasn't unlike Pop and Piper's skiff. "What are they doing?"

Piper could see what he meant. The boat had an outboard and they should've fired up the throttle by now if they didn't want to float back inshore. And just why were they moving about so much? It was so difficult to see in silhouette.

"There's Gaspar's inflatable in here," Serafim told her, coming out of the shed where he'd gone to investigate. "But the outboard's broken, I know that, and it's out of fuel."

Against the sea shimmering in sunlight, the taller of the two figures in the boat, made an abrupt movement to one side, setting the boat rocking. That would be Shine. The next moment he'd gone overboard with a splash.

Piper snorted. For a guy who was supposed to own a purse-seiner and reputed to be an experienced fisherman, that was a dumb thing to do. What a plonker. Couldn't he keep his footing when the sea was so calm and gentle?

The boat's throttle finally coughed in, and Piper expected Grady to swing round so he could pick up Tom Shine. But he didn't, he chugged farther out towards the open ocean and away from the man overboard. Never mind. Shine could swim in that millpond of a sea. She waited, but Tom Shine's head didn't break the surface.

She counted to ten. Oh bugger it. Someone was going to have to go and get him and that someone was her. She was dimly aware that Serafim made an unsuccessful grab at her as she shucked off her sneakers and dove into the rippling water.

The cold was a shock but after the initial tingling, her

body adjusted and the familiar sounds of being underwater filled her with as much pleasure as a homecoming. She let herself drift down, vertical, her hands above her head, the muted and bubbling sounds echoing around her. Long brown weeds swayed with the current, swishing like trees in the wind, and she expected to see wrasses nibbling at barnacles on the rocks and jetty walls. There was no life except for the swaying, thick-frond brown algae. But she wasn't down here to study the marine life; someone could be drowning nearby. She kicked out in the direction of where Shine had gone in.

As she swam farther, the ugly monster weed was replaced by algae she recognized from home: wracks and kelp glistened purple, yellow and crimson. The water hues became darker in the depths. Whispers and gurgles from below echoed back from the surface and rays of penetrating sun lit transparent shrimps and plankton in a jeweled halo. Was it in *The Water Babies* she'd read that the most wonderful things were hidden from view? Now she was seeing it and she laughed in delight, especially when the laugh came out as a large bubble that rose in a rainbow to the surface. Following it up, and breathing in a deep lungful of air at the surface, she took stock of her bearings. The current had pulled her out too far so she dived and started back nearer land.

She hit another patch of that weird brown weed that dominated the inshore area and this tract was larger than the other she'd swum over. At home she ate many of the algae: bladder wrack, sea lettuce and sweet oar weed which she fried to a crisp, but she wouldn't touch this stuff: brown and decaying yellow, dense, growing higgledy-piggledy, fetid and festering. Silent stripy fish flitted in and out creating a cloud of the muddy brown color she'd seen on the surface earlier in the day. Were those the fish Lili had fed her catering staff yesterday? The thought made her shiver. This weed might invite some kind of weird life but it also housed death, she thought as partly consumed fish, sardines she believed, floated past her, their rotting dismembered bodies reminding her of corpses left on a battlefield. Whatever this weed was, it didn't belong here and neither did those stripy fish; they were making this part of the ocean sick so that the water was sluggish and choppy under the surface as if struggling for air, just as she was. She kicked towards the beige-colored surface where she hoped she'd see a white-blond head. But there was nothing. If he had survived, he wouldn't last much longer without air.

She kicked down, forcing her way through the dense brown tentacles that grabbed at her ankles, vicious stuff that could've caught at his ankles too and held him prisoner.

It had. His body emerged through the muddy murk. Weed fronds enrolled his legs and those zebra-striped bug-eyed fish circled around him like vultures. His eyes were open but rolled back and a diminishing row of bubbles issued from his nostrils; he really was at the end of his resources, although she was surprised he'd lasted as long as he had.

Tugging at the fronds had no effect: they were as tough as twine. When she did manage to peel off a piece, a cloud of crimson, like blood, poured from the stem.

Pity she didn't have a knife, but this stuff wasn't going to beat her. Problem was, she didn't have much air left, and he looked like he had none at all, so she breathed the last of her air into his mouth before, her lungs bursting, kicking up to the surface where she took several deep breaths and then dived again.

She breathed more air into him, aware of how soft his lips were and, weird, how *warm*, filled her own lungs again and then went back among the swaying brown fronds, which she tugged and tore at until her hands were bleeding and swollen. As each piece broke off, the surrounding water filled with a red, viscous mist that mixed with her own blood. She was almost at the end of her oxygen when she finally unwound the last piece clinging to his ankles. The surface and air were her only thoughts as she kicked hard, scissoring her legs and grabbing his hair on her way up and pulling. They broke the surface together. As she sucked in air, he was limp and motionless.

She'd wrapped her hands under his armpits and struck towards the shore when she felt him kick. It was feeble, but it was movement. Then an engine sounded close by. Was it Grady coming back?

A white lifebelt splashed beside her, and she put it round Shine's body before grabbing another one. Within a moment she was lying on a pile of still-squirming sardines in the bottom of a fishing boat that didn't hold Grady but three fishermen who must have been returning home. Two of them worked on Shine who was face-down coughing up water. They were nearly at the beach when he choked out, "It's alright. I'm OK. Born with a caul… Can't drown. Impossible."

Piper didn't think she'd ever heard anything funnier, nor so ludicrous, and she couldn't stop giggling like a lunatic as a waiting crowd hauled the sardine boat up the beach. Even when she was on the sand, she snorted and curled over with laughter, her hands on her knees. "Caul," she gasped.

Many of the villagers, mostly women and young people who'd pulled the boat in, now held out blankets and mugs of hot sweet tea.

Serafim wrapped a blanket around her, and they watched while Shine vomited up water. But he was breathing on his own, that was the main thing. "Caul," she said again, sounding like an idiot but knowing it was relief at getting him ashore, mixed with the light-headed feeling of being drunk, the kind that being in the sea always gave her. Taking several controlled breaths, the sensation of euphoria began to fade and reality kicked in. In truth, the guy had been very close to drowning, probably within a few seconds. She tried telling herself that now perhaps he'd think twice before torturing animals and murdering people with drugs, but part of her felt admiration: not many would've survived being underwater for so long.

He was still coughing, now on his knees and holding out his hand to resist anyone's help, when the crowd parted at the sound of galloping hooves on wet sand. Piper moved closer to Shine so she could grab his arm in case he thought he could make a run for it, and, with her attention on him, she was only dimly aware of a grey horse rearing beside her. As she looked up, a figure stood upright in the stirrups.

Piper instinctively ducked, felt a sharp shove in her shoulder and then a hot lance of blinding pain near her neck. Someone screamed. Piper ate sand and found she couldn't spit it out. Nothing hurt but she couldn't move. In a moment a wave would break over her and that would be nice.

****

It was dark when she opened her eyes. Where was she? Just a chink of light spilled through a half-open door. Was that Tom Shine sitting over there, one ankle resting on one knee? *Caul.* She giggled, or at least she thought she did. What a load of crap. She must be dreaming or hallucinating, because Tom Shine wouldn't be here, he'd be in police hands by now after all the pain he'd caused poor walruses and otters and…stuff…and little kids…in school uniforms…forced to take drugs…And his lips were soft, he smelled of the sea, and he didn't like bullfighting. Someone with a smooth voice said, "Sshhh, it's all right." She'd like to hear some more of that voice. Stupid dream… Better go back to sleep.

CHAPTER TWENTY-TWO

"Tom, you been here all night?"

Leo opened his eyes and croaked a just-woken affirmative in the direction of Serafim poised in the doorway.

A glance at the figure in bed reassured Leo that Piper was sleeping peacefully. What would she say if she knew he'd caressed her cheek in the night and kissed her lightly on the lips when she'd groaned in pain? This was the second night he'd 'spent' watching over her as if he was some unwanted guardian angel. Some goddamn angel; the very thought of what she'd do if she found out made him move his legs closer together.

"Tom, the police want a word."

No surprises there; he knew they'd be crawling up his ass soon. With a quick look back at Piper, he followed Serafim out of the room.

****

Three hours later, being in Serafim's café was a relief after the claustrophobic atmosphere of the *Polícia Judiciária* headquarters in the local town. The combined fug of tobacco smoke, coffee, alcohol and fish in the café was as welcoming and familiar as coming home.

Several customers, who'd been ruminating over their coffee and tiny glasses of *mata bicho,* raised their heads as

Serafim and Leo appeared, and Prazeres came out from behind the counter wiping her hands on her apron, saying, "You took longer with the police than I expected, after all, you were only a witness."

"Because of his aliases," Serafim replied in a matter-of-fact tone.

Leo was relieved to hear the lack of recrimination in his voice.

At Leo's request, Serafim had been allowed to stay with him throughout the interview with the detective and the interpreter on condition Serafim stayed silent. He'd obeyed that order for the most part, except when the detective leaned forward over the desk until he was almost nose-to-nose with Leo and said, through the interpreter, "Who exactly are you? John Hughes, Tom Shine or…" he glanced at Leo's passport, "Leo Shine?"

"Leo Shine."

Serafim gasped.

The detective nodded, but his mouth was a crooked line of suspicion. "According to our colleagues in the US Federal Police, Tom Shine is officially missing, presumed drowned, John Hughes—who should've been at the event in *Herdade Albatroz* yesterday but canceled a day or so ago—is safely at home in Ohio and is sixty-five years old with no living children. And Leo Shine is on the international list of people suspected, but not proven, to be involved with illegal trafficking." He tapped his pen nib on the table several times while he scrutinized Leo. "So, perhaps you'd tell me why you're here visiting Luminosa?"

Leo's fists clenched at the words *illegal trafficking,* but he decided to keep an even tone to his voice. "I want to find out who killed my brother and father."

"That doesn't answer my question. What are you doing in Luminosa?"

Leo swallowed down his rising impatience and forced himself to speak evenly. "Trying to find who is responsible."

"What makes you so sure that the person or people responsible are in Luminosa?" The detective's voice was a monotone.

Leo shrugged before he said, "I've eliminated everyone else."

Serafim groaned again, earning himself a sharp look from the detective.

"Have you any suspects from your *private investigation*?"

"No."

"And what are you planning to do, Leo Shine, when you find out who you say is responsible?" For the first time, the detective looked up from his notebook and eyed Leo. Perhaps he hoped Leo was going to say he'd murder the person.

Serafim's face had turned the color of parchment and his eyes were bright with tears. A wave of affection swept through Leo. "I don't know, Detective," he said. "I just want closure and for that, I need to know *why* more than anything else."

"Strange you're here at the same time that some very unusual events occur in a place where crime is almost unknown."

This detective didn't know about Nelson's drug trafficking in the past then.

****

Once outside, Serafim pulled Leo into a back-thumping hug and a mumbled, "I'm so sorry, son, about your loss."

On the way home, Leo asked Serafim why Nelson had never been punished for throwing the Fletchers out of their house when they still had a right to live in it for another twenty years.

"It was a disturbing time in Portugal, Leo, and the Alentejo did have a number of large properties taken over by those who thought they had a right to them. We felt at the time it was better to have people in the Main House that we knew, rather than strangers. And the Fletchers did have their little house to move into so it wasn't like they were banished. They've always been part of the village and always will be. What's happened this weekend will definitely bring the property to the Royal Lands Foundation's attention now."

"Why hasn't it before?"

"Nelson is, or was, reputedly, very good at back-handers and, unfortunately, many people are very good at accepting them, naming no names."

Once back in the café, Serafim led Prazeres behind the counter and spoke to her in a low voice. Without saying a word, she came up to Leo and locked him into an embrace, so hard that eventually he had to say, "Can you quit hugging me now, as I'm having trouble breathing." But it was the gesture, not the force of it, which made his eyes mist in a way that shook his manly instincts. If she could, he thought, she'd lift him off his feet, but since she couldn't, he did it to her, her feet dangling as she shrieked in what he hoped was delight.

When he'd blinked away the last of his treacherous tears and his eyesight cleared, everyone in the café was on their feet, their hands stretched out to shake his.

He released Prazeres who gave her husband a quick nod. A message passed between them via some kind of mental communication, and Serafim left the café through the inside door saying, "I'll be back in a minute."

"I thought I might go see how Piper is at the hospital," Leo said. "I don't like she's alone there."

"She's not alone, Tom—sorry, Leo."

"It's not Lili with her, is it?"

"No, she's still at the police station where she'll probably be bailed later. She says she wasn't aiming at Piper, she was just mad at everyone. She'll no doubt plead temporary insanity which, as Etta says, is rich coming from someone who should have a sticker saying, *this way up* on her back. No, Piper's fine at the hospital and I'll go up later. We both can."

If Prazeres said Piper was safe, then she was.

The chain curtain at the door rattled, and Rosa-of-the-thick-ankles charged through them at such a rate Leo had to brace himself to take her impact straight on. "So you're Leo!"

"This place works on telepathy?"

"Smoke signals," Rosa cried, gathering him to her ample bosom.

He'd never been hugged so much in his life.

Her voice rumbled into his ear pressed against her shoulder. "I thought you were Tom too, but I didn't say anything to you because Serafim and Prazeres said they had the idea you wanted to keep things secret and were biding your time, checking us out, so no one opened their mouths. But now we can, even though you're not. Tom, that is. I'm so happy to meet my nephew, Leo." She squeezed him tighter.

"You are?" A warmth gushed through Leo as he untangled himself and stared at her. "You're my aunt? I never had an aunt before."

"You have." Rosa's laugh came straight up from her belly. "I've always been here. And an uncle: Serafim. Didn't he tell you?"

"Yes. You know, I thought he was a *primo* at first."

"Oh, you've got a cousin. Here he comes now, Rui, he's my son."

Leo remembered the young man's wide toothy smile, his instant liking for him, and it was Rui's boat Grady had jumped into.

Rui shuffled and dug his toes into the bare floor-boards. "I'd have talked to you before, but they said you were Tom and you were being cagey thinking we didn't know, and Uncle Serafim said we had to treat you carefully, if you get what I mean. And then just now Uncle Serafim said that you're Leo because Tom and your father…oh, I'm so sorry for your loss."

Within a few seconds, Leo was again surrounded by the café occupants and a few more who'd ventured in. But instead of hand-pumping, now he got sympathetic pats on the back.

Leo was torn between delight at being with seemingly understanding, friendly people and the traces of his misgivings he couldn't shake off that one or some of them could still have played a part in his immediate family's downfall. How he wished he could shake that feeling off.

But he had to admit it was good to have a cousin. "I'm sorry about your boat, Rui. Reckoned I could save it and never imagined I'd go overboard. Didn't see until almost too late that the dude had a knife. Guess I'm losing my touch, although Tom would say I never had it. "

Rui gave him a shy smile, and his mother broke in with her high-decibel voice. "Look." She pointed first at her son and then at Leo. "They have the same smile. You can see they're family!"

Rui rolled his eyes and then winked at Leo. "It came back. The boat. Last night. Came back around seven this morning on the tide. Empty but otherwise fine, like a runaway horse back to its stable. The police were all over it when we told them but didn't get any clues."

"What about Grady?"

"There's an air and sea rescue going on, but they haven't found him."

Leo pondered. "If he'd drowned, his body would've come back this way too, wouldn't it?"

A general shrug showed that the consensus was probably yes, but who were they to care? "I never saw nothing,"

Slippery Dick, call me Ricardo, said. "An' I come back in around eight this morning."

In the short silence that followed, Leo imagined everyone's minds were on the events of the weekend that had disturbed this otherwise peaceful village.

"Here, this is for you." Rui held out an object in the hand he'd kept behind his back since entering the café. It was a small oil-lamp, like a miniature hurricane lamp, with a glass shade sheltering a wick.

"He makes them," Prazeres said, nodding at the lamp Leo turned in his hand as he admired the intricate pattern carved on the tin base. "He's one of the few manual tin-makers left in Portugal. Like his father."

"I thought Rui was a fisherman."

"He is. This is his hobby."

It seemed everyone was busy doing something when they weren't fishing: whittling, wine-making, weaving and now tin-making.

Just as he was about to thank his new-found cousin, Serafim returned through the inner door with a folded piece of paper in his hand.

"I received this letter in February." Serafim didn't hand the paper over immediately, keeping it instead held tight against his thigh and glancing at his wife. Whatever signal she gave him made him reach a decision. "You said you came to find out who was responsible for Tom and George's deaths." He handed over the paper. "Read this where and when you like in private. Take your time. I just hope I'm not the one to blame, but I think I might be…"

****

A red buoy had come loose and bobbed on the surface of the waves. Sunlight glittered off the water, the surf smelled clean, and the sparse fronds of green algae that had been washed up looked like polished kelp. Prazeres had told him they used to have so much they could harvest it for fertilizer but nowadays there wasn't enough. Without doubt, Leo thought, its sparseness was thanks to the invasion of the brown stuff that had grabbed his ankles yesterday. He'd never seen a weed like the kind that had wound itself around him and held on. His air had just about run out when Piper managed to release him. He didn't remember much, but he had an idea he'd embarrassed himself by later twittering on about being born with a caul that Piper found highly amusing.

She was something else, that girl. He'd always reckoned he had great lung capacity—he and Tom used to have competitions to see who could stay under-water longest and Leo always won. But yesterday, she was down there almost as long as he was—with the added effort of having to call on her energy reserves to tear at the tough stalks with her hands—and by the time she pulled him back up to the surface (by his hair, he painfully remembered), she'd still been swimming strongly with no signs of fatigue, gliding through the water—in her element, as graceful as a mermaid in the water. He'd also noticed that her eyes, like the deepest ocean, were grey but at times they changed and became deep blue and green like the colors of an opal. She was an ocean child, sure enough.

Lili claimed she wasn't aiming at anyone in particular but, shit, that didn't excuse the woman. He couldn't recall exactly what happened on the beach; one moment he was coughing up seawater, then he heard horse hooves galloping closer and glimpsed crazy Lili on her big grey horse waving a spear which she plunged straight into Piper. The doctors at the hospital said Piper could've died if the spear had pierced her heart or a major artery. As it was, she had a torn shoulder rotary cuff, a painful injury and the reason why they'd kept her sedated overnight.

He'd felt as if Lili's spear had stabbed him in the guts when he saw the blood seeping out of Piper and into the waves breaking nearby. Serafim and Prazeres had stopped him from gathering up her fragile-looking body, wisely, he knew, telling him not to move her until the paramedics arrived.

Overnight the waves had carried the stains of her blood back to mingle with the ocean, washing the beach clean.

He shuffled one butt cheek to the other on the piece of driftwood he was sitting on and knew he was playing for time, trying to put off the moment he'd have to read the letter. What would he do if he discovered the cause of Tom's and his father's death really did lie at Serafim's door? He'd said he was afraid he was to blame. Leo had vowed vengeance and that meant he'd have to carry it out but, dammit, he'd grown fond of the place, the people, his uncle and Prazeres.

Life, he thought, could make you into such a screwball. It had a habit of leaping from one stomach-churning roller-coaster of emotions to another; one minute you had a family, the next you didn't; then you had a family again, then they told you the one thing you dreaded and you lost the new family.

He trembled like an animal in a cage; he figured he'd have to read the letter sometime. Best do it now.

Before he could unfold it, a tall lanky figure came up beside him and gave him a start. For a moment there he'd thought it was Tom, but it was Rui who toed the sand besides Leo's piece of driftwood. Rui wrung the hem of his t-shirt, which was funny because Tom used to do that too on the few times he was nervous, and Leo had been told he did it as well so it must be a family trait.

Great. Now he had an excuse to enjoy the beach for a few minutes more, able to put off the dreaded moment when he'd have to read his father's letter to Serafim. He patted a place next to him, and Rui dropped down on it.

"So your boat came back?"

Rui nodded.

"Which direction?"

Rui pointed north, around the promontory.

"The current's running the other way right now, but the tide's about to turn," Leo said, and Rui nodded. "Does it come this way at flood tide?"

"Mostly with the wind in its favor."

"So the tide was rising when the boat came back?"

"Yes, it was—couple of hours off." Rui eyed the letter Leo was bunching in his hand. "Hell of a situation. Don't blame you for wanting to clock someone, Leo."

What an understatement. Leo couldn't resist a quarter-smile. "Right now I don't have any reason to clock anyone." His hands rested between his knees, the letter dangling towards the sand. "Can you run the whole thing by me before I read this? So I have it straight from the very start? For instance, is it true what Victor told me? That Nelson was the middle man in the Caribbean to Ireland drug run years ago?"

"They say so. It's how he made his money."

"What was it, in the 70s? Before we were born."

"Thereabouts. My mother—your Aunt Rosa—remembers the men from the ships though, she said they came ashore once or twice—rough men she said, the kind you wouldn't want to cross, nor double-cross. *Tia* Conceição said they looked like sexy pirates." He gave Leo a wide-eyed glance, probably wondering if he should've said that final part.

Tia Conceição. How strange to hear his mother named that way. She'd been Rui's aunt all his life, and Rosa and Serafim's sister, but never Mom to Leo.

"What was she, eighteen at the time?"

"*Tia* Conceição? Suppose so. She was the youngest of the three so, probably eighteen or nineteen on the day she boarded the ship that had come to pick up Nelson's delivery. And sailed away on it."

"Didn't anyone try to stop her?"

"Nelson said he didn't realize what she was up to until it was too late and she'd scampered up the ladder and disappeared onto the ship. He tried to insist she come back but she shouted down from the deck to bugger off. The crew said if she wanted to stay, she could, so Nelson didn't argue any more. They weren't the kind to argue with anyway."

Leo didn't want to think about what the crew would've done to her and how long it would've been before she found out she'd made a terrible mistake. "What about anyone else? Weren't there any fishermen about?"

"Nelson always did the pick-ups and deliveries on his own with Gaspar helping him, but that day *tia* Conceição went instead. And no one else saw anything because those ships used to come into the bay on a dark moon, turn all their lights off and the whole transaction would be over in minutes. Gaspar must've been somewhere else because he wouldn't have let *tia* Conceição go with Nelson and certainly not get on the ship."

This was the first time Leo had a conversation with someone about his mother without the other person flinching, going very pale and leaving the room like his father always did, or going, "*pffft* for the bitch" like Tom would've done as he snapped his fingers in Leo's face.

"Why not?"

"See, Gaspar had a thing for Conceição."

"A thing?"

"Yeah. Like he liked her. A lot. Enough to track her down. I was told it was one of the few times he got angry with Nelson, angry enough to leave the village. They say he spent almost a year travelling from Ireland where they said the ship she boarded was heading. From there he tracked her to Miami where he found out she had a bit of a reputation..." he paused.

Reputation for being a spaced-out whore, Leo had no doubt, from the tone of his cousin's voice and small details he'd gleaned over the years exactly what Conceição had been, or even still was.

"No one knows the details, but he came home without her, without an eye and with that scar which he refuses to talk about, and, I'm told, not quite the same in the head as if someone brained him."

"Brained him?"

"Like he got injured and wasn't quite right afterwards." Rui pointed his finger at his temple and circled. "Loony-tunes."

"I couldn't quite make out what it was about him. He seems out of kilter to me. Isn't he too friendly with Lili?"

"It's the horses Gaspar likes. If they were in a fire and he had to rescue either the horse or Lili, there'd be no choice—he'd get the horse."

"So he's just a bit nuts."

"Not as in dangerous. Just never speaks much and stares at you in a funny way, that kind of thing."

Leo slowly sat back down.

"Anyhow," Rui continued, "when he got back from the States all bashed up, Gaspar did say *tia* Conceição had gone to Alaska because she'd met someone called George Shine, so he—Gaspar—gave up on her. Uncle Serafim found out where she was and went to Alaska, oh, soon after Tom was born, and he liked George. Said he thought if anyone could keep her well, then your dad could. Meaning off drugs, I think."

"Long enough for her to have Tom and me and then piss off."

Rui grimaced as if in apology for his aunt. "Suppose

that's a drug addict for you."

Leo watched the bobbing red buoy that had floated, just as he could've predicted, farther north on the current. Looking again at the promontory, he made some calculations in his head. "So I guess high tide was around nine o'clock last evening?"

Rui shot him a glance, perhaps at the quick change of subject, and it took him a moment before he nodded.

Leo let sand run through his fanned-out fingers. "Hard to think of that old guy Nelson as a drug-runner."

Rui didn't seem fazed by Leo jumping from one subject to another like a jack-rabbit; he just listened and nodded or shook his head at all the right moments. Perhaps he was picking up the vibes of how antsy Leo felt. "He wasn't always like he is now. Five or six years ago Nelson was a vital man. Then he married Lili who became more and more demanding."

Leo could imagine how she sapped that vitality and, because he thought Rui might appreciate it, he snickered. It was the right thing to do, because Rui echoed him. "And took all his money too. She didn't have anything when she met him, or at least wasn't well off."

"How'd you know that?"

"Because one day, after a few too many glasses of wine at lunch, she told *tia* Prazeres in the kitchen that she'd been a part-time model in Brazil. So *Dona* Etta looked her up online and found a picture of her in just her G-string. *Dona* Etta said it wasn't Nelson's leather jock-strap Lili was interested in but his wallet and that she was a bit of a slapper. *Dona* Etta said in her opinion Lili might graduate to trampoline artiste one day."

"Yes, Etta would say that." Leo thought of Nelson who was now a bent old man in a wheelchair. "But I guess his wallet wasn't a never-ending cash-cow and now the place is right run down. Trying to sell land that wasn't his to sell was a last chance gamble."

"Or hers. I don't know how much Nelson realized what was happening. He probably thought he was signing another check."

"All this weed and strange fish in the bay makes me think there have been some ships that have come into the bay and washed their ballasts out, with some toxic hitch-hikers on board. Why would they do that? If they were on the level, they'd do it in port where there's the right equipment to deal with it. You need a marine specialist here, otherwise that crap that's inland is going to take over."

Rui picked up a dried mermaid's purse and pretended to examine it. "We've been trying to deal with it ourselves. It's our way. But after what happened to you, I expect we'll need help." He sighed and threw away the egg-case toward the sea. "It's not easy for us to admit that. We normally take care of stuff like that ourselves."

The letter Leo still held crackled in the warm breeze. He took a deep breath and let it slowly out. "OK," he tried to keep his voice light as he unfolded the paper. "Time to get it over with."

Chapter Twenty-Three

Dear Serafim, He recognized his father's loopy handwriting. The letter was dated February, just over a month before the tragedy.

You know I wouldn't write to you like this unless I was desperate. You'll remember I told you last year I was worried about Tom who was showing more and more interest in his mother and her whereabouts. Don't get me wrong. If São was cured and contacted her sons as a well woman, I'd have embraced the idea, but I know for a fact that she isn't and I feared what contact with Tom would do.

Of the two boys I believe Tom has been the most affected since he had more time to know his mother, even if she never showed him much affection; Leo asks occasionally about her but never shows much interest otherwise. I've always taken the view she'd do more harm to the boys (boys! They are grown men) than good if she remained a drug addict, apologies as she is your sister, but I'm sure you'll agree. Addicts will do anything, even try and involve their own sons, to get another hit.

His father had been in contact with Serafim? This was news to Leo. Why didn't he tell Leo? And why didn't Tom tell him about wanting to know their mother? And did his father really figure that Leo never showed much interest? Feeling ridiculously like a child wanting to pout and stamp his foot in frustration at being left out and misunderstood, he read on.

And I thank you from my heart for offering to do what you can to help out if necessary. It looks like that time might have arrived. Let me give you the situation:

In the fall Leo did a stint as a skiffman on a herring seiner. Usually the brothers work together, but this time Leo went on his own, and while he was away Tom was a tad lost as he always is without his brother.

Leo stared at a seagull hovering in the sky, riding the wind. Since when was Tom lost without him? Leo remembered he'd told Tom before his stint that he could get him hired on the same herring boat as a deck hand, but Tom had retorted, "We're not fucking joined at the hip, you know. I can find my own jobs."

Leo had been surprised at Tom's words, since they always worked as a team, but he put it down to Tom having a new girlfriend at the time.

He was at a loose end, moping around the place.

Tom moped? Leo couldn't imagine it because the guy had grit in spades.

I'm afraid, Serafim, I grew impatient with my son and grumbled that Leo was working his butt off earning money to get the Goblin *finished while Tom just drifted. He blew a fuse and said that if I wanted money then he knew just the place to get it, and I'm ashamed I said things that I shouldn't such as Leo being twice the man Tom was. To cut a long story short, Tom left home, royally ticked off, only returning a few days before Leo was due back, when he proudly showed me a large sum of money, refusing to tell me where or how he'd earned it. In the next few weeks he seemed the same Tom except he said he was hankering after getting the* Goblin *ready earlier than planned.*

Leo remembered finishing his stint on the herring boat, returning home and finding life was going on as usual: Tom spent days nursing beers in the bar, demanding drags on Leo's cigarettes, spending nights out and coming back bleary-eyed, messy haired and jeans stiff with mud. Catting around, their father had called it. So no change that Leo had noticed. Did he walk around blind-folded? Seemed like it.

It was only one day, when he was in his cups, that Tom joked we should pay for São to get some teeth that I was horrified to realize that he must have been to Miami—how else could he know about her dental state? He must have gone there when he walked out during Leo's stint away.

Serafim, I am very afraid that the money he handed over when he came back was from some kind of pre-arrangement that he's agreed to and I am suspicious that he's planning something with the Goblin, *since he insists she has to be ready before March. I cannot stop imagining what happened when he found his mother and the people she mixes with. Knowing Tom, he will have boasted about the* Goblin *and he would've been easy prey for the Miami drug mafia. I can imagine they promised him huge wealth if he'd do one easy job for them, and to show him their goodwill they gave him some of the cash up front. Now he's committed and his temper is getting shorter by the day.*

Serafim, he'll try to get Leo involved who, knowing Leo, will do anything for Tom.

The solution will be to get Tom out of the country while I raise cash somehow to pay these goons back what they gave him. If I suggest he comes to you, he'll only rip me a new one. So, Serafim, would you find it in your heart to contact Tom directly perhaps by telling him you need him for family business in Luminosa, or that you've found some lucrative work for him to do (I will pay you back every cent)? Build him up with flattery, tell him no one else but he can do what you have in mind, and tell him his family are eager to meet him. It might just work. I know I'm asking a lot from you, but I do not know where to turn apart from in your direction.

Our ship, the Goblin, *will be seaworthy next month, thanks to Tom's moving things on a tad too quickly for my liking, and I just want my dream to come true and have my two boys being their own boss on our own ship. Both are accomplished fishermen, able to weather the worst of the williwaws, hard winters and dangers of their chosen profession. I don't want them to get wound up in the black drugs world, because Leo will if he thinks his brother's in trouble—he'll stick to Tom like glue. I feel I've let Leo down…the time I've always had to spend to keep Tom from going off the rails I feel Leo never received enough of my attention and it's made him a little withdrawn. He doesn't make friends easily and yet he's my boy with the most potential and the greatest heart.*

His father had attached a photograph, which wasn't the best quality. It was of Tom, but Leo could see the villagers would've mistaken him for Tom.

Leo put the paper and photo down and picked at a loose flake of skin on a fingernail as he stared out to sea. Would he have "stuck like glue" to Tom in this crazy adventure, like his father reckoned? Yes he probably would. But he'd have waited until they were in the deepest and roughest water—he may even have steered towards it—and then he'd have dumped the whole cargo overboard. Tom would've tried to stop him of course, but Leo had a few tricks up his sleeve when it came to overpowering Tom and would've got him tied up somewhere.

A movement behind him caught Leo's eye. Rui no longer sat beside him; he stood with a crowd, half the village it seemed. A few of them he recognized: Squidlips Gill, Gaffer Paulo, their wives with young children or babies who were surprisingly quiet; Serafim, Prazeres, Rosa and Rui were at the front with their hands clasped as they observed Leo, waiting for whatever would befall them, united and looking as fearful as if the Sword of Damocles was about to fall.

Despite his heart going at a hundred beats a minute and the sound of blood rushing in his ears, Leo took a deep breath and asked, "Why do you think you're to blame, Uncle Serafim?"

Prazeres stepped closer to her husband and squeezed his arm. He blinked and took a moment before he answered. "Because, Leo," he licked his lips, "I was worried. I mean, I wanted to help as much as I could but this story of your father's sounded like big trouble. Drugs and mafia. It scared me. You see, there's the village to protect and we don't get much trouble here and…" He paused.

"…and you thought Tom would bring it," Leo supplied for him, despair at the knowledge he was right welling in the pit of his stomach.

Serafim chewed his lip and concentrated on a dried starfish on the sand. "Yes," he said finally. "Somewhat ironic when you think of what happened this weekend, but anyway, Prazeres said when we got your father's letter that we had to do something, as he was my nephew and so on. So I sent one of those phone messages."

"An SMS," Rui filled in.

"…to Tom. I said we," he coughed, straightened his shoulders and tightened his jaw as if preparing himself for a confession that could only end badly, "I said we looked forward to seeing him here soon."

That would've been the message Leo had seen Tom reading the day Leo had been tinkering under his car. He wondered what Serafim would say if he knew Tom's reaction had been, "fucking *primos*."

"Yes?" Leo urged. "And?"

"That's it."

Leo processed this information. He stood and faced the group which, as one, moved in closer to Serafim. "So why does sending a text message make you to blame?"

Serafim twisted his hands in front of him. "I should've done more. Perhaps actually spoken to him, instead of that MSM thing. I should've done what your father suggested and told him we had work for him here. But I was…"

"*We* were uncertain," Gaffer Paulo corrected. "We had a village meeting with Serafim…"

"…in the café," Squidlips Gil added.

Paulo continued, "…and all agreed that we'd be delighted for Tom to visit but we couldn't in all honesty promise him lucrative work. We couldn't carry out what your father asked of us. It might have put the village at risk, all that talk of drug mafias. It was too dangerous. That's when we composed the message Serafim sent and let him decide for himself whether he wanted to know his family."

"I know it wasn't exactly encouraging," Serafim said.

"So when you turned up," Prazeres said, "we thought you were Tom. You seemed so ill at ease, it made sense. And as you arrived much later than we expected, we wondered if you'd come so you could hide from the police or something. It was a bit scary, but we tried not to show it. Your father said you—Tom, that is—was difficult so we decided that you wanted to be left quiet and that's what we did, let you find your own way about for the first few days and hope that you'd confide in us after. We never thought that…that…what had happened. And it never occurred to us that you were Leo."

"I'm so sorry, Leo, that I didn't do more," Serafim said. "With hindsight…"

Leo couldn't inhale properly; his breath was coming in small puffs as he watched his new-found uncle's bearded face tighten in despair.

"God, no, man. Guess in your place, I'd have done the same." Leo gathered his uncle in his arms and hugged until the Serafim's hefty body relaxed. But Leo's mind churned along with his stomach.

He'd found what he was looking for: an answer to who was responsible for the deaths and the sinking. Tom. And his mother.

He could only guess what his father had planned to do on that fateful day. Maybe he'd hoped to offload the cargo at sea too. Perhaps they were fighting over that when the wave hit; neither of them paying enough attention to what the sea was doing.

A pinging sound made him think he'd hit the right button. But it was Prazeres's cell phone ringing. She stared at the screen and then at her husband, her face, if possible, even more serious. "Jack Pepper *está cá.*"

The atmosphere couldn't have changed more rapidly if lightning had struck them. Serafim whirled round, crying, "*Deus.*" And the crowd jumped like stung rats. "We'll talk more," Serafim shouted at him as he turned to run down the beach. "Later."

Leo had no idea who Jack Pepper was or why the name caused so much consternation. His mind, in any case, was elsewhere.

The best place to clear it, he decided, and chew over events was at sea. He wandered towards the jetty where he found Squidlips Gil, Slippery Dick and Gaffer Paulo preparing to set sail for overnight scabbard fishing. The others who'd been on the beach were nowhere to be seen.

Leo peered into the storage shed where the fishermen kept their equipment. As he expected, it stank of fish, fuel, rubber and acrid bait. One wall was covered with a pile of plastic boxes, another with nets and buoys and a tangle of lines, hooks, haulers, ropes and rubber boots. And something pushed up in a corner piqued his interest.

He poked his head round the door where Paulo was loading the last of the ice.

"Can I take the inflatable that's in there out?"

" 'Course. The outboard needs fuel, and the boat might need air but still, I think it floats as long as you don't go far. Take care anyway, son. And keep a look out for Grady floating on the waves."

CHAPTER TWENTY-FOUR

Piper's head felt full of cotton-wool and her mouth dry. Her feet dangled over the side of the bed, and she winced at the stab of pain in her shoulder and arm, then slid her feet into a pair of hospital slippers and stood up. Holding on to a chair, she waited for the dizziness to pass before she picked up an empty glass from the bedside table and headed to fill it up at the bathroom tap.

It was taking a while for the cocktail of sedatives and painkillers to work their way out of her system, but the doctor, who'd been in to see her earlier, said as long as she took it easy for a week or so, she could be discharged later today.

She'd gleaned from the doctor's stuttered English that only one tendon in her shoulder had been nicked and treatment, as far as she understood, would be rest and physiotherapy.

Slaking her thirst with a long draught of water, she eyed her image in the mirror: pale, dark rings around her eyes, hair sticking up like a porcupine's in a gale. Looking like she did, there was no way anyone would've wanted to kiss her in the night. Boy, what a dream. Tom Shine had kissed her. That was just plain weird. Why would he want to do that when she'd outed him and pulled him up from the sea bottom by his hair? His lips had been as soft and warm as she remembered when she'd breathed air into him in the sea and, even though it had been a dream, it had moved her in a way she wasn't used to. *Painkillers and sedatives addled your brain, that was for sure.*

Something heavy hit the door to her room, making the wooden frame rattle.

She staggered out of the bathroom to see what the scuffle and shouting was all about.

"I want to take her back to talk to my father." That harsh voice sounded familiar. It was one-eyed Gasper's, she was sure of it. He wasn't quite all there in her opinion, and he was the last person she wanted outside her door throwing stuff about. She stood with her back against the door: he wasn't going to get in here.

"Yew think Oi'm goin' to let moi dawter stay with that psycho?"

Pop? That was *Pop's* voice? Jesus Henry and Margaret.

"Psycho? When you're nothing more than a pedophile!"

Another crash rocked the wall, definitely a chair.

"Are yew mad? Yew let that madwomen stab 'er. And *pedophile*? Felipa was seventeen! That does not make me a pedophile."

Piper's heart pounded as she rested her hot forehead against the cool door that vibrated with the force of the two men's anger.

"Let go of my arm!"

"Oi'll take moi hands off a yew when yew apologize, yew, yew…"

"I warn you, you murdering son of a bitch."

"Oi murdered no one! Yew fool. And yew're a foin one to tawk."

Being too dazed to consider what was happening, she stood at the now open door in her hospital robe and her bum hanging out. Hospital staff rushed down the corridor to find out why two burly, middle-aged men were shouting at each other and why Pop brandished a chair over his head, about to drop it on Gaspar.

Piper was *this much* away from putting her foot down and saying, 'If you two would just dampen down your rampant testosterone for a moment, I'd like to mention that the decision on whether I go or stay lies with me.'

But the first word, *if*, came out as a croak and nobody heard or took any notice of her. In any case, two policemen came along. They separated Gaspar and her father, sent Gaspar away—perhaps to a waiting area in the company of a nurse—and, after listening to Pop, allowed him to enter Piper's room with a nurse. She handed Piper her linen bag that she'd left in the stable the previous morning. "Man bring this for you. He say it yours."

"A tall man with whitish hair?"

"No. Short with beard."

Serafim then. That's who must've been in her room earlier. And the kiss? She snorted at the idea. Shame really, she rather liked the idea of Tom's kiss.

"This man your father?" the nurse asked.

Piper nodded, which made the room whirl. "Hey Pop." She sank onto the bed to try and get her mind in order. Was she still dreaming? How did Pop get here?

The two policemen returned, minus, she was relieved to see, Gaspar. They spoke in English, which was nothing like the villagers', and asked her what she remembered of the incident on the beach, and she told them the little she knew.

"She—Lili—in...how-you-say?" One policeman looked at the other for help.

"How abowt custody?" Pop offered.

"That right. Custard. She say she wasn't...you not her victim."

"She says she wasn't aiming for me?"

"Yes, she say she mad at all village in total and I think you were...there in wrong place. She say she not herself. We say she need *howyousay?*"

"Psycho treatment," Piper supplied.

"Psychiatric," Pop corrected.

When Piper thought back, she remembered Lili's wide, staring eyes which weren't focused solely on her; they had the glazed look of someone who was, well, just nuts, either temporarily or permanently.

"Exactly. We need to know if you want to…" The policeman looked at his colleague who shrugged.

"…press charges?" Piper was tired, exhausted by all this guesswork. "No, I don't want to press charges. On condition you get her some help and soon."

The policemen seemed to relax at her words; perhaps one night of Lili's histrionics in the police station was one too much for them. "She get help," they assured her.

"And what about Tom Shine? You got him in custody too?"

The policemen looked at each other before one shrugged. "Tom Shine. I know nothing of that name." And with that, they saluted and left.

Tom Shine had escaped? Was he still in the village?

The doctor was the next visitor. He shook his head when Pop said he was going to take Piper home back to the UK within the hour. "Not good idea. She has pain and big shock. Plane is not good for her right now. In maybe two, three days?"

"Pop. I'm not going home right now. There's too much I want to do in Luminosa. You said it was a danger, but everyone was kindness itself to me. I'm not going without at least saying goodbye." She also wanted to sort out Tom Shine. Now, just why did she feel a glow at that thought?

"Yew see?" Pop cried, pointing at her but talking to the doctor. "If she's well enough tew argue, she c'n travel. Oi want her home, safe 'n sound, loike." With his usual good-old-mates attitude, Pop flung his heavy arm around the doctor's shoulder and led him out of the room, murmuring in his ear.

Piper looked around for her clothes. She could put her jeans on, but her t-shirt was bloody and torn. The one she'd worn before would have to do, and she pulled the fishy smelling object out of her linen bag and put it on. When Pop came back, she'd make him take her back to Luminosa. She couldn't go away yet, she didn't want to so she wouldn't. Pure and simple.

Pop came back in, carrying her x-rays, followed by a nurse. His face cracked into his wide grin. "Here yew are, moi love. Yew tek these." He turned to the nurse who popped a pill into her mouth and helped her swallow it with a plastic cup of water. "Tha' old doc has said I c'n tek responsibility for yew."

****

Piper had an idea she was in a car of some kind, felt Pop settle her head against his shoulder and crooned an out of tune ditty:

"From Liverpool docks we bid adieu
To Suke, and Sal, and Kittie too
The anchor's weighed and the sails unfurl
We're bound to cross the watery row
For we know we're outward bound
Hurrah, we're outward bound"

Pop's rumble was a shanty she remembered from childhood, as comfortable as a security blanket. Of course, that could've been a dream too, she thought just before she sank back into oblivion. She only woke up when they arrived at the airport and Pop asked her for her passport.

She tried to shake the cotton-wool from her head. "I'm not going, Pop. I'm going back to Luminosa." She tried to get out of the taxi, but collapsed on the pavement. "Shit." Her legs felt like jelly.

Pop stuffed her into a wheelchair and wheeled her inside the terminal.

"I'm not going," she cried, her words slurring. "Pop, you take me back right this minute. What's Prazeres going to say that I didn't say goodbye?" And Etta? She'd only just met her and she missed her already. And, of *course,* she wanted to get to the bottom of Tom Shine. She giggled at that thought, his *bottom.* Damn, that hurt and she was so thirsty. She took the bottle of water Pop handed her and drank deeply. "Right," she said, attempting to get out of the wheelchair. "I'm going to the bus station and going back to Luminosa. They've got a criminal in their midst."

"I should say so," Pop said.

Then she remembered Pop saying something like, "No she innt drunk." She remembered getting loaded onto the plane and the scream of the engines as they took off. And she felt no pain. It only came rushing back when they were over the Bay of Biscay.

As her mind cleared, she ground her teeth. She would get some money and head right back at the earliest possibility, she told her father.

"Fair 'nuff."

"I mean, what's the rush? Why couldn't I say goodbye?"

Pop turned to her from trying to get his orange juice packet open. " 'Tis an emergency, Pip. Now's the toim we hev to tawk. Serious-loik."

"What is it? Money?"

"Old Todd, he lent me some. Anyway Oi got money from the car. Oi sold it."

"That's just dandy, but somehow not entirely surprising. You know we'll have to pay a fine on the van too? For leaving it at the curb at Heathrow like I did."

"Oi told the police it were stolen."

She closed her eyes. "You got any more pain-killers?"

"Oi do. But first Oi hev to tell you somethin'. One reason Oi want you home so quick was because of them old psychos in Luminosa. And another: Pip, it's abowt your ma. She innt, yew know, dead."

Piper decided she was still dreaming. This wasn't real. She shook her head to clear it and looked back at him. His eyes were as circular as two fifty-p coins and filled with tears.

"She's alive?" she whispered.

He nodded.

"All this time?"

He swallowed noisily and nodded. "But now she's dying, Pip."

Chapter Twenty-Five

The full story only came out the following day. The mental pain Piper experienced was greater than her physical, but she was grateful for the tablets Pop gave her so that she could escape from the world for a while without having to try to make sense of it.

After a night of drug-filled dreams, she woke in her old bed in the draughty cottage. On shaking legs, she descended the creaking stairs to find her father rocking backward and forwards in his scruffy armchair, and sea-water in the kitchen. "Tide were higher than ever, last noit, Pip," he said when he saw her.

She sat on the sofa and made herself as comfortable as possible, shivering at the damp that swamped the air. "Tell me."

****

Eighteen years old and tired of doing odd-jobs aboard leaky fishing boats operating out of Lowestoft, Jack Pepper decided he wanted to see the world. There were plenty of vessels leaving the port so it was just a question of signing on for one, long distance fishing, cargo—didn't matter much—get off in whatever port caught his fancy and then sign on for another vessel.

"Oi sailed the seven seas, Pip." He counted off on his

fingers, "The Black Sea, Caspian, Arabian, Indian Ocean, Red Sea, Mediterranean, Atlantic, Pacific, Adriatic, Baltic."

More than seven, but never mind.

"Oi had a high owd toim but four years later, Pips, Oi felt loik comin' home."

He would have been twenty-two then and he'd done all that by the time he was her age. She couldn't help but feel a pang of envy and more than a smidgeon of anger that he'd discouraged her from spreading her wings or going where her heart led her.

He decided to go home when he was in Santo Domingo where he'd grown tired of fiestas. At the port of Barahona he found a cargo ship carrying bauxite, destination Portugal. One of the crew had been offloaded as being too sick to work, so Jack Pepper was hired at the last minute as an able-bodied seaman.

"So, first question, Pop."

"Off yew go then."

"Are you Norman Pines or Jack Pepper?"

"Well, now tha's a difficult one. Both. Born Jack Pepper, changed name to Norman Pines."

Brilliant. She was Piper Pepper.

He continued, recalling the journey across the Bermuda triangle with its huge swells and storms. "Oi was mostly helmsman," he told her with pride.

She knew the strong Gulf Stream could push a ship off course with ease, so that was some job.

He was concerned about the cargo shifting and couldn't understand why the chief mate wouldn't let him down to the hold to check on it.

They came back via the Azores and refueled in Madeira. "But they never let us crew go offshore which Oi thought hard. But no crew ashore were orders and were obeyed. It were a strange ship with a quiet crew who were loik ghosts, they were. No arsing abowt or becoming mates loik on most ships. Everyone just went about their tasks and then in the little toim they had orff, just slept. Oi were glad when the Portuguese coast shewed up."

That was when they slowed until nightfall before anchoring in a small bay. It was a pitch black night with a new moon. "Oi were on day shift an' when that ended, they said only necessary crew on deck and everyone else stay down below. But it were hot down there so Oi crept up. Oi was by now more'n' suspicious somethin' were up, so Oi took care not to be seen."

He made it to the deck where he found the cargo hold open and a small fishing boat with a wheelhouse tied astern. Curious, Pop made his way to the hold where most of the activity was taking place. The few night-crew climbed down a ladder from the cargo hold, carrying boxes that they handed to a man in the small boat.

"That weren't no metal bauxite, Pip, in them small parcels. Drugs, Oi knew immediately—seen enough o' the stuff in moi travels and how they pack 'em. Well, Oi didn't want no truck with that game, Oi decided it was roight mawkin' for getting on that ship and all Oi wanted were to get orff it fast."

Security on board the cargo vessel must've been very lax, Piper decided when she heard that Pop picked up a large box of packages and clambered down a ladder with the box perched on his shoulder so that it shielded his face. Luck was on his side that day; no one noticed him and if anyone found one crew member wasn't on the vessel, then they only discovered it later. Nor did anyone see him crouched behind a pile of boxes now stowed on the fishing boat.

"There were only one man on board—middle-aged man Oi later knew as Nelson. Didn't take long afore they finished off-loading boxes and the boat set orff for the beach."

Hidden from view by the cargo, it was easy for Pop to

slip off the gunwale with barely a splash once they were near the shore, and he swam in the opposite direction so he arrived on the far side of the beach. From what he could see in the unlit world, he was standing within a short distance of a small village of white-painted cottages running along the main street.

"Starless and bible-black." The image conjured up Dylan Thomas's words from Under Milkwood in Piper's mind. "The houses are blind as moles."

In the next few days, Jack Pepper would discover that the place was lit by generators and, normally, the little village would be lit up because those cottagers whose husbands, brothers or sons were due back with the fishing fleet would still be up, ready to feed them. But in those days, just one or two a month on the new moon—or dark moon as they called it—it was traditional to take the night off and go to bed early. And that night was one of them so the only illumination was a dim light set into a cave-like structure in the rocks at the far end of the beach where the fishing boat he'd been on was being unloaded.

Jack Pepper's aim was to find a main road and hitch a lift to Lisbon which, he knew from the navigational maps on board the ship, was just up the coast to the north, maybe forty miles or so. His clothes would soon dry in the warm night air.

But he hadn't gone more than a few yards along the cobblestone street before a cottage door opened, "an' this apparition rushed out, goin' loik the clappers." Pop's face took on a dreamy look. "Bright sunlight, Pips, tha's what it felt loik just to look at her."

The girl was sweet-scented, small, with two little dimples high up on her cheeks. Piper touched her own as Pop carried on. "She laughed at me, she did. A soft giggle and then in the dim loight from the cottage I saw she blushed roight to her roots."

" 'Spect Oi look funny," Jack Pepper had looked down at his dripping self.

"Wet," she agreed, stifling her amusement with her hand. "Listen, I'll take you to Serafim's café so you can dry off."

"Not the Serafim you know, Pips. 'Twas his dad then. Owd feller, he were."

Pop was in two minds whether to continue his plan and get out of there, or whether to stay a while longer with this stunning girl. He decided to stay.

In the café, the "owd feller Serafim," without asking questions, gave him a room and dried his clothes, saying they enjoyed having visitors and didn't get enough of them. The next morning, Jack Pepper went back to the cottage the girl had emerged from, but it turned out she'd been visiting a cousin. The girl's name was Felipa and she lived up the hill. Following the directions they gave him from the cottage, he trudged up there and, "lo an' behold, there she were, comin' moi way. Her sweet face turned to the sun like a *girasol*—tha's a sunflower." They walked back together to the beach. "She said she couldn't live without the sea and she had to come every day. Anyway the fishermen was expectin' her. Oi didn't know what she meant then."

Down on the jetty it was a beautiful morning over the sea, gentle waves lapping against the keels of the moored fishing boats and sunlight reflecting off the waves onto the bright walls of the fishermen's cottages. Felipa spoke to a couple of fishermen who were loading their boats with buoys and nets before she returned to Jack.

"Fancy another walk?" She held her hands behind her back and her doe-like eyes gazed at the ground just by his feet, suddenly shy.

They dawdled and she showed him the vineyards, some weasel droppings in a nearby field, colorful jays flitting in the branches of cork trees that blushed when stripped of their bark. Piper imagined they were diverted by other activities too, but kept her peace.

By the time they'd scrambled up the steep path to the top of the cliffs, Jack Pepper knew he was in love with this lemon-scented girl, and he also discovered why the girl helped the fishermen. As they lay on their stomachs, chewing on leaves of fragrant wild herbs, they drowsily watched the bobbing fishing boats now well offshore.

"I told João he needs to head to the west if he wants sea-bream," she said, the skin around her eyes crinkling against the glare of the sun. "That cherry color, that's where he'll find them. Look at that! He's passed over a shoal of *corvina*." She glanced at him, her dimples deepening. "But I expect you think I'm mad, seeing colors in the sea, don't you?"

Felipa and Jack had three idyllic days together in Luminosa; they trekked the fields disturbing hares, martens and even a wild boar that tore out of the undergrowth at twilight. She took him out in one of the skiffs to catch mackerel, leading him to the largest shoals he'd ever encountered, and they swam in the cold Atlantic waters.

"It were really too cold for me, but she were loik you, Pips. She could hold her breath for minutes and never wanted to come up once she gone down. Said it were magic down there. Scared the shit…excuse me…loife out a me when she stayed down too long. Just loik you."

But what Jack Pepper didn't know was that Felipa was disobeying her father who expressly forbade her to talk to the fishermen. If she saw colors, then she had to tell him and he'd tell the fishermen which way to go.

"Why was her father like that?"

"Said it were common-loik to tawk to fishermen an' she were above them. Didn't allow 'er to even go near the sea. Kinda broke Felipa's heart that did, but she still did it."

"What about her mother, my grandmother?"

"She'd died two years before of somethin', probably from living with tha' owd git."

"Did she, my grandmother, love the sea? And see colors?"

"Oi think all the females in the family could for generations back."

It was the third day that Felipa's father found them on the beach grilling mackerel on a portable grill that they'd set between two beached boats in the hope of not being seen. Felipa later told Jack Pepper she'd confided her feelings for him to her brother and that was why her father had come looking for her.

"Weren't pretty, Pips. Things he said. Loik Oi was the type who drilled anything tha' moved. Oi recognized him right enough as bein' the bloke who was taking delivery of tha' stuff from the trawler an' Oi told 'im Oi'd tell the police on 'im about the drugs an' he threatened to set the drug mafia on me. Cut me hands orff and maybe more when they caught me, tha's what he said they did. He were violent to Felipa too, pulling her too rough for moi loiking, trying to make her go back to that big owd house which she told me she didn't loike because the English family weren't there no more, and wished she could live with her cousins in their cottage, near the sea. So Oi hit 'im. Square on the nose. Blood spurtin'. Weren't pretty, Pips, no." He wrung his hands, staring into middle distance. "Oi hurt 'im, Oi did." He spoke in a quiet, regretful voice.

While Felipa's father was bent over holding his bleeding face, Jack and Felipa grabbed each other's hands and, without saying a word, raced up the hill together to the main road. A passing car stopped for them, and the driver told them he was going to Lisbon if they wanted a lift.

****

As Pop finished his story, Piper moved for the first time, wincing at the pain in her shoulder but now resolving not to take any more drugs. "I think," she said carefully, "that I would like to see my mother now."

CHAPTER TWENTY-SIX

Serafim hadn't been kidding when he said the inflatable didn't have much air in it, and the engine gave a grumpy rumble as if it hadn't been cleaned or maintained for a good while. No matter, it floated and that's all Leo wanted right now: to be on the water, to feel the rhythm of the Atlantic swell and currents. The waves broke early here, near the promontory, but farther south they broke on the beach. It would be a good place to surf.

There's music in the deep:

It is not in the surf's rough roar…There's quiet in the deep.

His father's voice echoed in his head.

"Why'd you keep all that was happening from me, Dad?" Leo murmured now at the glittering water that whispered against the deflating rubber. "We never had secrets, the three musketeers."

His father's written words to Serafim returned: I don't want Leo mixed up in this…he'll stick to his brother like glue.

Wasn't that what brothers were for? He could've got Tom out of that mess but then it seemed Tom wasn't as transparent as Leo thought. Who'd have thought his brother was so obsessed by their mother, that he'd really stoop so low as to take on that kind of task for her. Their fucking mother. She was to blame for everything. She was the one he'd been seeking to reap his revenge on. The bitch.

He was drifting north which wasn't ideal since he was losing sight of Luminosa beach. He turned the throttle on the outboard but it barely responded. "Why didn't you trust me, Tom?" he whispered.

Trust Saint Leo?

Was that Tom's voice or was it his own sub-conscious talking? *Saint Leo?* Tom had never called him that before. True, he'd talked his brother out of getting a nose ring (it would get caught on a net), and tried to advise him to tone his fighting technique down a tad (kicking a guy's butt three times when he was down just wasn't right), but Tom had replied, "You gotta fight dirty. You fight fair you only gonna lose 'cos they'll take advantage of ya."

Crap, the outboard wasn't responding at all well, choking like a moose in a noose. With a final burp of smoke, it stopped. He tried full throttle, but the engine didn't even cough. Maybe he could try cleaning the plug, but it would take a while to dismantle the outboard and the current heading north grew stronger, he was already drifting beyond the promontory. For the first time he noticed there wasn't even a damn paddle on board. Had he lost his mind? That should've been one of the first things to check.

He was well round the promontory now, still floating north on the ebb with yet another half hour before the tide turned. When it did, he was pretty sure it would push him south again. He'd just have to wait it out because Paulo and Gil's longliner was not much more than a dot on the horizon by now, and they couldn't see him. What about the search and rescue? If they were still out looking for Grady, Leo hadn't seen any sign of them.

Perhaps if he tried riding the waves towards those narrow caves along the shoreline, he could shelter for a while. A movement in one of them caught his eye at the same moment the inflatable farted the rest of its air into the sea and sank even lower. The weight of the useless outboard didn't help matters, but while he vacillated between whether he should leave it on or just drop it, he sank waist-high in the water.

Time for a swim, then. His body prickled against the chill. Jesus, the water was cold, something he'd hardly noticed yesterday. He struck out for the cave where he'd seen movement—it didn't take a genius to know who was in it.

If Grady had fallen overboard this time yesterday then he was lucky the tidal stream was running in at just over a knot, Leo reckoned, in the direction of the cave. Leo didn't even attempt to use much energy swimming because he knew the water would land him, express delivery, right near the shelter. By now he'd adjusted somewhat to the temperature so he wallowed, barely kicking, and thought of the way Piper had flowed towards him when he'd been trapped in the weed. The smidgeon of envy he felt at her underwater skills encouraged him to dive deep, trying, but failing he knew, to imitate her easy style, so smooth and deceptively effortless.

Bubbles of his breath rose to the surface like soda-water as he swam for the small cave. Through the rippling water he could see a pair of trembling legs in blue pin-striped pants, up to the shins in water. Not so dapper now, then.

"Thank God. Help me," Grady gasped as Leo emerged, eight or nine meters away where the coastal-shelf dipped sharply. "Please don't leave me here." Grady's dark hair, which had been gelled back yesterday into a quiff, now dripped like rats' tails down into his eyes.

"Think again, bud." Leo treaded water.

"Damn you," Grady snarled through his chattering teeth.

"Still got the bad attitude, Grady?" Leo spat out salt water, and then peered under the surface for a moment before re-emerging. "Lost your shoes?" Yesterday Grady had worn the shiniest shoes Leo had ever seen.

"For Chrissakes, man. I am numb from the waist down,

I have lost all feeling."

"Been standing in water all night then?"

"Of course I have, isn't it obvious? And the water doesn't seem to get any lower than this."

The guy would be experiencing his second low tide now, but even so he needn't take that *I'm-talking-to-Mister-Stupid* tone.

Leo rubbed his chin, scratching at the stubble. He gazed at the waves flowing in, judging how much longer they'd have before the water level rose again. "Who'd a thought? How'd you lose the boat?"

Grady gripped the rocks beside him, his hands trembling. His face was grey under the spray tan. "I…I fell overboard." It could've been the cold and weakness that made his voice waver; it sure couldn't have been embarrassment at his ineptness, the man didn't have a self-doubt in his body. Leo was right, because the next moment Grady was leering like a skeleton. "A bit like you fell overboard yesterday."

"Thanks for stopping to help me. Appreciated it."

"Shouldn't have tried to fight me, should you?"

"Shouldn't have pulled a knife on me, should you?"

Grady set his jaw, perhaps to try and assert his position. "Now listen, whoever you are. And just who are you? Hughes or that other person the girl shouted yesterday. Tom something?"

"Name's Leo Shine. I'd offer my hand but I'm using it to stay afloat here."

Grady shook his head. "How many names you got?" he asked as he watched the waves rolling in. "It's going to get higher again, right? The tide?"

"Tends to do that on a regular basis."

"Then I have to get out of here, because let me tell you, I was up to my neck last night before it started dropping."

"Is that a fact?" Leo said, pretending to be surprised.

"Now that's a bummer because high tide this evening will be round about nine and, oh man," Leo wiped his hand through his hair, feigning desperation, "I heard rumors that it's a waxing gibbous moon." He made it sound as if this was dire news, even though the flood tide would be a little lower tonight.

"What's that mean? Sounds like a monkey."

"You could jump up and down, I guess, for a while, try to keep your head above water. Or try and float. Water's a tad cold, though, and hypothermia's a bitch. Now, it's been good shooting the breeze with you, but I guess I'll head on back round the promontory, back to the beach, and I suggest you do the same."

Grady swayed and sank a few inches, his eyes widening, arms flailing. "Take me with you. I'm not the best swimmer. To tell you the truth," (that'll be a first, Leo thought), "I can't swim at all. When I fell overboard last night, a wave brought me in here and smashed me against the rock, this one here, which I managed to hold on, otherwise I'd have drowned. I reckon you could do it, you know, help me, like those life-savers do on their backs. If you'll do that, I'll make it worth your while. I'm a very rich man, you know."

Leo scratched his chin again, grinning inwardly at the thought of Grady riding on his back. What did he think he was, a dolphin? "Hmm," he ruminated. "It's tempting but with the tidal stream running this way, I guess I'll have a struggle myself, going all that way. I mean, I'll do my best, but I might have to drop you mid-ocean if I get too tired, you get my meaning. Then you'd be on your own."

Grady's face returned to its former haggard look, now wrinkled and fallen in on itself like a rotten apple. "Are there sharks? There aren't, are there?"

Leo treaded water. It *was* getting colder, and he couldn't help but be a bit sorry for the bastard standing in the water all these hours. "Basking sharks." He had no idea if they were off this coast, but this sounded like it might scare the crap out of Grady. He wasn't going to let the guy off too easily.

"Are they dangerous?"

"Very, if you meet one with an attitude problem." They normally ate plankton but, still, it was good to think that Grady was now pissing into the sea. "By the way, didn't you see a helicopter out looking for you earlier?"

Grady looked away, biting his lip. So, Leo concluded, the guy really was scared of being in the authorities' hands, to the extent he'd stand in cold water for hours on end.

A larger wave swept in and sloshed Grady, splashing his face, making him squeal. The guy was freaking out. Leo would have to get him out of there in the next half hour; otherwise, Grady would go into pure meltdown the higher the water level rose. It was possible, with the turn of the tide now, that Leo could tow him to the beach, but it would be risky with Grady panicking half-way. And the cold would get to them both because it would be slow-going.

"OK," Leo said, relenting. "I'll see how to get you out. Hang in there a while."

Grady made a feeble attempt to strike out to join Leo but immediately snatched at the rock behind him again. "I'll give you anything."

Leo swam full circle and treaded water. "Whatcha got?"

"Anything."

"Money?"

"So much you can't imagine."

"You trying to say Lili and Nelson had that much to hand over to you? Because, far as I could see, the other old folks you were trying to rip off sure hadn't passed across a cent."

"I'm not talking about their money or that broken-down house. Those investors this weekend were merely going to pay deposits which would cover the land price and the money owed to the mayor."

"Kickback for subverting state regulations, huh?" This guy never gave up trying to fool folks that he was squeaky clean.

"Listen, I help communities like this rundown village. Think of the employment my project will create?"

"Assuming it ever really gets built. And I guess if you ask the villagers, I know what their preference would be."

"This project is peanuts compared to my usual entrepreneurial ventures and *that's* where I have money invested. In any case, I'll still profit from this weekend's fiasco." Grady glanced at a small niche in the rock where a piece of paper rested above the water line. "I have the paper signed by Nelson. I'll sue him for breach of contract and, I tell you what, I'll halve the compensation with you."

Leo thought the paper in the niche must be soaking wet and wondered how much writing on it was still legible. "Bullshit. How about being honest for once in your life? You ever tried giving that a whirl? You prey on gullible people that you like to get tanked."

Despite the cold he must be feeling, Grady turned red. "Listen, you scum, who gatecrashed under false names— kettle, pot, black Shine. I went to Harvard, I run a hedge-fund in Singapore, I worked for many years for Sachman... Gold..." He released one white-knuckled grip on the rock and pinched the bridge of his nose, trying to find the name.

"Uh huh." Leo shook his head. "Gotcha. The cold water must be addling your brain. You ran a hedge-fund in Switzerland, that's what you told them at the meeting. You're just full of crap, Grady. Why not call your private plane and ask them to come pick you up? Tell them you're in the second cave on the right. Bye." With that, Leo turned and swam with a strong crawl straight out to sea, riding the current. Whenever he turned his head to breathe, he heard Grady's pleas growing more distant.

It was hard going so he turned on his back to get his breath. The cliff rose high above him, throwing him into shadow. As he stared to the left up at the escarpment, he chewed the inside of his cheek. Yep, that would do. He turned over and swam back to the cave where Grady's face was greyer than ever.

"What? Didn't the plane answer your call?" Leo asked as he reached Grady who was now submerged up to his waist. He needed to get out of there pretty soon. "But first, one thing. How'd you find out about the Carneiros? And the land?" If it proved *this* guy had anything to do with the *Goblin's* involvement in trafficking, however obscure, then Leo would leave him here.

Grady's teeth chattered as he answered, stumbling over the words. "My work brings me to the Iberian Peninsula, my work as a *hedge-fund...*"

"Yeah right. So we'll wait for the search and rescue. All right by you?"

Grady sighed. "I am often entertained by clients and, one day, I was in Miami meeting some influential people who," he paused for a moment before continuing, "who told me about Luminosa."

Miami. Where his train-wreck of a mother lived. "Would these *influential people* have been involved in, heaven forbid, any shady business?"

"Such as?" Grady looked offended.

Leo treaded water, considering his best line of attack. "How did they know about Luminosa? And tell me the truth, if that's not a word totally outside your vocabulary."

"And then you'll help me out of here?"

"Yep."

"Take me somewhere no one will see us."

"Do my best."

Grady clung to the rock, his knuckles white. "They told me that a year or so ago they'd tried to re-start a business connection with someone they knew in Luminosa, something about dropping off deliveries here. All to do with trade routes you understand."

"Of course."

"Well, long story, short, the person they contacted was—and this is between you and me," he tapped his nose, "was Nelson. But who replied to their approach was Lili. According to my source in Miami, she agreed to take on a couple of deliveries with an associate of hers who had a small boat to make the pick-up."

"Gaspar?"

"Possibly. Anyway, both times the deal was struck Lili failed to come through. My connection in Miami was rightfully upset, but Lili's excuse was that her associate had refused to cooperate."

"Grady, I would say that knowing Lili, that she agreed before asking Gaspar. Then, when it came time to take delivery, Gaspar refused. If these friends of yours in Miami are the ones I think they are, I'm surprised they didn't come to visit the village all guns blazing."

"Shine, anyone I work with does not operate that way." Grady rolled his eyes, the asshole.

But then, Leo realized, the Miami mafia would probably have other, subtler, methods to punish: washing out ballasts filled with toxic marine ooze on a dark night in a bay rich in fish stocks would be one; sending Grady to wreck Lili and Nelson's lives would be another.

"How did you get her to meet you?"

"That was easy. A quick note to tell her about how talented I'd heard she was as a bullfighter and an invitation to join me at a fight in Campo Grand in Lisbon."

Is a butterfly not attracted to crap? "One last question.

You ever been or had contacts with Alaska?"

Grady's lip curled and his complexion became even whiter as if Leo had asked him to gut a pollock. Alaska might be cold, foggy and rainy but it didn't deserve that reaction. Leo loved the mist that nestled at the base of snowy mountains, the hiking, skiing and sailing, and the beauty of the tundra. "Guess not?" he ventured.

"No. I never have," Grady replied with a sneer. "Mr. uh…Shine?" he said through gritted teeth. "I've enjoyed our conversation, but do you think we could get out of here now?"

"Now here's the deal," Leo said, still treading water. "We'll get up the cliff. Or at least part of the way if we can't get all the way up. But at least we can wait there for the ebb tide."

"How can we climb out of this?" Grady whimpered as he surveyed the rock surface of the walls. "I tried that yesterday but the rocks are too smooth and I slipped off and hurt my arm."

"We need to swim a little to the north—that's left from here." Leo pointed, away from the village. "There the cliff face is easier to climb. The rocks look craggy to me, so I reckon we'll have footholds."

"But do I have to swim to get there?"

"Two choices: swim or stay here. You decide, unless you're Jesus Christ and can walk on water."

Another high wave swept in. "I'll swim," Grady said after he'd spluttered and wretched on the salt water he'd swallowed. "But you'll have to help me."

"Chill a mo'. I didn't tell you the deal yet. If you want my help out of here, you give me that paper." Leo pointed to the little niche in the wall. "If it's the same one that Nelson signed."

Grady chewed his lips before replying, "How about, I

give it to you when we reach land and safety? Deal?"

The paper was probably already ruined, but signatures were signatures and who knew what could survive and still be evidence? Leo shook his head, treaded water and held out his hand. "Nope. It's now or never." He kicked so that he drifted farther out.

"No wait!"

When Leo had the paper in his hand, he glanced at it and then tore it in two, then four, then six. Tiny pieces floated on the surface. Grady looked at them with a spark of hope, as if he'd like to gather them and stick them together later.

"Now give me your shirt, Grady."

"My shirt?" He gazed at the material sagging from his torso. "It's a Hermés dress shirt."

A hermit shirt? As in crabs? "Take it off. Is it cotton?"

"Well, of course…"

"Good, makes it stronger." Leo reached under the water and tied one sleeve round Grady's waist, and the other one around his own. Then he grabbed Grady's trembling wrist and pulled. The knot around his waist came loose.

"It's not working!" Grady squealed like a stuck pig and grabbed the rock again.

"Dude, I am busting my balls here, trying to help you. Take your fucking hands off the wall and hold the knot I'm tying."

If a higher wave hadn't rushed in and pried Grady's hands off the rock, it might have been more difficult to make him let go.

"Don't do anything, except float on your back," Leo told him as they set out. It was slow-going, but they were making headway as Leo towed Grady through the water. What a great way to spend an afternoon that any tourist would describe as glorious.

Grady squirmed, making Leo break his stroke and a

wave struck him full in the face. "I'll let you go you do that again," he spluttered. "Just float for Chrissakes. Relax. Man, you're shivering like you got St. Vitus Dance."

He surveyed the cliff-face they were passing; the rocks were either still too smooth, or there were no easy places to gain a hold. He was getting cold too now, and tired which was bad news. If they couldn't find the place he'd spotted… Wait. "Here it is."

Holding Grady's wrist and fastened together by the shirt, Leo pushed him in front. "Clamber onto that platform. There." He steered him towards the small rock projection. "Grab the tufts of grass there."

Grady tried, Leo would give him that, but the guy hadn't the strength for levering himself up. "Guy like you with those pectorals, thought you spent hours at the gym," Leo said. "Let me try." With one hand still holding Grady's wrist and the other grabbing the jutting rock, Leo climbed over him, a tad too intimately for his personal liking, but still, needs must. He let go of the wrist and grabbed Grady's pants at the waist and hauled, his muscles straining. The shirt came loose and floated away.

"Oh my God!" Grady squealed, scrabbling at the slippery rocks.

"Chrissakes," Leo muttered, hoisting himself up to another rock where he got a hand-hold before dragging the half-drowned man up with him, sure he was scraping the poor bastard's chest and abdomen on the sharp rocks. It was a struggle as he held on to Grady's belt and levered himself up further, but he managed to scramble onto a ridge and pull Grady up beside him.

"You've broken my tendons," Grady whimpered, rubbing his arm.

"And it's not over yet. You gotta get up there."

Grady's stare followed Leo's finger pointing up the

sheer cliff face.

Despite his bravado, even Leo wasn't so sure they'd make it. He'd done rock climbing in Alaska with Tom. But then he'd had shoes, spikes, strong ropes, crampons, even a harness. Now he didn't even have the shirt to tie them together. He eyed Grady's pants, they might do and so would his own jeans. The day was going further downhill with every passing minute.

Or perhaps not. The putt-putt of an outboard had never sounded more beautiful. Nor had the sight of a fishing skiff, complete with cousin Rui at the tiller.

"Hey!" Leo waved.

"Over here," Grady cried, obviously uncaring now who was going to pick him up.

Rui guided the boat towards them, and Leo steadied Grady's arm as he wriggled on the ledge. "Take it easy, you'll fall into the sea, you jerk. He's still got a way to come."

Little did he know how prophetic those words would be.

Maybe it was instinct, or maybe he'd spotted or sensed a movement from above. Whatever, something made him lean to the side and as he did so, several rocks, some pretty big, fell from the sky and hit Grady smack on the crown of his head.

As he heard the splash of Grady hitting the water, Leo looked up and saw the top half of Victor Fletcher's head peeking over the edge of the cliff. "Whoops," he said.

Chapter Twenty-Seven

Ever since she'd been a child, Piper had dreamed of finding her mother alive. One day, a beautiful smiley woman with shiny smooth black hair would knock on the door, her arms full of presents. "I lost my memory," she'd tell a young Piper, "and have spent all this time roaming the world looking for my identity which I have only now remembered." She'd nod with understanding when Piper told her other kids teased her for being small, or talking about colors in the sea, or for wearing old clothes, or for smelling of fish. Her mum wouldn't say, *Oil go an' sort them owd mawthers owt"* and stomp up to the school in filthy, blood-stained wellington boots that left a trail of fish scales behind. No, her mum would sympathize and pat her and give sound advice such as not to poke anyone in the eye again, or that Piper's right hook was just a teeny bit too strong for ten-year-old boys to withstand, even though she was only eight.

Piper still kept that dream alive. Since she'd found the photo, she had a smiling face to imagine too and, for some reason, recently her mother wore a hat with a pheasant's feather in it, and smelled of freshly laundered sheets.

****

Piper and her father now walked up the cedar-lined drive to the entrance of a beige-stone building, complete with sash windows. They passed a sign that said 'hospice' and Piper murmured, "*Humankind cannot bear too much reality.*" T.S. Eliot had been spot on.

"Don't expect too much," Pop told her for the millionth time, holding tightly on to her hand as they walked through the glass main doors into a silent lobby that smelled of antiseptic and beeswax. He'd already told her that her mother was in a continuous vegetative state.

Their feet squeaked along the corridor, while staff members managed to glide along with barely a sound. Many greeted Pop either as Norman or Mr. Pines.

"Yew get the check awlroight?" he asked a bulky woman in a blue uniform who appeared like an apparition at a door that they passed.

"Don't you worry about that," she replied, her voice soft as silk.

"Don't yew worry…" Pop imitated, mocking her, once he and Piper were out of ear-shot. "She'd be givin' me a roight bollockin' if she hadn't received it."

Piper's heart was beating fast when they stopped in front of a closed door, and Pop turned the handle.

Her first impression was how peaceful it was in the room with just a regular puffing sigh of the breathing machine and how white, although the walls were covered in pictures, photos of sunlit beaches, ocean views. One wall was devoted to photos of Pop and Piper; photos she thought had been lost, or never remembered being taken. There she was as a baby, toddler, child, pre-teen, teen, young adult, recently. Most of the photos were candid; she'd never pose voluntarily for a camera. But the collage on the wall would be the first thing her mother would see if she opened her eyes. Piper had asked her father earlier if her mother ever did.

"She used to. Not recently but in the early days. But she never saw nothing, they said, she didn't follow objects, it were just a blank stare. Still, Oi kept the photos going."

He'd also told her that over the years scans had been taken, PET studies carried out which had shown there was still residual cognitive function in the brain cortex to one stimulus: pain. Nothing else. "But it showed she weren't dead. So Oi lived on hope, Pips, that she'd wake up."

"Did she ever know me? Hold me?"

He'd paused for just that little bit too long before answering. "She did, Pip." The brain hemorrhage had occurred shortly after the end of her labor when she'd lost consciousness. "She most certainly held you. Oi saw it moiself. Saw her expression of love."

But that long pause told Piper that he wasn't quite telling the truth.

She took her first look at her mother. The figure in the bed was so small she barely made a mound under the blanket and was curled into a fetal position. Pop took one of her clawed hands. "Hey," he said, in his softest voice, the one Piper loved most. "Flips, Oi 'ave Piper with me. She wanted to meet you." He nodded for Piper to take her mother's other hand.

It wasn't soft as Piper had imagined it would be but rather rough, bony of course, the skin paper-thin. It lay in Piper's palm like a cold dead fish. "Hello, Mum." She'd imagined saying those words so many times and here she was actually speaking them aloud. "I've come to see you." Daft thing to say and she wanted to say more but a lump lodged in her throat.

"We been to Luminosa, Flips. Tha's roight, Luminosa. And all's well."

As Pop rattled on, telling one porky after another about how marvelous the trip had been, and bustling around the bed, tucking in the already tucked sheets, avoiding the tubes entering and exiting, Piper studied her mother. Despite her gauntness and pallid expressionless face with her slightly blue lips dry and parted, Felipa had an ethereal air; she was dainty and fragile, her hair as fine as gossamer. A strange feeling of utter calm washed over her as the thought entered Piper's mind that her mother was the most beautiful woman she'd ever seen. "I love you," she whispered. "I always have."

****

Over the next few days, the visits to the hospice became a regular part of their routine. On the way, Pop always held Piper's hand tightly as if glad to have her with him.

"What I can't understand, Pop, is why you didn't let me see her before."

He had, he insisted, "When yew was a bitty babe," during an experiment to see if the sound of the baby's cry would stimulate Felipa. But it didn't. "Then yew got older and it upset yew." By older, he meant around two years old and Piper thought that wasn't the time to set a standard for the rest of her life; at two she'd probably scream the house down if she didn't get the red smartie. "Later, Oi was worried yew'd yak about it to your little friends. And word would get round."

What friends? And she was sick of this so-called yakking business that he brought up on a regular basis as if she was a walking-talking machine that never zipped her mouth up. She'd once had her head pushed down a toilet at a school by her *little friends* in an attempt to get her to speak. But he was oblivious to that event, just as he was to her nickname of Buttoned-up Phil.

She was saddened to know that Pop's understanding of her verged on nothing at all.

"What were you doing when you stayed away for longer than you said? Those times when the fishing job was just two days and I didn't see you for nearly a week," she asked. The hospice wasn't that far away from the cottage.

"The toimes she were real ill, Pips. Been a few toimes they thought it were the end and Oi stayed here by her bed. Others Oi were so tired Oi slept in the car. And there were once or twice, Oi have to admit, Oi needed some comfort… A man needs…aw, Pips,' he ran his hand through his hair in seeming embarrassment, "don't yew make it more difficult for me to 'xplain."

She wasn't going to blame him for needing comfort, but it explained why, with the expense of that and her mother's care, they never had any money.

"Wish you'd told me, Pop."

He studied her for several seconds before he looked away.

If her mother did make any movement, then Piper missed it; the only change was that one day her mother was lying on one side and the next the other with an oxygen mask covering most of her face. The doctor told them her pneumonia was worsening, and although they were pumping her full of antibiotics there wasn't much hope.

"Should we tell someone in Luminosa? Like her father. Is he still alive?" Piper asked Pop a week after they'd arrived. It niggled at her that she never found out what she'd gone there for in the first place: to speak to people who knew her mother, to find out if she had relatives. She'd got half-way with Prazeres and Serafim, but they didn't get the chance to tell her anything except that Serafim was some kind of distant cousin.

"Why were you fighting Gaspar at the hospital?"

" 'Cause he hates me."

"Why?"

Pop's lips thinned together like vices and two veins swelled in his temples as his dark, button-like eyes stared at her. Finally he said in a carefully measured voice, "He's your uncle, that's why. Felipa's brother."

Jumping Jehoshaphat. Jesus, her mind had gone into overdrive, like she had no control over it. Had she heard right? Did Pop say Gaspar was…no, he must mean someone else. "Who did you say was my uncle?"

"Gaspar."

"Then, Nelson is my grandfather?" Holy shit. The old geezer who'd cheated darling Etta out of her rightful inheritance? The old poop who'd tried to sign away the villagers' beloved *Herdade Albatroz* without a second thought? And *Lili?* Oh, don't go there…

Pop held her arm as he led her to the broken-down sofa. Once seated he said, "Yew got some questions. I think it's toime Oi answered, don't you?"

It was time a long, long while ago. "Why did Gaspar call you a pedophile?"

Pop's eyes narrowed as he said, "He were an idiot, he were. Felipa was seventeen when Oi met her, eighteen when yew was born. An' didn't he have eyes for Conceição when she were only sixteen? So he were a foine one to tawk."

"Conceição?"

Conceiçao, Pop explained, had been a girl in the village. Pop hadn't met her; she'd "already gawn to America three or four years before. Got caught up in the drugs, apparently. Terrible for a young 'un."

Pop told her that, broken hearted, Gaspar had gone after Conceição but had come back looking like he did now. "Just look at 'is face, and never quoit roit in the head yew ask me, 'cept Felipa said he were loik that only when he came back. He were bitterer 'n a sour lemon. But that owd Gaspar, he did love his sister Felipa, Oi'll say that for 'im an' she did 'im too, but she had no truck with 'im trying to force her home."

Pop knew Nelson adored his daughter too in his own way, so, "When yew was born I told 'im he had a granddaughter. Seemed only roight and Oi thought it moight heal things between us. But he threatened to beat me to pulp and take Felipa back to Portugal." Pop examined his thumbs as he formed his next words. "Tha's why Oi told 'im later she were dead. Then he threatened yew—said yew'd murdered her along with me." He rubbed his hands through his hair, sweat dripping from his forehead. "Oi don't know. Oi never knew if Oi did the roight thing telling 'im that Felipa was dead. Just thought at the time he'd leave us alone."

But Nelson hadn't. In his rage he swore he'd find Pop and Piper.

"Oi didn't want to frighten you, such a little kiddie. But should Oi have told 'im the truth about Felipa? Thing is he were mixed up with that drugs business…and mafias and the loik."

Piper hugged him. Her mother was receiving good care: she was clean, comfortable, warm; a doctor visited every day; she was being pumped full of antibiotics to try and treat the pneumonia. What more could be done? "You did right, Pop." But a thought germinated in her mind that Pop may blame her, even subconsciously, for his wife's condition.

CHAPTER TWENTY-EIGHT

Pop and Piper were there when Felipa died. A scan showed no brain stem activity at all now, so all the machines were turned off and catheters removed, and Pop and Piper waited, each holding a hand, while she slipped away like a candle burning down.

Felipa Pines's funeral was a small event. The only people besides Pop and Piper to attend the service in the cold church were the doctor and three members of the staff from the nursing home. Pop had wept into a filthy hanky at the pulpit and recited that his beloved wife "had slipped away into the next room." Piper's face ran with tears because she'd never seen her Pop cry before and because, unlike him, she had no familiar name to call her mother by.

In the following days, Pop didn't stop weeping, a never-ending supply of tears flooded his face and filled the craggy lines with white salt.

The wind still howled through the cracks in their flint cottage in the dunes. The night of the funeral the tide washed through the front door and flooded part of the kitchen, leaving behind a fishy, briny smell which Piper then spent hours trying to cleanse. The sea-birds still squawked at the pounding waves, oyster-catchers shrieked in the marshes and the honeysuckle bush scratched at the window pane, but the sound of her father's inconsolable weeping dampened the pleasure of familiarity.

She tried to get him to talk about her mother, hoping memories might cheer him up. "Tell me more about Mum, Pop. When she was pregnant with me what was she like?"

Talking to her did help for a while. His voice brightened when he told her Felipa had enjoyed her pregnancy. "All the negatives about it, Pip: throwing up, big ankles, and chewing on pencil rubbers. Couldn't get enough 'em. She sang to yew, cradling her belly, that old song she loved: *cheira bem, ela é boa*... Don't think them were the roight words, but she changed 'em 'cos she knew somehow that yew was a girl."

With tears stinging her own eyes, Piper listened to his every intake of breath, nuance and tone of voice as he recounted how her mother had knitted and crocheted bootees, cardigans—so many they "lasted yew til yew was two they did. She said she was the luckiest woman alive."

Piper gathered him to her, a huge bear of a man who had to bend to rest his wet face on her shoulders. "And now I'm the luckiest," she told his hot, bright red ear. "Was it my fault, Pop? That she died?" she voiced the question that had been echoing through her mind ever since he'd told her about her grandfather's accusation.

"Aw moi pet. No." He wagged his great head. Felipa had suffered from pre-eclampsia: a dangerously high blood pressure during pregnancy. He told Piper she'd seen a doctor when she arrived in England and had her pre-natal tests, but they'd said her readings weren't important, even though she complained of headaches, and her hands were swollen. "Oi thought it best for yew not to know your mother as a human vegetable instead of the woman she really was: the brightest star in the universe, full of life and fun."

To try to break him out of his sadness, so he wouldn't spend the night sobbing, she took him for long walks along the shingled beach, explored marshes stretching for miles in all directions where pheasants clicked and clucked in the fields where a lone windmill rose above the reed beds. But he was no longer interested, it seemed, in the endless sky alive with clouds of jackdaws, finches and sparrows.

"Wish we could go crabbing again," she told him. "I'll get out once my shoulder's better." She hoped he would try to find a job—their own boat was gone, sold to cover the funeral costs. "There's plenty of dab out there. And we have to pay Mr. Todd back for lending you the money for your airfare and taxis."

He agreed but didn't do anything about it except to sit in his sagging worn armchair and stare at the cracked floorboards where his slippered feet rested.

In the next few days his depression lifted a little as she cooked him food he told her reminded him of Felipa: a fish stew with plenty of garlic, peppers and *piri-piri,* followed by a spicy crab stir-fry with coriander and paprika. He found his appetite and lapped it all up, even licking his plate, and smiled for the first time since the funeral.

With her father so fragile, she tried to put all thoughts of Luminosa behind her but, once in a while, she visualized a white-blond man's dark eyes observing her with a look that made her tingle.

To take her mind off him, she asked her father, "Do you think we'll have to move again soon? The tide's going to wash us away."

"It sure is, moi girl."

She put down the knife she was using to chop parsley. "We moved so much, didn't we? I never understood why."

"There was good reason."

"Tell me," she said, leaving her chopping board and sitting on the creaking arm of his chair in front of the log fire in the fireplace.

They'd been living in Fleetwood, Pop told her. Felipa and him. They'd chosen to live there after arriving from

Portugal because Pop could still get daily fishing work. When Piper had been born and her mother already in a coma, he came home one evening after visiting Felipa at the hospital, having picked baby Piper up from the neighbor he'd left her with, and had climbed the stairs to their own flat to find the front door open. He thundered back down to the neighbor, almost threw the baby at her before he pounded upstairs to confront three hefty men, "their faces all caved in, Pips, loik feral animals." The neighbor had called the police but by the time they'd arrived, Pop had been held down while the three took turns to kick him wherever they could. Knives had come out but not used because sirens sounded in the distance and the men, all with foreign accents, had left down the fire escape after telling him they'd be back to finish him off and the baby with him.

It didn't take much elimination to work out who was behind the attack. After all, Pop didn't piss that many people off and not to that extent. Without waiting to get his bruises treated, he'd taken Piper, caught the first train leaving, changed six times until they found themselves in King's Lynn. "Fate brought us here."

"So you're not from Norfolk? How'd you get the accent?"

"Mebbe Oi exaggerated the accent at first to mek people think we was from here and it koind of sticks now. Oi tried everything to run from them ruffians. They destroyed all our furniture, Pippy." And dropped her cot from the window to the pavement below. "Your little bed was shattered, its legs spread out loik a squashed spider." He swiped at the tears once again pouring down his cheeks.

"And Mum?"

"Well, Oi assumed Nelson thought she were…you know…*no more*, loik Oi told him." Pop moved her to a home in King's Lynn, and changed all their names by deed-poll to Pines, and his own from Jack Pepper to Norman Pines. "Yew do understand, don't yew Pips? Oi couldn't lose yew nor think of yew hurt. Oi always was so scared."

She understood. If anyone tried to injure her Pop, she'd do her utmost to turn the attacker into a stain on the floor. No contest.

"And that's why you told me not to talk about myself."

"Oi couldn't trust no one. The world's a small place and tawk's dangerous. Specially as yew inherited your ma's gift of seeing the colors on the water. That really is special, yew know."

Serafim had told her it was special in Luminosa. Oh how she missed the place and the people in it. Now that her father had cheered a little, she thought she might try to contact Prazeres.

CHAPTER TWENTY-NINE

October no longer held the blinding heat of September in Luminosa, but the place was still so different to what Leo experienced in Alaska at this time of year. He loved where he'd lived, even the snow-blocked roads and the shorter days, but the fall colors would be over now; the temperatures would be so cold it would chill the core of his heart, and here he could still wander about in his t-shirt at six in the evening.

The familiar scents of baking and cooking filled the air, the cluck of chickens sounded in the yards, bells clanging around the necks of cows and goats in a nearby field. Television static competed with babies crying, children laughing on the beach. An old woman dressed in black waved at him as she cradled a baby and humming some sort of a cappella folk song to her grandson, or great-grandson, he forgot which.

It had been a good day. He'd been out on the Atlantic early fishing for corvine and red mullet in Flattie Fred's boat and they'd brought back a reasonable catch by five. He now lived in his Aunt Rosa's house where he spent pleasant evenings eating her filling suppers and chinwagging with his cousin Rui. They'd already started plans to discuss if they could build a *Goblin II*. Ideally they'd like a wooden 35-footer which wouldn't come cheap even with the help of the other villagers in constructing her. But she'd be a thing of beauty, Leo had no doubt. And to earn a little more, he'd promised Rui he'd be a willing apprentice at tin-making, follow Rui's instructions and not make wise-ass cracks all the time.

In the distance, right at the end of the main drag, past Serafim's café and in a small cottage that sat almost right on the beach—in contrast to the rest of the cottages that were set farther back—and next to the cliff, Leo could see Nelson, his face turned to the sun, taking the last of the rays.

Two days after Grady had been arrested, the Carneiros moved out of the Main House and into the white cottage, blue-edged like the others, but this one was detached, a few feet away from its neighbor and right on the end, three doors down from Serafim's café. It adjoined the side of the cliff that rose high at the end of the beach. This cottage had always been theirs but they were, as Etta said, "Furious as buzzcocks about leaving the Main House. But they have no choice. It's not theirs, never was and the Royal Estates are coming soon to check the place out."

Today, for the first time, Leo came across the old man, Nelson, sitting out on the stoop in his wheelchair in the sunshine, gazing vacantly at the neighboring cliff.

"What's your name, young bastard?" he'd asked Leo in his wavering, old-man's voice.

If the old guy hadn't been Piper's grandfather, Leo wouldn't have answered, but he decided to be civil. "Leo Shine."

"Young bastard will do for you."

And that was about as far as Leo's contact had been with him since then.

He'd seen Lili. She'd had her passport taken from her and had been released on bail pending trial, accused of attempting to sell land that didn't belong to her. Lili was a shadow of her former self, having, according to Gaspar who had moved in with them, to sell her horse and any cattle that Nelson still owned. Today she sat, as she had all day yesterday, on the wall in the cottage's small yard, her dark hair stringy and her face pale and listless. If she saw Leo as he passed near on his way in to Serafim's, she didn't acknowledge him.

Her attitude didn't bother him and didn't spoil his pleasure at being in the village. He may miss Alaska at times, but what did he have left there except memories? And, as Squidlips Gil told him yesterday when Leo voiced his doubt about returning to Alaska, "You can't do that, you're part of the village now. Stay on a while."

Leo had been left speechless because he didn't feel he deserved their loyalties, not after he'd treated them with such contempt and pretended to be someone else, twice.

Just after Squidlips had said that, Leo found out what being a villager meant. It might leave him with the comforting thought that he belonged somewhere, but it also involved having to attend the Luminosa Kangaroo Court (as he called it). And that was why he entered Serafim's café now.

Serafim's was packed. Leo wished he was elsewhere, anywhere, even bent into a 100-knot williwaw wind would do.

A somber atmosphere filled the café instead of its usual festive one. But, apparently, one of their own had broken the village code of conduct which wasn't at all acceptable. The culprit had to be tried with Leo as the main witness.

A row of chairs had been set out in front of the counter for Serafim, Squidlips Gill, Gaffer Paulo and Slippery Dick. Serafim was dressed in black, while the others were still in their fishing gear even down to the rubber boots and yellow wet-gear. To one side Etta sat, resplendent in a fluorescent yellow coat, her blouse and scarf competed in a dazzling mixture of patterns and tones of crimson. Even her glasses frames were red.

At her side sat Victor in his tweeds, glowering at anyone who'd catch his eye, for he was the one on trial.

Leo never imagined Victor would've allowed this to happen and that he'd dismiss it as simply a feudal ritual. But,

Serafim earlier told Leo, this was the tradition that had been set up by the Fletchers themselves centuries ago, and Victor himself often attended the trials, usually as the judge. Since the Fletchers were, and considered themselves very much still to be, an integral part of the village, Victor couldn't refuse to participate just because he was the one on trial. "Probably didn't even occur to him," Serafim told Leo.

The rest of the villagers packed the café, acting as jury and facing the judges.

Etta patted the free seat next to her when she spotted Leo. He had just sat down when Serafim clapped his hands for quiet and announced that Leo would explain what had happened on the day in question.

Reluctantly, he got to his feet, glanced through the rattling chain curtain at the door and looked longingly towards the jetty where a couple of fishermen unloaded their catch.

Leo cleared his throat. "On that day, September 21, Mister Grady and I were on a ledge half-way up the cliff round the point out there. We were hoping to climb up and reach the top, but to tell you the truth I didn't reckon that Grady would make it. He'd been standing in cold water all night and was very weak. Just when I'd given up hope, Rui appeared around the promontory from the direction of the village in his skiff. Just a moment later some rocks fell down and hit Mr. Grady."

"Thank you, Leo. When you looked up, who did you see?"

Leo fidgeted with the hem of his t-shirt.

"Go on," Etta urged. "Say the words. Move the lips and waggle the tongue, it's easy."

"Victor," Leo whispered.

"Who? Speak up, man."

"Victor Fletcher."

Serafim, his face as grim as the Reaper's, turned to the

named culprit. "Victor Fletcher, what do you have to say?"

Victor got to his feet, holding his lapels as he addressed the group sitting in front of him. "I admit I was on the cliff-top, but I would like you to take into account that I was under much stress at the time."

"It's true," Etta interrupted. "It was so bad, he kept trying to get me to lick light switches."

"Thank you, my dear. This Grady business had just happened and I was furious that we—the village, of course I mean—might lose the *Herdade* thanks to a mere scam."

"Because the bleedin' mayor's rotten to the core and is as rich as a fat chef's fruitcake from the handouts the Carneiros paid him."

Everyone tittered at Etta's choice of words.

"Exactly, my dear."

"That has nothing to do with this case," Serafim said. "Nelson Carneiro cannot mentally be held accountable."

"Who was talking about him?" Etta asked.

"Lili has been disowned by the village—which is punishment enough—and will be mentally assessed in due course, and Mr. Grady is being tried by the nation, not by the village. Everyone in the scam case will be duly punished. Our village court that is in session today is different. We are trying to discover if Victor Fletcher is guilty of deliberately trying to drop rocks on Leo—one of your fellow villagers—while he was assisting Mr. Grady."

"All those involved with that farce, trying to sell the land, are rogues, cads and confidence tricksters," Victor grumbled, "for bringing the *Herdade* to its knees."

"Victor," Dick said, his voice falsely patient, "we're trying to ascertain if you intended to injure Leo."

"How many more times? Leo and I were working together. Maybe I did think he was Tom at the time, but that's a fair enough mistake since everyone else did too."

Leo looked at the floor, wishing it would open up for him. He should've been honest right from the beginning. "It's true," he said. "Mr. Fletcher has apologized to me several times and assured me he wasn't aiming at me. That's why he said, 'whoops.' "

Etta sniggered. "Mr. Fletcher. This boy's as polite as Pippy. She called me Miss Fletcher and I didn't know at first she meant me."

"I admit," Victor said, his chin in the air, his eyes challenging, "I wanted to harm that cad Grady. Imposter, charlatan. I'd have gladly drowned him. Of that I am guilty. So do what you will with me."

Grady would've drowned if Leo hadn't dived in and dragged him up by his gel-greasy hair (boy, that hurt, he knew) before Rui hauled him into the boat with a fishing hook. Once he'd vomited up all the seawater, Grady had sworn like the most hardened crab-fisherman and nothing like the smooth-talking financier he pretended to be.

Rui was the next witness, but he had little to add except, "The rocks could've easily hit Leo if he hadn't moved."

"If they had," Leo added, "it would've been considered as friendly fire."

Leo, Rui, Etta and Victor were sent outside while the villagers deliberated.

"Grady had no hedge-fund; he had no dosh; he's just a goddamn fleecer and all he talks is posh bosh."

"Thank you Etta. That was lovely, my dear. Now keep quiet."

"I made that up, you know. Just now."

"Obviously. Good grief," Victor said, looking towards the Carneiro's cottage, "does that woman do nothing but sit on that wall all day?"

"Not coping too well, are they?" Leo asked.

"Gaspar does whatever he needs to for Nelson like he

always has and Nelson—well he's just Nelson so not much change there. Shame Pipsqueak didn't want to press charges against Lili—I hate anyone who hurts that girl."

So did Leo.

"Lili should've been prosecuted," Victor said. "All very well to plead insanity…"

"Crazy as a bag of chips." Etta turned to Leo. "Have you heard anything from Piper? How she is. I do think about her so often."

Leo glanced at her in surprise. He also thought about Piper, but he said, "I don't think she'd call me, do you? I reckon I ticked her off big time."

Etta took off her glasses, leaving a red mark on either side of the bridge of her nose, and huffed on them. "Codswallop. The way she went all sparkly when she looked at you? She was like a little flower opening in the rain."

Leo was speechless. Was she kidding him? Piper? She'd looked at him as if he was a run over cat. That thought threatened to turn his soul to stone. "No, Etta. I reckon that was her look when she wanted to deck someone. At that time, it was me."

Etta looked up from her frantic polishing. "You think? I saw her face light up in a sudden wonderful smile when we arrived. And she wasn't looking at Victor."

Longing flashed through Leo, a feeling he'd been trying and mostly managing to resist, and he felt the full force of wanting her. "How can we…I mean, do you reckon we could find her?"

Before Etta could reply, Victor growled like an angry dog. "By the way, I hear there're moves afoot to deport Grady to the US to be tried for his crimes. He should be tried here first, serve his sentence in a Portuguese jail, then he should face trial in all the other countries where he should serve the prescribed time and, finally, he can relax in the comfort of his lovely cell in the United States."

Leo wasn't too sure about the comfort or loveliness of a US jail, but he did like the idea of Grady being hauled off to country after country to serve his time out.

"And we all know why the system here is reluctant to delve too far into his crimes in this country…"

Before Leo could bring the conversation around to Piper again, they were called back into the café because the kangaroo court had reached a verdict.

"Victor Fletcher, it is our unanimous belief that the rock throwing was deliberate but only to hit Grady, not Leo, so we'll be lenient because you hit someone none of us liked anyway, and he wasn't from the village. It is our considered opinion that you, Victor Aloysius Fletcher, have been found guilty of putting one of the villagers at risk, though. In this case, Leo Shine, who could've been injured by rocks thrown by you, even if it wasn't deliberate. You are therefore sentenced to take the village children on nature hikes twice a week to teach them about our natural habitat just as the Fletchers used to."

"School children?" Victor's mouth twisted and he closed his eyes. "And this will be for how long?"

"As long as this court deems adequate."

"As long as they can stand him, more like," Etta whispered to Leo.

CHAPTER THIRTY

The coach station in Lisbon hadn't changed in the past two months, certainly not as much as Piper had. Arriving at the same late hour, she sat in the same spot she'd spent the night last time. Today, though, she knew what to expect when she arrived in Luminosa and knew that she'd be welcomed.

Finding any kind of contact number had been a nightmare, and she'd constantly hit dead-ends, but finally she was given a land-line number for *Herdade Albatroz*. As she dialed, she hoped like mad Prazeres would be working in the kitchen that day and answer the phone. But it had rung, unanswered.

Her own mobile phone ringing now startled her.

"Pips, it's me. Yew got there awright then? Sorry Oi didn't answer when yew called. No signal in moi cabin."

"Hey Pop. Are the Chief Mate's quarters comfy?"

"Oi'd sleep in a hammock just to be back at sea."

She knew what he meant. "Safe journey. Bet the weather up there is a bit colder than here."

"The old North Sea is chippy-choppy."

Less than a week ago, he couldn't have surprised her more by telling her he'd seen a vacancy for Chief Mate aboard a beam trawler operating in the North Sea out of Holland. Within a few days, the job was his and he signed on for the season.

"Since you're going to Holland, then I'm going back to Portugal," she'd said, swallowing her astonishment because until then she'd imagined she'd be taking care of a depressed Pop right into her old age.

"Fair 'nuff," he responded, rubbing his hand over his bristly hair. "Reckon yew could give that Gaspar a kick up the wossname if he starts anything. And that Nelson's just an old bugger now. No good to man nor beast."

After what Pop had told her about Nelson and Gaspar's vendetta against the two of them over the years, she wasn't preparing to have anything to do with them and if they tried to hurt her, she'd hurt them back ten-fold. The best course of action was to stay away from the Main House altogether. There were plenty of friendly people in the village who'd be prepared to tell her about her mother. Excitement rose in her chest mixed with relief now that she was free to ask whatever question she liked.

Now she'd find out how life really was in Luminosa. Hopefully, the drama of the investment party had died down. Prazeres had told her about the *festas* that happened on a regular basis amongst the villagers, and Piper would like to see those in action. 'Course, there wouldn't be a white-blond haired, lanky guy to make her heart sing because he'd have long gone. But who cared about that? She didn't, that's for sure. Did she?

Shaking herself for thinking such daft thoughts and knowing she couldn't afford to spend much time, or money, on this little holiday, once her curiosity was satisfied in Luminosa, she'd probably return to Norfolk and find fishing work. Or maybe further afield. The world was hers.

Her eyes began to close as she daydreamed on the coach-station bench. She almost missed a small figure dashing up to her. For a moment she felt disoriented but then she realized the kid had picked up her bag from beside her and fled into the shadows.

She took off after him.

Piper's chest hurt as she forced air down to her burning lungs, but she wasn't going to let a little kid escape with her bag and money she and Pop had scraped for. God, the kid ran fast, he was a budding Usain Bolt. Her rucksack on her back didn't help. It bumped against her bum and back with every step she took. She yelled, but the kid put a spurt on.

She made it across a busy street unscathed, entering an unlit area of graffiti-covered, half-demolished brown-brick tenement buildings, some with sagging roofs close to collapse, others with their windows and doors boarded up. Trying to watch where the boy was going, she dodged forlorn heaps of rubbish and fallen masonry.

Maybe the kid got tired, she didn't know. Whatever, he slowed down under a sodium light which gave her a chance to catch up and, once she was within distance, she lunged to grab the back of his t-shirt. The greasy material slipped through her fingers. He darted away, tossing the purse into a dark alley that separated two buildings. Piper skidded to a halt—she couldn't care less about the kid, she wanted her bag: the one being clutched to the chest of a skeletal, zombie-like figure who loomed out of the darkness of the alley. The murk made it difficult to see, but she thought the person was a woman because she was wearing a ragged dress, even though the person had no shape, being rake thin. Under the sodium light, her unhealthy yellow skin stretched across her face like cellophane, while her mouth was a badly painted scarlet slash. She must have been bald because a cheap-looking nylon dark wig perched skewed to one side, revealing a wrinkled scalp. And no teeth either, it seemed, as she stepped closer mumbling and chattering without saying a word that Piper could understand.

Piper had no idea where she was, only that the streets reeked of sewage that poured from the alleyway where the woman emerged.

Piper held her hand out. "Give me the bag."

The woman hid it behind her back like a child. "No," she said, an English-speaking vagrant.

"It's mine."

"Yeah, it's a girly-girl purse. Whatcha got in it?" The woman scuttled backwards, taking small steps and casting Piper swift glances, reminding her of a rodent. "Cash?" Her scarlet-painted mouth widened into a cavernous grin that disappeared as she raked through the rest of Piper's belonging. "Fuckin' nothin' else!" She threw out Piper's mobile-phone that smashed on the rubble in the road.

Piper sprang at the woman. With more agility than she seemed capable of, she twisted away and made a bee-line to an open doorway. The woman had the advantage since she apparently knew of a pathway through the piles of putrid matter that blocked the door, whereas Piper stumbled through knee-deep junk that threw up the stench of mold and rotting food and stuck to her jeans with a stinking ooze. Piper tore up a staircase, each stair creaking and crumbling, closing in on the woman who squealed like a stuck pig.

"Conceição needs a hit," the woman mumbled as they reached a cracked door that was halfway open. She leaned against it. The wood gave way and she fell inside.

"Give it back," Piper said, following her in. It would be easy to knock the wits out of her; she looked frail, old and wizened like a rotting apple as she lay back on the holey wooden floor. She raised her dry nut-brown face an inch or two to stare at Piper, first with one blood-shot eye closed and then the other. Both were outlined in a mixture of smudged and cracked black liner and blue eye shadow. "Where're you from?"

Maybe talking to her rationally might relax her enough for Piper to grab the bag. "I'm from England. Norfolk. What's your name?"

"Conceição-for-all-you-could-give-a-shit. You could be Portuguese, the look about you." The woman sat up, her legs splayed with Piper's bag between them.

"I do have a bit of Portuguese blood. Half actually." Piper tried to sound friendly, and she edged forward, waiting for her opportunity to make a grab at the bag. "My mother's family comes from a little village called Luminosa."

It never occurred to Piper that this would make any sense to the woman, but Conceição shook her head violently back and forth, front and forwards with such force that Piper winced as the bones in the woman's neck creaked. Had the name upset her?

"Luminosa?" Piper whispered, trying again.

Again, Conceição swung her head that seemed far too big for the stalk of her neck. She squeezed her eyes so tight the skin showed white in the creases around them, her hollow mouth opened but no sound came out, just a snake-like tongue writhed and flickered in the crimson cavern. She skittered backwards and collapsed against a cracked wall that creaked and showered her in a blizzard of plaster, but she paid it no heed, staring at Piper, her eyes wild. "Luminosa, Luminosa. I'm dead meat 'cos of Luminosa."

Piper edged closer, positioning her hand to snatch the bag. "Tell me why," she said, hoping to distract the woman.

"Thought I could be something in the world instead of rotting in Luminosa. And I was. But then fucked up big-time. What did I do?" Conceição babbled. "Give 'em false information, they said. I didn't. Send them on a wild goose trip, they said. No not my fault." Her rough, blistered hands rubbing together sounded like a paper bag scrunching up. She tilted her head on one side, looking like a wounded bird. "I was screwed, cheated. Said they'd deliver. They didn't. Family too. Fuckers. Next week. Monday? Friday? Yes, yes next week. No drugs. Court date. Miami. I got warrants."

She looked up at Piper as if demanding sympathy and didn't notice she'd let Piper's bag drop from her thrashing hand.

So as not to startle the woman, Piper slowly reached down and took it, hugging it closely. Poo, the smell of garbage and sewers wasn't only coming from the room they were in and the woman too. Now Piper's bag reeked of it.

Conceição pushed off the wall, unaware, or uncaring, that Piper now had her bag. "Screwed over. I was." She stood, swaying.

Piper took a step backwards. Maybe she should just make a silent escape. She hesitated. Why had the word Luminosa had such an effect on the woman?

Conceição spat into a pile of rotting vegetation, cabbage possibly. "What a fucking load…"

Clutching her bag tightly, Piper thought she could overpower this poor woman if necessary. *Leave,* every cell in her body screamed. Yet, Conceição's reaction to Luminosa intrigued Piper. She moved to the broken door, half-in and half-out, in a position to make a run for it if necessary, and keeping space between her and the woman. "My mother was from Luminosa. Her name was Felipa Carneiro."

Conceição's weird head-shaking began again and the stunned look in her eyes faded. Glazed eyes caught at Piper's heart as Conceição's wig tilted further over one ear. Was Conceição lost and needed help finding her way back to Luminosa?

"Serafim," Piper tried another name.

"Brother." Conceição's lips barely moved as she said the word but Piper heard it.

"Brother?" Never in a million years would Piper have guessed that relationship.

"Serafim," Conceição said, rocking from one foot to the other. "First Gaspar, then Serafim."

Wait half a moment. "Gaspar's your brother too?"

Something was off kilter here. Gaspar was Piper's uncle, but Serafim was no relation, or a distant one, so where was the connection?

Conceição blew green snot down her nose and cackled. "Brother. Gaspar?" she scoffed. "No way. Gaspar wanted to get in my pants. Gaspar wanted to take Conceição home to Luminosa. *I love you soo much. Come home.* I set him up, the fucker. Gave him a suitcase of Aunt Hazel, and the sucker thought it was my clothes he was delivering to an address." Conceição spat again. "But the asshole opened it before he arrived."

Piper wasn't sure what Aunt Hazel was, but it didn't sound like a relative, least not a cozy one.

"He chucked it away in a dumpster! What a loser. So the Big Boys cut him up for that, whopped him good they did and he crawled back home to Daddy, not 'xactly the way he left. Big deal. Then comes George Shine who says, *you're so beautiful.* They loved me, both George and Gaspar. I am such a *doll.*" She preened obscenely, opening her legs and pulling her skirt up to show her lack of underwear.

It was not the most beautiful sight in the world, and Piper turned away. "What about Serafim?"

"He comes to Alaska to take little sis home too, but he liked George Shine. Thought he'd be good for Conceição. He took a shine to George." She howled with silent laughter, arching her back with the effort.

Shine. Piper's heart missed a beat.

Amusement forgotten, Conceiçao paced the room with short, staggering steps in her too-high heels, keeping close to the crumbling walls and hugging herself as if cold. As she circled, she kept up a ludicrous monologue, "…giving hard looks and who laid this bitch and who laid that. And they hit me in the stomach and the kidneys. They're fullashit. No cursing!" She had such skinny elbows and knee joints disfigured with arthritis or rheumatism. On one of her rounds, while in her phase of spouting gobbledygook, she collided with a mattress that leaned against a wall. With a tug, she pulled it down bringing with it a shower of debris, a piece of which fell near Piper's foot. It was a small clear pipe, the type she'd seen a crew member—who'd been offloaded in Porto—use at night to smoke, she'd been told, crack cocaine.

Conceição, her eyes shining in the dusty murk, continued, "I asked for a coupla bucks and they said go fuck yourself, honey. I gotta job, you lowdown…" She pulled at her dress and leered at Piper who backed away.

Piper's instincts screamed for her to get out of there. It was just…George Shine? The name was familiar… "Tell me, Conceição, tell me about George Shine."

"Look, shitkicker. I gotta job. Bitch."

How the hell could she get this woman back on track? "I'm sure you do."

"In Miami, I could've been somethin'. Maybe was at first. Yeah I was. But you seen this?" She pointed to a square tattoo just above her right ear. "Conceição's been marked by the Big Boys. Tattooed coupla months ago. You know what this means? Huh?" She pointed at the tattoo again. "Means, I've upset the big boss and hard. Dead meat they said if your kid and husband don't deliver. And the bastards didn't. But I still had some of the money they gave me upfront for fixing the deal." Her wrecked face creased into a toothless black-gummed smile. "I got me a wig, got a passport and got a plane to Lisbon. Here I am. But still not safe from them. They found me." She wrung her hands. "They know where I am. I know they do. They'll hurt me just 'cos those suckers failed the mission." She touched her tattoo again and cringed like a dog about to get kicked. "Maybe I go to Luminosa. Maybe you take me?" She folded her scabby hands in her lap and half-whispered, half-sang in a child's voice, "Albatroz.

Lavender's blue, dilly dilly, Lavender's green. When you are king, dilly dilly, I will be Queen."

"Who told you so, dilly dilly," Piper joined in, "who told you so. 'Twas my own heart, dilly dilly, That told me so. Did Etta teach you that?"

The woman rocked, leaning against the wall, as they sang together, her eyes half-closed. "Albatroz... Tony, no asshole, *Tom*. And, and...George. They failed with deal *I* set up, bastards. But not Leo. Do not involve Leo. I told them that, you know." She peered at Piper. "Leo is the baby."

There it was: Tom and George Shine. Should she, Piper, tell her that Tom wasn't dead, that the last time Piper had seen him he'd been up to some game in Luminosa? Is that why she wanted to go there?

"Was George your husband?"

"Only, only, only, 'cos he knocked me up with Tony... Tom. You don't survive in Miami with a kiddy, kid, kid. Bastard Tom. Only discovered I was up the shoot when it was too late to have an abortion. But not Leo. Leo wasn't like that."

"You have two sons?"

"Tony...Tom, *shit*, and little Leo. Do not involve Leo in the sting, I told them. Let Tom do it for his mommy, he owes me for not making him a bastard. Just Tom. And he came to see me in Miami and said, *'Mommy I love you sooooo much. Gimme money and I'll do this simple thing so the bad men don't hurt you.'* " She used a falsetto to imitate what must have been Tom, except Tom didn't talk like that, Piper knew, Tom had a smooth deep voice.

Conceição continued, "He promised he'd do it and not tell anyone else. *I have a biiiiig boat, Mommy, and I'm such a good sailor.* But then he called me and said Saint George Shine insisted on helping. Well, fuck 'im I said. Fling 'im overboard when you're out there. But they didn't deliver. Not one or other. Fucking ruined it for me."

They didn't deliver, and Conceição had two sons. As an idea blossomed, Piper put her hands to her temples. "Did Tom and Leo...were they alike? White-blond hair, dark eyes."

Conceição shrugged. "I ain't seen Little Leo in over twenty-five years. George Shine had hair like that and Tom did when he came to Miami to fix deal. Bastard let his momma down."

Was it possible that the man in Luminosa had been Leo? "Was Leo born with a caul?"

"Leo," Conceição repeated with a wide smile. "My little boy. *O meu menino.*" She folded her arms and rocked as if she held a baby and hummed what could have been a lullaby. "I wanted Leo. Something I could plan that would go right for once."

The light from the window reflected on wetness at the corner of Conceição's eye for a moment before her manner changed again. She opened her bony, scarred arms wide as if to drop whatever it was she thought she was holding. "Leo's caul. I sold it." Then she went off at a tangent again. "Those shitkickers don't deliver, Conceição, we're gonna slit your goddamn scrawny throat because that was the deal—no delivery, then I get tattoo. Goddamn George, the Mother Teresa of Alaska." She slapped her tattoo. "Thanks a fuckin' bunch. This says, death sentence." Her voice became jerky, her hands constantly rubbing together or waving, unable to stay still. She eyed Piper's bag. "Need money. More. Give me that."

Piper remembered the newspaper article she'd taken from John, Tom, *Leo's* ruck-sack. The coast guard had confirmed the boat...*Goblin,* she thought...had sunk with all souls and there'd been no other ship in the area. How could George Shine or Tom have survived?

Should she tell her? The woman should know why the deal hadn't worked out. Piper wanted to, yet was unwilling to touch the woman's hand that was covered in suppurating abscesses. Instead she put her bag down by the door in case she needed to restrain the woman with both her hands, and got as close as she could manage without retching. "Conceição. The boat sank."

Conceição stopped mumbling for a moment, but several seconds later she started again. "Lowdown fucking losers. Sail boats all their lives. They don't sink."

"It was hit by a rogue wave. The papers said they drowned, Conceição."

"Fuckers, fullashit. Fullawater. What a loada crap." She cackled but then was silent, her mouth working on its own accord. "They drowned?"

But before Piper could respond, Conceição looked up, her eyes darting from side to side as if she was listening.

Piper listened too but heard nothing. But then Conceição pushed past her through the door with such strength that Piper lost her footing and fell. She'd have tumbled down the broken stairs if she hadn't managed to grab the crumbling bannisters. By the time she'd found her footing again, the woman had disappeared through the mountain of rubbish at the doorway and out into the night.

Bugger. Piper had left her bag and ruck-sack in the room, but when she went back for them, her bag was lying on the floor open and the money in her wallet gone.

On shaky legs, Piper stood under the only sodium lamp and tried to get her bearings. Had she made a mistake about Tom Shine? And, Jesus, was that the guy's mother? Piper was light-headed, unsure of what she should do in this fucked-up rat-infested place. A couple of dim figures emerged from the gloom but disappeared back again, and a cockroach showed too much of a liking for her foot, so she stamped on it. With the sound of the crunch, her senses returned and she could hear the rumble of traffic in the distance. That was the direction she should take.

It wasn't long before order returned to her world: cars whizzed by, cafés turned on their lights, getting ready for the day's business, and trucks had started on their deliveries. She didn't know where she was, but well-dressed people hurried along, perhaps on their way to work. The fresh scent of approaching rain filled the blustery early morning air, so different from the sewage-stench in the alley. Looking back at the labyrinth of apparently abandoned buildings she'd just left, doubt filled her again. Was it Leo who'd been in Luminosa that weekend? Come to think of it, no one had mentioned Tom Shine, she'd just assumed from the newspaper cutting he was Tom. If he was Leo, then when she saw him, he'd recently lost his father and brother and, if Piper could believe Conceição, he hadn't been involved with the trafficking. It also sounded like Leo never knew his mother—like Piper. But, unlike her, his mother was still alive. Just.

She'd been so wrong about so much. If it was her mother back there in that dump, she—Piper—wouldn't want her left to die, would she? She owed it to Tom…Leo, rather. Leo. She liked that name; it suited him with his eyes…

It was already light by the time she thought she was back under the now unlit sodium lamp. The place looked worse in the daylight: scarred, traumatized, wounded and on its last legs. Not unlike Conceição.

She forced herself to go back up the broken stairs, unwilling to discover what awaited inside the room. But there she was, Conceição, slumped in the far corner, a cuff about her arm and a syringe stuck in a vein. It had been barely half an hour since Piper had seen her but right now she looked dead.

Piper inched forward to check and then jumped as Conceição gave a snort. She was still alive then, but having difficulty breathing. Piper felt a flutter of a pulse.

CHAPTER THIRTY-ONE

Leo fought the sea. It took both his and Rui's strength to hold the wheel firm as the boat swayed on the tidal currents that ploughed against them and, together with the wind, tried with the force of a ten-ton truck to push them off course, as if trying to tell them they were going the wrong way, that Luminosa was the other way. A tingling of energy shivered down Leo's left side and it was reaction rather than consciousness of building energy that made him turn the boat into a huge wave looming down the starboard side that could capsize them.

The wave lashed the bow rail and knocked the boat sideways, shifting the bulk of their heavy load of catch to the port side, causing the boat to list heavily.

"Life jackets," Fred ordered, donning his, as he and Rui rushed out and down the ladder to help Dick prevent the rest of the bins of stored fish from moving.

They'd been out on Flattie Fred's boat since before dawn when the sea had been, in Fred's words, "flatter than Lili's arse."

"It'll pick up—the sea, I mean," Leo had responded and, just after midday, when the nets were full of fish, was he proved right. He was at the helm heading into the rising troughs. The sea had picked up well, but not enough to make the catch something to be proud of.

"Hundred kilos," Fred said, coming into the wheelhouse,

blowing on his hands. "Once upon a time we'd get five hundred just five kilometers out. Wouldn't need to go twenty." He pulled at his lips as he watched Rui and Slippery Dick in their slickers, pouring fish out of the nets, up to their ankles in the flapping silvery creatures. "Miserable catch and don't give me that sustainable fishing crap that you got in Alaska. I *know* there's a whole bunch of fish down there, just can't find them."

"Wasn't going to mention a thing," Leo replied. "Rui and me, well, we call you the patron saints of sustainable fishing. Right sized nets and webbing, keeping to quotas."

"No more than we've always done and I know you do too. Was only kidding. We're lucky to have such a long coastline so we must be the guardians of it. Trouble is, the problem isn't keeping to quotas, it's trying to meet them."

"Yeah, it sucks," Leo responded just as his fingertips tingled, something he hadn't felt for a while, and a brief rush of energy made him look closer at the ocean. "Wind's picking up," he said. The sky was cloudless but even so there was that heaviness that weighed on his mind, a foreboding that didn't sit right with him. "Reckon we should set the nets and head back in."

"You think so? The weather forecast said offshore winds today."

Leo stepped off the bridge and let his instincts run free. "Wrong," he said when he returned. "The wind's about to change. It'll blow inshore any time now. Cold too. Low pressure's building and fast." That meant a storm was brewing that could hit with a startling speed. "Dark moon tonight and that's a wild wind. I don't like that combination."

Fred rubbed his strawberry-colored nose and glanced at Leo. "You think so?" He checked the radio and listened. "They're still giving moderate with offshore wind."

"Shit can happen."

" 'Kay. I'll go tell Rui and Dick to set the nets and then we'll head in."

What a difference in attitude to the skipper's on board the *Alaskan Star* who'd have risked twenty-footers, stayed in his warm wheelhouse and ordered over the hailer instructions that the crew were to stay on their feet. Today Fred was down there with his deckhands, Rui and Slippery Dick, helping them to finish their work as fast as possible so he could take them back to safety.

"If Leo said the weather is turning, then the weather is turning," Leo heard Fred say as the final buoy went over the roller.

Leo hoped he was wrong about the weather, but the pressure kept building in his head, making it buzz, and the tingling had reached his chest.

Dark clouds billowing on the horizon told him the low pressure system was charging in from the west. With any luck, it might ride the westerly jet stream and miss them, heading up to the Bay of Biscay instead, but the chances of that were small and, Leo couldn't deny it, whatever they were in for loomed inland. The weather forecast had changed and now was giving out shipping warnings.

The crew were down on deck gutting fish and throwing them into buckets of ice while trying to keep their balance on the increasingly unsteady deck, when a signal came over the VHF.

Trying to get himself heard over the squawk of seabirds following the boat and the crash of waves against the bow and fighting to keep a steady wheel, Leo shouted to the men below. "Paulo's in trouble. Engine failed, batteries failing. He's two miles west."

Rui, Dick and Fred looked up, and Fred barely hesitated as he thumbed towards the west.

That would be against the tide and not a good idea

with the weather picking up, but Leo turned the wheel to change course. Another fisherman was in trouble and there was no question about not heading against the weather so they could help.

The sky darkened by the minute and the force of the water gripped the boat, rocking it violently as it descended into ever higher troughs formed by the strong tidal current. Leo concentrated on his course, secretly flattered that Fred, who had stayed on deck securing anything movable, trusted his boat to him. It wasn't going to be easy. Even in calmer seas, towing a stricken boat back to Luminosa without damaging either boat would be difficult, but in this maelstrom it might prove impossible because now they couldn't avoid the full force of the storm surge. Maybe they should find shelter together somewhere?

Fred and Rui came into the wheelhouse. "ETA to Paulo twenty minutes," Leo told them, making a course adjustment.

A static message rattled from the radio advising all ships in the area to head for shelter against an unexpected but imminent storm-surge, news that made Leo bite on his lower lip but otherwise ignore as they headed farther out, away from the shore.

The next message was an emergency Coast Guard signal to use, but Leo knew they wouldn't use it unless things became dire. Coast Guards saved crew, but not boats and Paulo's boat was his lifeline: they'd save it together if they could. If they could spot it because it was getting darker and the radio signal was fading fast along with the batteries. Pretty soon he'd have no lights.

Leo strained to see something that resembled Paulo's boat on the horizon. He shook his head and silently thought they were too late. But then, their radar picked up a silhouette about half a mile off.

"There she is!" Dick called from his look-out position

on the deck.

The small longliner listed a good forty degrees. Leo pulled out the throttle and as they neared, they could see the crew tied together and ready to launch their inflatable life-raft. "Put the bumpers and buoys over the side, I'm going alongside," Leo said. "Save having to pick 'em out of the water."

"No, no," Fred said. "We'll tow 'em so they'll stay onboard and distribute the weight. Can't lose the boat."

There was no arguing with the skipper, so, against his better judgment, Leo pushed back the throttle and let the swells maneuver them nearer Paulo and his waiting crew.

CHAPTER THIRTY-TWO

The local casualty department was not the nicest of places to spend a Saturday morning. Outside the main door, Piper lifted her nose to take in the fresh, rain-drenched air. Grey clouds scudded across the sky filled with flocks of seagulls heading inland away from a gathering storm. It smelled lovely after the antiseptic and wee stink of the hospital.

An ambulance came roaring up followed by a police car, lights flashing, sirens howling. To give them space, Piper went back into the hospital to see if Conceição had regained consciousness.

Piper had been questioned about how she'd found Conceição and she'd told the truth.

"Do you know her name?" a receptionist asked.

"It's Conceição but the surname I've no idea," she replied. If she was Serafim's sister, then she might be...God, Piper didn't know. "Oh wait! It might be Shine. Conceição Shine."

The receptionist tapped her front teeth with her pen before she nodded and wrote down the information. "And where's she from?" she asked.

"Well...Luminosa, I suppose, originally."

"Never heard of it. Is it in Portugal?"

Piper tightened her lips. "Definitely."

"But you're not a relative." The receptionist tapped her teeth again.

Piper considered. "Don't think so, unless maybe a fourth or fifth cousin counts."

"Bit distant. Who can we contact if we need to try to find out her next of kin?"

"Serafim's café in Luminosa? Nelson Carneiro? No, I don't know the number." Piper didn't know anyone else. "Can I see her? Is she all right?"

"A heroin overdose, especially in her condition, will take time for her to be 'all right.'"

A harassed and tired-looking doctor hurriedly told her later that Conceição was being 'stabilized' but that many of her organs were in danger of shutting down thanks to her long addiction, but if Piper wanted to, then she could take a quick look at her.

Inside a cubicle, a maze of tubes entered and exited the small figure on the gurney and only her head was visible, the rest covered by a sheet. The scenario reminded Piper of her mother but instead of the ethereal, fragile beauty of her mother, Conceição, who had lost her wig, looked like a wizened monkey.

Piper took her hand, and she half-opened her eyes. It took a moment or two for her to focus on Piper. "I remember you," she whispered, pausing between each word to take a breath. "Do you know Leo? I was dreaming of him."

"I think probably I might know him."

"Can you tell him he's *meu menino lindo*. Truly. Never wanted to hurt him. Born because I wanted him. Something of mine. Wanted to take him with me when I escaped, but George forced him away from me and said I was a lousy mother. I wouldn't have been, not to *meu menino lindo*."

It took Conceição several minutes to get these words out and they left Piper stunned. "What does *meu menino lindo* mean?" she asked a nurse.

"My beautiful child or son."

How Piper would have loved to hear her mother call her 'her beautiful daughter.'

Piper had no idea whether Leo Shine was still in Luminosa or not. If she'd known he was Leo and not Tom, things might have been a little different between them and she would have tried hard to contact him from the UK. She found herself touching her lips with the tip of her finger, in just the place where the memory of his light kiss still lingered. In any case, in her place, she'd like to know that her mother was in a hospital in Lisbon. She'd better get to Luminosa quickly.

****

The coach crossed over the river to the south bank where the landscape became flatter in a jumble of fields and car factories. Unlike the heat haze that shimmered before, this time the sky was a seething mass of dark grey clouds while a bitter wind gathered strength and whipped the cork-oaks and olive trees from side to side.

Like the other time, Piper sat back in her padded seat and fell asleep, only waking when they arrived in Sines where she changed to the old jalopy of a bus to Luminosa. This too was buffeted by gale-force winds as it wound along the coast road, heading south. The sea pounded on the rocks in a savage show of temper, and spray hit the bus windows. She was the only passenger today so no one offered her goats' cheese sandwiches or sweet, eggy cakes.

Half-way down the hill to Luminosa, Piper paused to look at the silvery, heaving water against the dark lavender sky churning with grey clouds. A storm of huge proportions brewed out there and the swell of the sea grew by the minute. None of the fleet had gone out by the looks of it: larger boats were moored on the lee side of the harbor breakwater, and a dozen or so skiffs had been hauled up, and piled on top of one another on the narrow road fronting the beach. Fishermen sure didn't need a barometer to know when bad weather was on the way. Not that they needed intuition today either, anyone with half a brain would've been able to tell what they were in for in the morning, so no one should have gone out.

In any case, the inshore fishermen wouldn't have too much work at the moment because the sardines and horse mackerel were spawning off to the west at a point a mile or so off. It shimmered with the aura of mother-of pearl, strong iridescent colors, rising and then falling with the crests and steep troughs, brighter from being reflected against the lowering sky.

Down at the far end of the beach, just beyond the piles of fishing boats, hurricane lamps lit up both the dull afternoon and dozens of people who were digging in the sand. Children and dogs ran around the grown-ups so that barks, laughter and chatter filled the heavy air and drowned out the crash of the pounding waves. The closer Piper got, the easier it was to make out what everyone was doing—filling sacks with sand.

One of the figures on the beach looked up, straightened, dropped a sack and hurried over at a heavy trot. "Piper!"

Piper felt like she was floating, drawn towards the group and Prazeres like a magnetic force she had no wish to resist. How lovely to see them all, even though she didn't recognize everyone. With a sigh of pleasure, she fell into Prazeres welcoming hug.

Prazeres then delivered her up into grizzly-bear Serafim's embrace that made her think of Pop.

"Tell us, dear," Serafim said, now holding her at arm's length so he could study her. "We've been wanting to know but could never find you. Gaspar said he thought you lived in Norfolk, but didn't know where. Etta tried a number Victor had for your taxi-service but no one ever answered. Tell us now, how is your shoulder?"

"Nearly perfect, thank you. I already have full movement. But I have more to tell you." They needed to be told about her mother because, as far as they knew, Felipa had died at Piper's birth and she felt they should know the truth. By the time Piper related the story of her mother, the crowd had gathered around silently. Even the children, who'd been circling her with cries as loud as fireworks, stopped, their excitement cooling as they drew round her.

Even though she put Pop into the best possible light as she retold her tale, telling them that he'd acted for the best and had kept his silence to protect her, Piper, she still expected accusations about him to fly. She had already planned her small speech on the rattling bus and had reached the decision that if there were generalized incriminations against her father then she'd have no choice but to take herself away from the village again. It was only right that they knew where her loyalty lay.

The few seconds of silence that followed the end of her story felt like an eternity, and she braced herself for the worst. But there was no need to worry.

"We'll say a Mass for her," someone said as everyone began to file past her, some gave her a kiss on both cheeks, others shook her hand and everyone gave her a brief hug.

Trying to hide that her eyes had filled with tears, Piper faced the sacks abandoned on the beach. "What's happening?"

"Sandbags." Prazeres told her. "We're in for a tidal surge—one that wasn't predicted, I might add. The wind changed unexpectedly and is now blowing inland. The tide will be a high one tonight and the weather forecast is giving flood and storm warnings. And we've two boats out."

"But the weather…didn't they realize they shouldn't

have gone out?"

"They left before dawn and it was clear then. The sea was calm and the forecast good. It changed so suddenly. Most of the fleet was near enough to come home immediately they got the message," Prazeres said.

The sea, which was beating its chest in a show of bravado, was not one Piper would like to be out on in a boat right at this moment. "Are those two boats coming in, or going to find shelter somewhere?"

"We last heard from Fred that they were going to help out Paulo who was nearby and in trouble, but that was a while ago. Since then we've lost contact." Serafim said, chewing his lip and pulling on his beard.

"Have you called the Coast Guard?" Silly question, really. Of course they would've called them.

Serafim sucked his lips in as he stared out at the sea where every wave was a gray swell, full of malice. The wind had picked up to a moaning gale that flung wet sand at them. "Paulo won't want to lose the boat. If we call the Coast Guard, they'll just help the people…"

"My Fred and Rui are out there," Rosa said in a quiet voice. "I wish they'd come back."

"And Paulo, Rob and Gil," someone else continued. "And Ricardo. Oh, God help them."

"They'll be all right," a large woman in black said. "Leo's with them. If anyone can read the sea, it's him. He'll bring them back safely."

Leo. The very person she needed to see. And he was out in the kind of storm even the hardiest of fishermen ran away from screaming. "God, no," she whispered.

"Well," Serafim broke the ensuing silence, "it's no good worrying." He turned to call out to two boys sitting at the café door, "You two listen for the VHF—if there's any message call me instantly. I have my mobile here in case they get a signal and can call."

Piper stared at the tumbling horizon. Please don't let Leo get lost at sea like his brother and father; that would be so cruel. Out of the corner of her eye, she spotted a figure sitting on the wall by a cottage that was farther away and isolated from the village; it stood some yards away from its neighbor and was the one nearest the sea, the only one actually sitting on the beach, attached to the adjoining cliff, almost as if it had been carved from the same rock.

On a wall that surrounded a small yard at the side, Lili sat staring listlessly at the sea. She looked older and had lost weight in the short time since Piper had last seen her; once smart clothes now hung off her frame that looked about as cuddly as a bundle of sticks. Her face was swollen and her eyes glazed as if someone had put her on a special diet of pills.

Prazeres broke into Piper's thoughts. She indicated the sacks of sand. "Let's get back to work and get the cottages protected, it'll help take our minds off those still out. Best to keep occupied at times like this."

Leaving her rucksack in Serafim's café, Piper returned and set to. Sand and salt filled her eyes, ears, nose and mouth in the next hour as they all worked to fill sacks that were then passed up the beach to those people stationed along the first line of cottages. Piled up sandbag barriers grew to protect against the flood tide and keep water out of the cottage doors. When Piper finally stood, stretching her aching back as she wiped sand from her eye, she noticed that Lili hadn't moved or offered to help, even though they'd systematically moved along and now piled sandbags higher in front of the final cottage—Lili's.

"Have a little rest," said Prazeres. She also rubbed the small of her back. "We'll be finished soon, and I'll go in a minute and make us a hot punch with some of Gil's *agua-*

dente." She shaded her face with her hand and scanned the horizon. "Please God, bring our men back safely."

She voiced what everyone was thinking.

But a sudden downpour spoiled Prazeres's desire to go to the café. Lili scurried inside her cottage, and Prazeres, Piper and the other sandbag fillers barreled to the cliff-face next to the cottage. As they sheltered under the cliff's overhanging ledges, Piper decided she couldn't keep Conceição's story to herself any longer, even though Leo wasn't present. Something had to be done about the woman lying alone in hospital.

She pulled on Prazeres's sleeve to move her away from the rest of the group and then told her what had happened from the moment Conceição had loomed out of the dark alley, clutching Piper's bag, to when Piper had left her in the hospital. "They said they were going to put her into an induced coma for two days," she said. "So I thought this was the right time to come down and tell you all. What do you think?"

"Oh, my dear girl, you have been through so much. What an experience. I think…" Whatever Prazeres was about to say was cut off as the door to Lili's cottage flew open and Gaspar loomed in the entrance. They were so close Piper could smell damp wool from his tweed jacket and cap, and boiled cabbage from God-knew where.

"Hello Gaspar. Uncle." Piper didn't want to wind him up, but the glaring eye and stern expression, so different from everyone else's in the village, annoyed her. Just like Lili he chose not to lend a hand in helping with the sandbags, despite the fact his cottage needed shoring up against the tide more than anyone else's, and they'd worked hard to build the sturdiest barrier they could there.

"I heard you talking about Conceição."

Yes, he probably would have. Piper should've been more

careful about keeping her voice down. After all, Lili had gone into the cottage, so Piper should've realized he lived there.

"Did she talk about me?" Gaspar asked, his expression static as if frozen.

"Yes." It was true. Conceição had mentioned him; she'd said he was a loser.

"Where is she?"

Piper felt a childish urge to say, "Where is she, *please?*" Instead, she replied, "Santa Maria Hospital in Lisbon."

"I'm going." He turned and slammed the door in their faces.

"Oh hell," Prazeres said. "Who'll look after Nelson now?"

"Lili?" Rosa ventured.

"She's no good," Prazeres replied. "She'll just stand around vacantly and watch his boils grow. Or sit around more likely."

"So Nelson and everyone else are living in here, are they?" Piper asked.

"Yes, they moved out soon after that eventful weekend. Lili's waiting for a psychiatric assessment and has had her passport confiscated. No date has been set yet and she just seems to have shut down. Etta told her to take a course of some kind while she was waiting to keep her brain active. She suggested finishing her degree in Advanced Eye-makeup Application. But Lili just stared at her as if Etta was a lunatic."

The door opened again and Gaspar, with his default expression of disinterest, stepped delicately over the sandbags, dislodging one or two and not putting them back.

"Can you keep an eye on Nelson?" he asked Prazeres.

"Oh brilliant. Just what I need."

"I'll do it," Piper said and met Gaspar's gaze with defiance. He was the first to give way and he turned away with a slight nod before walking off.

"Didn't take much to persuade him, did it?"

"Probably a relief to get away from Nelson for a while. I know he's a miserable old so-and-so, but Gaspar does take good care of Nelson, you know."

"He had a thing for Conceição, didn't he?"

"He did, and look where it landed him? Still, if he wants to go and see her, who am I to tell him it's a bad idea?" She took a step towards the cottage. "Well, I'd better go and see what Nelson needs."

Piper placed her hand on Prazeres's arm. "I'll come with you. I need to meet my grandfather."

Prazeres gave her a long look before she said, "I'll introduce you."

CHAPTER THIRTY-THREE

Prazeres tapped on the blue door that Gaspar had closed behind him when he left. Lili opened it, and her gaze flickered over them without any visible interest.

They waited for her to say something, but she focused on an object over Prazeres's shoulder.

"Aren't you going to ask us in?" Prazeres prompted.

Lili shrugged and opened the door wider.

"My shoulder's much better," Piper said, unable to resist, "thank you for asking."

Lili finally let her gaze fall on Piper. "*Eu…*" She hesitated for a moment. "At the time, I not know, or care, who I hurt. I sorry. I was *howyousay* someone other than I. Not me, if you understand."

Piper had never expected an apology from Lili, but it was one Piper could accept.

They entered the cottage straight into a tiny living room with a flag-stone floor, a dark wooden trestle table with a bench on either side and a couple of deep armchairs set around a small open fireplace. The fireplace gave little warmth and it was chillier inside than out—nice, Piper thought, for a hot summer's day but not for today. She shivered and looked around the dark wooden-beamed ceiling, white rough-plastered walls which were simply adorned by a couple of hanging painted plates. Pretty basic for an ex-lord-of-the-manor.

A crash which sounded like an angry wild animal trying to get out came from behind the closed door of an adjoining room. Then the cracked and chipped door opened and an elderly man clattered through at a speed no doddery old guy like him in a wheelchair should be able to achieve.

Lili didn't seem at all surprised since she had no reaction, just sat in an armchair and gazed at an empty fireplace. The man's loud entry must be a regular event.

Who could this be except Nelson? If Piper had been nervous at meeting her infamous grandfather for the first time, it quickly turned to a morbid fascination—the kind that makes people stare at the aftermath of car-crashes.

He was dressed in a maroon fitted Regency velvet jacket and snakeskin boots, his silver hair sprang in all directions like an explosion in a cotton-wool factory, and his red complexion matched his jacket.

Prazeres must've seen Piper staring because she said in a low voice, "He wears that every day, sometimes adding for effect a round smoking cap with a tassel."

And wears it all night too, probably. The crumpled jacket was stiff with spilled, dried food and its original crimson was turning in patches to the color of rotting meat. His rheumy eyes gazed at them in his mashed up wrinkled face which held an expression of a toothless bull-dog sucking a lemon.

"Leo calls him crazy with a side of fries," Prazeres said without lowering her voice. "But he's old, that's all, and I suppose pretty much ga-ga."

"*Onde está o Gaspar?*" Nelson's voice was as raspy as two rusty nails rubbing together.

"He's gone out for a while," Prazeres replied in English. "*O que?*"

"Gone out," Prazeres yelled. "He's deaf," she told Piper.

Piper stepped forward. "Hello," she said, her heart beating wildly, and braced to avoid any violence on his part. Who knew how he'd react at seeing her?

The old man slowly faced her, moving just his head. Nearly a minute went by in which no one said a word; Prazeres and Piper just exchanged equally heavy stares. Then, the old guy's face cracked into a smile.

From the downturned lines on his face, and what she had heard about her grandfather, Piper would guess that his usual smile was either full of scorn or contained a fair amount of menace, anything but amusement. But this one had a touch of pleasure and bewilderment mixed in.

"Felipa?" he asked out of the corner of his mouth, which seemed to be the only bit of it that worked.

A gasp escaped from Prazeres as Piper stepped forward and knelt down in front of the wheelchair. "It's Philippa," she told him, emphasizing the first syllable rather than the middle one as he had.

Nelson turned to Prazeres who was chewing her lip until Piper thought it might fall off. He addressed her in Portuguese.

"I didn't tell you Piper was here," Prazeres replied loudly, "because I didn't know myself until a little time ago."

"Did anyone tell him I was here two months ago?"

Prazeres shook her head.

"Or about Lili and her lovely spears?"

Lili took her gaze off the fireplace to look at her and frowned. "*Não,*" she said. "He not know." And, from her dirty look, Piper gleaned that she assumed no one would ever inform him.

A wave crashed with extra force on the beach, seemingly just outside the door. Shock-waves rocked the little cottage, and Prazeres looked anxiously at the door.

"Go on back to Serafim," Piper told her. "I'll bring Nelson along in a moment to the café. Let me just talk to him."

Prazeres slowly opened the door and peeked out. The

heavy wave had indeed ended just a few feet away and now withdrew in a hiss of tumbling surf. Would the tide get any higher? Surely not. "I'll bring him in a moment. Promise," Piper repeated. "And her too." She nodded at Lili who had returned to commune with the fireplace.

Prazeres hesitated, perhaps torn between leaving them on their own or returning to her husband. Then she nodded at Nelson and said, "He's safe, I mean he won't attack you or anything like that, but don't listen to what he says if he starts ranting. He has a tongue like a holly bush. I'll see you in the café in a minute."

"Don't be too long." Nelson wagged a finger at her. "My dinner's due. And today I fancy a *caldeirada*."

"He'll be lucky," Prazeres whispered to Piper. "He'll get some of my pork and like it. And he'll eat it in the café because I'm not bringing it here today."

"And the floor needs a good sweep."

They both looked at the pristine flag tiles, at the gleaming white plaster walls, and the shining wooden ceiling.

"Bullshit," Prazeres whispered as she stepped out, fighting the whipping wind.

She'd barely closed the door behind her before Nelson reeled off a string of Portuguese. He wasn't talking to zombie-like Lili, he was talking to Piper.

Kneeling beside his wheelchair again, she asked, "Could you speak English to me please?"

"Why should I? You are Portuguese through and through, Felipa, which you should remember and be proud of. Your fixation with everything English is not normal. Just like the rest of Luminosa." Whether he realized it or not, he'd reverted to English.

She took his hand. "I'm your granddaughter," she said gently.

He eyed her carefully before bursting into a throaty

laugh that turned into a coughing fit and he needed to be thumped on the back to recover. "Oh, Felipa, Felipa," he gasped when he found his voice again, "you always try to joke with me." His face darkened and his voice grated as he said, "And I don't like it. You respect me, as your father. And do as I say." He pointed a rheumatic knobby finger at her before staring around the room. His gaze finally settled back on Piper again, and he frowned as he said, "You are a lovely, lovely girl."

"Thank you." Patting his worm-veined hand and noting how freezing cold it was, she decided it was pointless to insist on being his granddaughter, because the likelihood of him accepting it seemed zero. Or sub-zero. She rubbed his cold hand. "It is very chilly in here. We need to get you warm."

As if waiting for that cue, the wind hurled itself at the closed shutters on the windows and rattled them like someone trying to get in. Gravel or sand blasted at the walls with a slashing sound that Nelson responded to, listening with his head tilted to one side, his mass of hair bunched up against the back of his wheelchair, his expression puzzled as if he'd lost his way.

Even Lili stirred herself to glance at the window.

Nelson's hand shook in Piper's as he said, "I like to sit and think and wish and hope. You know? Rain is cold but tears are hot."

She pondered this, wondering if it came from a literary quote or not.

"I mean," he said, perhaps seeing her thoughtful expression, "rain takes a long time to reach us because they belong to the skies but tears are immediate and belong to us alone."

Her stomach clenched in sympathy. "Oh you don't cry do you? You mustn't cry." She knew what he meant, although she had determined years ago never to weep, even when the tears welled and threatened to overflow.

"I do cry," he admitted, nodding. "When I think about things that make me sad."

She couldn't stop herself from gathering his frail body in her arms. "Don't be sad," she whispered in his hot ear and felt a twinge of satisfaction when his arms wrapped around her waist. A clock ticked the seconds away as they clasped each other. "My name's Piper," she whispered.

"And you're so pretty, Piper. Who did you say you are?"

Before she could form a reply, the front door caved in under a tremendous force. It held for a moment, just long enough for Lili to scream and Piper to leap to her feet. She acted instinctively, darting to the back of her grandfather's chair so she could wheel him out of danger. But they had no time.

A wall of green water broke first through the small window, then smashed through the door, flattening it, and roared in with the force of a loaded lorry.

As water threatened to take her feet from under her, she gathered her grandfather up—he was no heavier than a loaded crab-pot—and carried him through the door to the bedroom. "Lili," Piper cried over her shoulder. "Come on!" She held the door open with her foot as Lili waded through past her and then, by pushing hard with her bottom, managed to close it behind her. They were in a bedroom with a tiny window that she thought was big enough to allow each of them to get through one at a time.

She set her grandfather carefully down on the bed as water swirled in through the edges of the closed door, and she tore at the latch on the shutters until they opened. "Go first, then you can catch him when I pass him through to you," she cried to Lili who, perhaps for the first time in her life, obeyed an instruction. She levered herself up to the window and her skinny body slithered through it.

Piper lifted her grandfather off the bed. By now the

water was up to her waist and she pushed him up onto the sill. He clasped her arms, unwilling to let go as he perched there, so she was forced to push him and close her ears to his cries of pain and complaint at her undignified manhandling. There was no other option.

Please God, don't let Lili skedaddle without waiting for Nelson. To Piper's surprise, bony hands reached up and pulled him through. As he fell, Piper heard a splash. God, the garden must also be underwater.

Now it was her turn to scramble through the small window and push herself off the ledge. She landed beside Lili who was trying to lift Nelson but was making a pig's-ear of a bad job. Maybe she was too weak to keep his face from falling under the surface. Piper took him under the shoulders and lifted him clear of the rising water, relieved to hear him take a gasping breath. Now, just how were they going to get out of the garden and away from the water?

Another howl of raging water coincided with a deluge hitting the cottage door, the frame cracked and the door gave way. The water level rose up to her chest. The force of the underwater swirl at her feet tried to drag her back towards the tumbling cottage but she fought it, using most of her strength to keep Nelson afloat. Lili also strongly pushed against it as she slogged towards the wall, the top of which was still above the water-level. Lili howled something in a language totally unknown to Piper.

Where was the woman heading? She was familiar with the place so she must know of an escape-route, and there was no other choice but to hope she did. Piper followed her, the water ever higher and her arm muscles screamed at the struggle to keep her grandfather as far out of the water as she could. Even so, his lower body remained submerged.

She blinked, her face running with salty moisture and wished she had a free hand to wipe it away as it dripped into her eyes. Lili was tugging on something that moved. Yes it did. Something that opened. A gate and now a gap opened just wide enough for Lili to slip through along with a gush of water that lowered the level on Piper's side for a moment. Piper made to follow but a wave caught her from the back, knocking her forward with such power she let go of Nelson for a second before lunging and grabbing him again. She had to make it to the gate.

A blast sounded from the other side of the cottage, as violent as a gunshot, followed by the noise of rubble breaking and the groan of splinting wood. But, worst of all, another wall of water thundered straight for them. This wave would swallow them.

Laying her grandfather on his back, with his head pointing towards the gate, and, thank the Lord, Lili's white face peered back at them, she pushed at his feet, propelling him onwards. "Swim, Nelson. Swim," she cried just a mere second before the wave swamped her and took her back with it.

The mighty being is awake! Whether she consciously thought these words or whether the notion was just there, she had no idea as she was tossed, grabbed and submerged in a world of green that had no master except its own whim.

"Piper!" That was Lili's voice she heard. Lili called again, but the wave swept Piper away and Lili's voice grew fainter. Funny that Lili would be the last person she ever heard.

CHAPTER THIRTY-FOUR

Everyone had donned foul weather gear and life-jackets. Rui stood just outside the bridge on tow watch, Dick waited down by the secured tow-line that he'd caught on the third attempt; Paulo's boat was now reliant on Fred's. Leo held the wheel, and Fred was still trying to reach Paulo again on his cell phone. "I think I'm getting a bit of a signal again."

"Watch out," Rui cried, "she's quartering."

Leo slowed, heading into a wave and hoping Paulo could keep his boat steady with the meager steering he still had. What neither boat needed right now was to take a wave over the starboard bow. They'd already ensured that Paulo's load was securely fastened aft, the bow rising high to help stabilize her. He also still had bilge pumping working, but not at full rate.

"OK, she's turned," Rui reported.

"Keep going," Fred confirmed, the relief clear in his voice. "Careful and slow."

Despite the cold in the wheelhouse, as all heating had been turned off to conserve power, Leo wiped away sweat that threatened to drip in his eyes.

The wind and waves were chaotic and it took all his concentration to read a pattern in the height and duration of the churning water so he could time his course in a way that Paulo's boat could follow without rolling.

"I got him!" Fred announced, triumphantly waving the

phone before discussing with Paulo whether to head nearer land and anchor there, or whether to keep on for Luminosa and trust their luck would hold out. "Trouble is," Fred said, "it's getting darker by the moment. We'd best head in now, there's a good harbor shelter in Albarran. It shouldn't cause any problems maneuvering…"

Static over the VHF and Serafim's disjointed voice over the sound-waves interrupted him. Serafim crackled for several seconds before he was cut off, leaving Fred and Leo staring at each other. "What did he say?"

Fred shook his head. "It was difficult to hear, but he said something about tidal surge, I think. He said *flood,* I'm sure he did." Fred picked up his cell phone and gabbled into it for a moment before that too lost its signal.

"Paulo agrees. We have to get back to Luminosa," Fred said as he threw the phone down, the tendons in his neck taut and swollen. "Rosa is there alone. Rui will say the same. We have to. A tidal surge! To get us there quicker, Paulo will have to discharge his load to make him lighter because he has his parents to worry about. I'll see if I can signal to him."

Leo nodded and turned his attention back to the waves. He'd gained a lot of ground in Portuguese this last month, but he wasn't sure if he'd misunderstood when he'd heard Prazeres's voice in the background during Serafim's radio-call just as he mentioned the *inundação.* Hadn't Prazeres called, *A Piper está presa em casa com Nelson e Lili.* That definitely meant, "Piper's trapped with Nelson!" He added just a tad more throttle, as much as he dared, before he called for Fred to take the wheel because he wanted to watch the sea closer.

****

Not more than just over half a mile from shore Leo felt a terrifying, but not unfamiliar, freight-train-like force of energy surging from the south-west. Growing like a migraine developing, the strength of its sheer potency filled his head, and both his arms burned as if receiving constant electric shocks. "Turn," he cried to Fred at the helm, his scrutiny never leaving the long waves with their dense overhanging crests. "Veer. Stern to the wind. Now! Pull out the throttle. Do it!" He glanced quickly at his cousin, Rui, who peered through the door, his white face shining out from his hood, trust and fear reflected in his young face.

If the crew on Fred's boat felt they were having the ride of their lives, Leo couldn't imagine what it was like for Paulo's. Without any question, Fred had obeyed Leo's command to veer and although they were still heading into the waves, now they were on another current and turned away from Luminosa, going at the fullest speed. Behind, Paulo's boat tumbled and plunged in the troughs. Once again on the cell phone, he told them his crew was on standby to launch the life-raft and had tied themselves together again.

The pull on the tow grew taut to screeching point, and Paulo's boat listed at a sickening angle to port. With every wave pounding over its side, it settled lower in the water as its tanks and hull were flooded.

There was nothing Paulo and his crew could do other than launch their orange life-raft which meant Fred now needed to heave to and pick them up.

Jesus, Leo prayed. This was going to delay their progress out of the path of the giant wave that was still heading their way, filling his brain with a pressure that was about to burst. If he looked at his fingertips, he reckoned he'd see sparks from the energy gathered there.

Fred's engines roared as he tried to keep steady and make sure the life-raft that was coming ever nearer didn't get caught by the propellers or the side of the boat and overturn. They used up ten minutes of valuable time for the rescue operation, and by the time Paulo, Gil and Rob were aboard with them, Leo could hardly think with the monstrous compression hammering inside him. Whatever was bearing down on them, it sent out enough power to make him explode. "Return to the previous course, Skip, I reckon," he shouted at Fred as Paulo staggered, soaked and dripping, onto the bridge. It was the skids for his boat, and Leo knew that if no huge wave materialized, Paulo would never forgive him for making Fred change course. If they hadn't, both boats might well be entering Luminosa right now.

Although Leo would rather that the wave didn't exist, after five minutes it appeared, almost out of nowhere it seemed. The wind still screamed and the surrounding waves peaked at an average of fifteen feet, but the larger one loomed vastly higher than the rest. The force of it made Leo want to scream.

The outline of Paulo's boat was still just visible as the wave caught, tossed and pummeled it as if it were a tiny mouse a lion was playing with. Fred forced his boat to pound away from it. They were now against the sea going at full power, both engines screaming. Paulo groaned as his boat succumbed, broke up and sank, stern first within a few seconds. And still the wave continued its relentless path, gathering speed and strength. Leo tried to make out in the dark how long it stretched: a good thirty meters to the north, he thought. Just a little more and they'd be just about at its outer edge and still heading away from it. But a smaller wave, coming at them in a different direction smacked into the bow, slowing them down. Without that, they'd have escaped and the wave would've missed them. As it was, they were grazed by the end of huge wave's swell and buffeted by the smaller wave's onslaught. Fred's boat went through every motion; it pitched, rolled and yawed violently, its cargo crashing from side to side, threatening to smash through into the chaos of water.

"Another one." Rui pointed ahead, just to starboard. Leo joined Fred and together they grappled the helm hard to starboard so that the rudder turned the boat to port, pointing her into the gathering wave which, although still collecting energy from the previous giant one, was not as high. The boat bucked but not enough to prevent Paulo's crew, Rui and Gil from keeping the cargo settled on deck.

Once stabilized again, and now in a brief lull, Fred cut the power to ease the overworked engines, and the six men silently stared out at the dark sea. Leo looked his fellow fishermen over. They looked dazed and were no doubt as bruised as he was from the battering they'd each taken by trying to stay upright.

"Well," said Paulo. "We had no choice. It was either lose the boat or never see my family again."

"We'd never have towed you through that," Fred confirmed, which made a combined rush of relief and sympathy flow through Leo.

His mind had begun to clear of the heavy weight that had filled it to bursting point, his arms felt lighter again and he didn't have to force himself to breathe. He looked at Fred who was wriggling at the helm. "You want a pee?" he asked. "Want me to take the wheel?"

"I want a crap." Fred rubbed at his face fit to scrub the skin off. "And, yes, I want you to take the wheel because I want to get to Luminosa as fast as we can. That wave was heading towards the village."

Piper, Leo thought, fear filling the space left by the fire-power of the giant wave.

****

They'd gone back out so far, they were now a mile from

Luminosa, and the sea looked like it was made of ski-slopes with the white spume blown off the surface by the shrieking wind. Leo concentrated on the waves, timing their entry with the least turbulence.

Eventually, and it seemed like an eternity because they had to chug along far slower than they'd have liked, they were within sight of the village. But they weren't prepared for what they saw through binoculars as they neared. It was clear the tidal surge had broken through the sandbags piled high in the doorways of the cottages. Boats had come away from where they'd been positioned on the road, and some were hanging over the sea wall and bulkhead, and a trawler had been deposited clean over the side of the jetty.

"Jesus Christ," Fred breathed.

Leo maneuvered towards the harbor breakwater and tried to choose a set of waves that might take them inside. But with water levels so high and the sea so chaotic and high, what was the point? They couldn't moor safely. "How about we wait by the breakwater and anchor down?" he asked. The boat would be at risk from the turbulent tide, but would not get smashed against the rocks or jetty.

Fred nodded, rubbing his chin and unable to take his gaze off the village. "We'll lay at anchor and hope that when the seas recede the anchors aren't pulled out." He shook himself visibly. "Whatever. Right now our priority is to get ashore."

Leo agreed and silently set up a prayer for the villagers on land. And Piper. *Oh please let Piper be safe.*

Rui poked his head around the door. "Life-raft?"

"Yep," Fred said, and the other six men breathed sounds of agreement. "The boat's got heavy rope warps which we'll attach to a loop in the anchor chain when it goes over the bow."

"Fine by me," said Leo.

They prepared to deploy the life-raft on the lee side of the boat for maximum protection, which wouldn't be very great, and Leo hoped they could judge the sea from there.

Fred stayed back and looked at his wheelhouse with a sigh.

Leo patted his shoulder. "You'll see it again," he said, wondering whether the next time they did, it would be driftwood.

"Off you go," Fred ushered them down the steps. "Cap'n's the last one off."

"We'll be OK with Leo," Rui said with a trembling laugh as he tightened his life-jacket. "He was born with a caul."

"Yeah," Leo straightened Rui's straps. "Born with a caul. It's a right help. You stay by my side, kid." He gave him a reassuring clap on the back. What a load of bullshit, but if it kept his cousin optimistic then what was wrong with that?

Once they were crammed in, Leo cried, "Who has got surfing experience?"

No one, the silence told him.

"Me neither. Ah well," he said, "It's time to give it a go. Always a first time."

The breakwater gave little protection from the plunging waves that, Leo knew, were perhaps the most dangerous thanks to the steep, sloping beach and sandbars which didn't make Luminosa the safest beach for swimmers.

"Watch the waves," Fred said.

"Take one that has a shorter interval between the next," Leo confirmed. They didn't want to get caught in too long an undertow and get dragged out again.

They waited.

"Here it is," the men shouted as one. And they were off.

It was like being in a clothes dryer getting tossed from side to side. Sitting high on the raft, they held on for dear life while Leo used the oar as a rudder. But the wave broke early, sending the raft spinning in the air and landing upside down on a receding wave. Leo counted heads as they broke the surface; they were all there—shivering so hard their teeth chattered. In the glacial waters, Fred must've become disoriented as he began to swim the wrong way. But Gil caught the back of his life-jacket and pulled him back. They managed to grab the raft that had righted itself and clamber back in. Once seated again, and their wits returned, they discovered they'd all drifted nearly back to Fred's anchored fishing boat.

The second attempt sent them rolling violently again, over and over this time, banging into each other, arms and legs entangling, cursing fit to bust.

It seemed far too long, and Leo lost his sense of direction and wasn't even quite sure which way was up when a violent bump made his teeth rattle as he was tossed head over heels. He wondered if they'd hit driftwood or wreckage and whether they were going to get dragged out again with a holed raft. Then he bit down on sand, a full mouthful of it, just before he thudded against a solid object.

CHAPTER THIRTY-FIVE

Piper curled into a ball, clasping her head to avoid rubble and debris injuring her too badly as the force of the water battered, dragged and bashed her against objects she couldn't see. Over and over she was bowled by a forceful current that would take her wherever it wanted for it ruled the waves. Now and again an upward surge took her from underground springs that shot her briefly to the surface before it yanked her down where she could no longer see scudding clouds, nor feel or hear the gale. Her world became a whirling kaleidoscope of muddy greens, browns and a sandy mist that blocked her view of the raging turbulence above of surging, crashing waves.

When she felt her lungs would burst, another upsurge took her to the surface for a quick breath before it forced her back down. With air to last her a short while, she turned a somersault and then did another just because she could.

She lengthened her arms, spread them out ahead of her and she kicked. Or tried to but something entangled her legs. Once again she curled, this time to pull off whatever was caught around her. She knew immediately when she ripped at it that it was the weed the villagers said was not native to their shore, the one that had nearly caused Leo to drown. Bloody stuff. In a fury, she tore at the weed until, leaking a dark crimson substance into the water, it floated off in pieces to join the rest of its kin. Now that she looked, she saw great clumps of the stuff, bunches of it being battered higgledy-piggledy through the water, uprooted by the relentless fury of the water, some of it being washed ashore, some hurled out to sea where it was thrashed and mangled. The way it was being flung about reminded Piper of a child in a tantrum over an unwanted toy and who just wanted to smash it to bits.

Once again, an invisible force hoisted her back to the surface where, like a roller-coaster, she was propelled through watery loops and turns, up hills and down again until a wave enfolded her and catapulted her through the air, which was colder than the sea had been. "Stop playing bloody ball with me," she yelled. "Flipping heck!"

But the sea was in no mood to listen and within a moment, the wave that carried her sped towards land.

****

Someone was whimpering, another groaning and yet another pleading for God to help him. Maybe it was one man, maybe it was many. Leo had no idea as stars danced against blackness. He had a tremendous headache and it was fucking cold.

Shaking uncontrollably and his heartbeat thumping fit to explode, Leo felt around him. Sand, mostly. A body. It was warm...ish.

A crash that made the ground he was lying on tremble rumbled in his ear and cold water slapped him in the face. His head cleared. Piper! The village! Like a blind man, he felt around him again until he moved his hand up a low wall. The beach wall. With twitching, weak muscles, he pulled himself to his feet as another crash sounded near him. A light blinded him.

"Leo?"

"Serafim?" he stuttered in reply.

"God, man. Give me your hand. Gil? Paulo, Fred? Oh thank God. Can you get over the wall? Rui? You all here?"

Serafim held a huge searchlight, shining over them. Covering their eyes against the glare, each of the crew members slowly got to their feet. There was Rui. Leo put out his hand and together they clambered over the wall, a task that seemed as difficult as climbing Mount Hunter. Once they stepped out of the light's beam, darkness engulfed them along with embraces from villagers who crowded around them. From the other side of the wall, Serafim shone the searchlight out to sea.

Leo looked around. "Piper?" he gasped, still trying to catch his breath.

"Piper's still out there somewhere," Serafim said.

"What?" No. The hope, rising inside him when he saw so many of the villagers, died.

Silence followed the strong light beam as it searched the monstrous waves still sledge-hammering onto the beach. Backward and forward along the length of the beach, each unrewarded sweep was accompanied by a louder groan from the crowd. Out, beyond the breakwater, Fred's trawler was silhouetted dark against the navy blue sky, riding the peaks and disappearing into the troughs. It was the only bulky object in the water, for nearer land there was nothing except debris.

"Piper!" Leo called. "Piper," he shouted again.

****

There's quiet in the deep. Maybe it wasn't a thought, more like a feeling. Piper was beyond thinking, down there where all was just echoes. Peace and quiet. No choices. No hope.

"Piper!"

Something that sounded like her name filtered down to her, distorted but still…her name.

Several voices were calling, she decided. But one was the loudest: deep and resonant, an American accent. It reminded her of rough wool and the scent of surf in the air. Her body reacted and she kicked, but the weed bound her legs and the more she tore off, more of it clung to her.

****

The search light swept the beach another time, from the cliff at one end to the swamped quay at the other, and back again. Everyone was calling, *Piper, Piper*. A sense of hollowness overwhelmed Leo. The ruins of Nelson's cottage were visible and it was clear that if anyone had been trapped in there, they'd have been swept out to sea. No one could have survived.

"Nelson's OK. And so is Lili," Serafim told him, looking over his shoulder as if reading his thoughts.

Just Piper was missing then. Leo cupped his hands around his mouth and yelled as hard as his tired lungs would allow and followed the light again.

Wait. He squinted at a dark object on the beach. "Go back, Serafim. Back. There. What is it?"

Everyone peered in the direction, and Rui leaned forward to get a better look. "Looks like a piece of driftwood. Or a clump of weed."

"It moved, it moved! That's not debris or driftwood. It's alive," Serafim shouted.

"Piper!" Leo yelled.

Leo set off, sprinting ahead of the others who were thumping and skidding on the slippery sand behind him. The dark form was still again. Could it be a large dark fish of some kind washed up? Oh damnation, another wave was coming, one vast enough to swamp the unknown form and take it (or her) back out to sea again in the backwash. He put on a spurt.

But, unlikely as it had seemed to Leo—given the size of it, the wave broke early, just gently washing over the end of the dark shape. As he darted along, Leo could swear the wave nudged it towards land, out of the water, towards safety.

****

Piper forced her gritty eyes open. It was dark but the pandemonium of noises hurt her ears: people shouting, feet thudding, waves crashing, wind howling. What the chuffing hell was binding her body? She wanted to get up but felt she'd been wrapped up in tight bandages like a mummy. Blinking to get rid of salty water dripping in her eyes, she thought she saw a pair of very dirty sneakers materialize right beside her. Her gaze went higher, following soaking wet jeans clothing long legs, a scruffy leather belt round a neat waist and a bare torso that made the thought, *so that's what washboard abs look like* zip through her mind. A smooth chest, muscular arms. The wet jeans hunkered down beside her, and her ears filled with the sound of rushing blood as Leo Shine's face, so well-remembered, and hair hanging in lovely rats' tails, came into her view. The sight sucked the breath out of her and for a moment all she could see were his wide eyes drifting over her.

"Piper?" he whispered. His face was ashen and a knot of tendon stood out on his neck.

"I'm not dead," she murmured back.

His face lit up, and he fell forward onto his knees as if they'd buckled under him. "Get this stuff off her," he cried to someone, tearing at the weed covering her legs. That voice. The one that had held the power to lure her out of the sea against all odds. "It's that fucking weed. She's covered in it."

Within a minute she was in his arms, her own arms and legs wrapped around his body as he lifted her. She breathed his breath and an electric current surged through her. She snuggled in, moving her face against his neck. "You don't know how good that feels," she said.

****

Piper woke in a narrow bed with the sunshine pouring through the open window onto her eiderdown. As she gathered her wits about her, she wondered if she was in the middle of a rainbow. A swirl of fairy-lights and crystals caught the sunshine and reflected its rays in a multi-colored, sparkling chimera that danced across the ceiling. There, they mixed with the chandelier that transmitted the colors to the walls. These were covered with shelves, books and an assortment of bric-a-brac from pug-dogs to Toby Jugs, golden, fat and thin Buddhas, and even a wooden clog. She might see myriad colors on the sea, but even they looked muted in comparison with the glare of this room.

"Have you lost your wits? The furniture is half mine. I'll leave you your half." Victor Fletcher's gravelly voice echoed outside the door.

Piper pushed the covers back and got up, cautiously creeping past railings packed with color-coded frothy, fluffy clothes, hats and trailing scarves. She peeped through the door. Etta glared at her brother who rubbed his stomach.

"You don't need to hit, my dear," he groaned. "That's violence."

"I'll give you violence. Half," she spat at him. "*Half?* None of it is yours, you nincompoop. None of its mine. You have no family jewels. It's the State's now. We donated it as spoils of war. Spoils to spoils, state to state. Now," she prodded him in the ribs, "when I go back to the *Herdade* later on today with the Royal Estate people, just tell me I'm not going to find anything missing, am I?"

"Missing?"

"Like some little beetle called Victor has sold off anything? Hmmm? I know exactly what's there, you know, and in exactly which place in the priest's bolt-hole: the Shivan carpets, Chippendale chairs, French commode, probably late eighteenth century, Louis-Philippe lacquered cabinet, painting—possibly Goya early period. Spice chest…" She counted off each item on her fingers. "Three tapestry oak chairs, probably Louis XV, four Regency armchairs, an armoire, two pairs of sconces and the fabulous lavabo that I love as well as the table that extends and the consoles."

Victor stretched upright and sighed. "Everything's there because I haven't touched it. And Nelson or worse Lili, never found the bolt-hole."

"Good, then I'm sorry I hit you in the wossname. The Royal Estates would've been very upset to find anything missing."

"Good morning," Piper said, unwilling to interrupt, but unable to avoid it.

"Pipsqueak," Etta cried and pulled her into a hug. "You're awake, but my darling girl should still be in bed. You nearly *drowned*." Etta's eyes turned as round as half-crowns behind her yellow-framed glasses.

Piper extracted herself from the beads and scarves entangling her. "No I didn't," she managed before being engulfed again. "I was OK," she finished, her mouth muffled by Etta's bosom.

"I'm so, so sorry about your mama, darling. So sad. We didn't know, you know, about her. But we did try to contact you."

"She did," Victor confirmed and patted her, rather hard she thought, on her back.

Once again, she unwrapped herself from the continent of Etta. "Thank you, I know you did. And I tried to contact you too. Tell me, what's going on here? What are you two fighting about?"

Etta clapped her hands with joy. "You'll never guess. The Royal Estates were here just two days ago looking at the *Herdade*. They spent all day inspecting the place, the grounds and listening to how things work and have always worked around here. Then, you'll never guess, never in a million years..."

"Just tell the girl, my dear."

"They want to turn it into a *Casa Museu*. That's like a living, breathing museum. They're coming back today to discuss things further. The farm would continue, horses and goats and whatnot. The whole caboodle would carry on in the same way, and the villagers go about their business but now the house will be run properly. And guess what?" She ignored Victor's sigh. "They were talking about me being a custodian. That's..."

"She knows what that is, my dear, she's not a dunce."

Change of tune, Piper thought.

"And me, my dear. I'll be one too. A custodian."

"Not if I tell them you wanted to sell some of the furniture they won't." Etta frowned at her brother, but then beamed at Piper. "It is so funny. They never found it, you know."

"She's talking about Nelson and company."

"Indeed I am, Victor. They lived there all that time and never found what we'd stashed away in the priest's hole. If Lili had known, my God!" She threw her hands in the air. "Napoleon's commode would've gone under the hammer in no time and the place filled with decapitated bulls."

Piper grinned. "That's wonderful, wonderful news. I hope it all goes ahead."

"It will, it will."

A toilet flushed, and Piper turned to Etta in query.

"It's only Leo, darling."

A door opened and there he stood, in a bright white t-shirt and clean jeans, barefoot. All she could think of were those legs that went on forever, and his bare torso from last evening. As he stared at her now from the doorway, his mouth curving into a dimpled grin, a flame of pleasure shot through her.

He approached, his lithe way of moving—not unlike a lion that had just been fed—drew her eyes straight to him. "How are you?" he asked, his gaze only for her, his eyes dilated.

"I'm so fine. Wonderful. I was tired, that's all. How are you? Did you hit your head?" She lifted her hand towards that wonderful glimmering hair but stopped halfway, embarrassed.

"He's got a terrible bump," Etta said, mussing Leo's hair.

He dodged, and took Piper's hand. "Do you really feel OK? You look better than you did last night when we brought you up here."

"You mean you didn't watch over me last night, my guardian Angel? You're losing qualities."

His tanned face became a little darker, and he looked away, murmuring, "So you knew?"

Piper snorted but grinned. "Mostly. Thought I'd dreamed it, actually. Now I know it was true." She squeezed his hand to show she meant it in a nice way. "How's the village? Has much been destroyed?" She hadn't taken much notice the previous night and only remembered being carried in Leo's arms along the drowned main street.

"I've been down there this morning," Leo told her. "It is a mess. The Civil Protection services came along last night to evacuate people, but in fact, apart from the…the…" He hesitated as he checked her.

"…Nelson's cottage," Piper supplied. Nothing could've withstood the might of those waves hitting it. And she'd seen it washed away.

"And the one next door. That was Gil's place, but no one was in it. His family was all down near the jetty waiting for us to arrive. And Serafim's café got some water damage, but Prazeres has swept it all out and says it'll be...what tickly-something?"

"Tickety-boo," Victor supplied.

"And Nelson? My grandfather?"

"He's staying with Elsa, along with Lili. And the *bombeiros* are out in force, washing sand and debris back off the road to clean up the garbage. As usual, everyone is lending a hand. I didn't see Gaspar, though."

Piper licked her lips. "No. Gaspar isn't there. Leo, I need to talk to you."

Chapter Thirty-Six

It would've been a magical journey to Lisbon if Leo wasn't very nervous and anxious about meeting his mother. "I don't think I can do this," he said to Piper three times in a row.

"OK. Let's just take it step by step," she told him, hoping it would calm him.

As the hired car sped through the Alentejo, glowing golden today under clear azure skies, Piper said, "I feel terrible that I jumped to the conclusion that you were Tom."

Leo tapped a finger on the wheel for a moment. He had one hand on the wheel, his other elbow resting on the open car window. "I don't blame you for that. If I was Tom, I don't think I'd like myself very much either. Except I did like him. I loved him. I still do, if you see what I mean. That make much sense to you?"

"Perfect."

"And I never thanked you for saving my life that day Grady pulled a knife on me and I fell in the sea and got caught in that goddamn weed."

"He pulled a knife on you?" She stared at him, taking in every feature of his face. "I didn't know that. Jesus." There was so much she didn't know and so much she wanted to find out about this lovely man. "I heard you went out after him and got him the next day. I heard the whole story about the rocks and stuff. I'm sorry I pulled you up by your hair." She raised her hand and this time, ran it through the soft locks as she'd wanted to before. It was worth the wait.

Her action, though, prompted the first of what would be many stops on that journey. Leo pulled in by the side of the road and stared at her. "You're like a diamond that attracts the light," he said and leaned forward until their lips touched and, just as she'd expected, his lips were sweet and gentle. His fingers traveled her body with such care and skill they brought her warmth and such pleasant tingling as their bodies weaved together and the car rocked with passing heavy traffic.

Fancy him wanting to kiss a hobbit like me, Piper thought, when they were on the road again. Now, there should be no more secrets, no more lying.

"Tell me about her again," he said for the third or fourth time. "From when you were in the bus station and the kid stole your purse."

She would recount it a million times, leaving nothing out, if that was what he wanted.

Once inside the massive Santa Maria Hospital, Leo's face tightened and his lips thinned with worry. She held his hand tightly as they made their way through the labyrinth of corridors to the ward where they'd been told Conceição was being treated. A nurse told them to wait for a moment outside the ward, so Leo sat on one of the plastic chairs in the corridor and patted the seat next to him. He shuffled nearer to her after she'd seated herself. "Are you cold?" she asked. He trembled against her so she put her arm about him and pulled him closer, wishing she could transmit warmth, optimism and hope to him by osmosis. A steady stream of hospital personnel, visitors, and patients clumped past them, up and down the corridor.

When a nurse in blue scrubs came through the door beside them, they both jumped. "*Senhora* Conceição has one visitor now. Only one permitted. You her son? Then I tell this man…wait a moment."

She returned with Gaspar in tow. She nodded at Leo but shook her head at Piper, reminding her that one patient could only have one visitor.

"Will you be OK?" Leo asked Piper, frowning at Gaspar.

She nodded her confirmation and gave him a kiss on the forehead. "I'll be right here waiting for you."

With a quick squeeze of Piper's hand, Leo slowly got to his feet and followed the nurse inside.

Gaspar stalked up and down the corridor, ignoring Piper. He looked terrible. His face was more yellow than ever as if he hadn't slept, and the creases on his face were deeper. Piper wondered if he'd walked the full hundred miles to the hospital in the storm. His clothes, or maybe it was him, smelled of boiled cabbage. He stood to one side of the door to the ward, facing the flow of passing people, his fists clasping and unclasping, his back bowed.

"Uncle?" Piper half-stood, her hand on the back of the chair.

At the sound of her voice, he turned his head. Tears welled up in his one eye and poured unchecked down the scar in his hollow, gaunt cheek, into his mouth, dripping onto his tweed jacket.

"Uncle?" she asked, a lump forming in her throat.

Then he focused on her, taking her in—*drinking* her in, with the intensity of his stare. Blindly reaching for the chair beside her, the one Leo had just vacated, he slumped down and buried his head in his hands and sobbed quietly.

Piper had no idea what to say. She put her hand on his shaking back and let him cry his heart out.

The flow of people didn't cease, no one looked at them or offered comfort; maybe this was a common scene in hospitals where unmitigated grief was the norm and unless the mourner keeled over in a faint or with a heart attack, there wasn't much anyone could do to relieve their pain.

Piper rubbed her hand on his back in slow circles until his anguish eased and his sobbing stopped. Several minutes passed while he mopped his face and eye with his sleeve. Then he slid back in the chair, sitting straighter. He raised his head and faced her, his lips working but no sound coming out.

"How is Conceição?" Piper asked.

He swallowed hard and wiped his nose on the back of his hand. "Bad." He dried his eyes again on the sleeve of his dank jacket and returned his gaze to her. He nodded slightly. "Felipa."

"I'm not Felipa and you know it. I'm Philippa. Prefer Piper, actually."

"I know you're not...her. You're the image of her, though."

"So they say." His relentless stare made her uncomfortable.

"She hates me, you know."

"Who?"

"São." He nodded his prematurely grizzled head in the direction of the door of the ward. "She just told me. But it wasn't a surprise, because I know very well she always did. I'm just too pig-headed to accept the truth."

"She did some awful things to you in Miami, didn't she?"

He remained silent while he mulled over whatever was going through his head before nodding. "I tried to persuade myself I'd just walked into the middle of a pitched battle. I was such a fool. Of course I knew she'd told her...her *pimps*, her suppliers, that I was trying to get her to come home and this was their way of telling me I wasn't welcome." He laughed without mirth. He continued, "You know, even though she was terribly confused in there, right now, she knew who I was, and she told me to piss off." He paused. "I loved Felipa too. My little sister. They all leave me."

"Maybe you should learn to let go." It seemed harsh to say, especially as she'd never been able to say it to her own father.

Gaspar frowned as if processing her words, then returned his gaze to her face, scrutinizing it.

Piper shuffled. "I mean, you can't go around threatening people. Just 'cos they leave you." She stiffened, expecting him to lash out. He'd heard the worst from Conceição and now this. He was a dangerous man. Pop had said so.

"Those people I sent to your Dad?"

"How could you have done that?" she whispered, anger filling her to the extent she wanted to get up and loom over him, threaten him as he'd threatened them.

He scrubbed his hand over his face. "It went wrong. Far beyond what I'd told them to do."

"You told hoodlums to come and hurt us." She tripped over the words, unable to hide the disgust in her voice.

"I didn't want them to take it so far. They were only supposed to teach your father a lesson. Beat him up a bit."

Her anger forced itself like a lump into her throat. She stood, towering over him, unable to control herself now. "I'll say they did. They hurt him. They threatened to kill me, a baby." She was pleased to see him pale even more. His face resembled parchment. "And then you pursued us. We *ran* for our lives all the bloody time, Gaspar, *Uncle* Gaspar. From one place to the next. No proper schooling, no hope, no childhood. That has been my life."

As she spat every word, he gasped and raised his hand to his mouth. "No," he whispered. "No. I never…Fel…Phil… Piper, I swear. That one time. When I knew they hurt your father and smashed…smashed…"

"My little bed."

He lowered his head, studying the floor to which he then

spoke. "Just that one time. I called them off. Never again, I said. Never again. Enough suffering. Just that once. I never pursued you. Never."

Piper gaped. Was that the truth? Had they tried to keep one step ahead of someone who wasn't even *walking* after them? "Oh, Pop," she whispered and this time it was she who put her hand to her mouth. "We always thought…Pop was convinced you…" She met the stare of the broken man beside her who was wringing his hands.

"I didn't mean…Piper…I didn't. Just once. Then, when they reported to me, I was furious. If I'd had a gun, I'd have shot them. But they were bad people—people who were always around Nelson, wanting to get the drug trading going again. I spent so many angry, angry years, Piper. Years I regret. I lost any love I had, became like a stone."

Sympathy began to overtake her fury and hurt, but she wasn't going to let them go yet. "You were pretty violent in the hospital when he came to get me just two months ago."

"Yes. I came to the hospital because I wondered if you were Felipa's daughter. I saw you at the Main House when we took that Grady upstairs and at first I thought you were Felipa. Such a shock. For the first time in so long, I felt a link to a person who wasn't a horse." He laughed, but it was a harsh sound. "So I came to the hospital to see if you were all right. And Jack Pepper…well the sight of him made me… stupid. He had everything—he had taken Felipa, he had you." He looked down at the floor. "I never expected my…my niece to ever come to Luminosa." He looked up at her. "I'm glad you did even though I'm going to be haunted forever by the thought of what I did to you." He clapped his hands to his knees. "I'd better get out of your way."

She put her hand out to stop him. "Wait. Let's sit down again. You see," she paused, digesting what he'd just told her. "Am I like her?" she asked at length.

His gaunt face broke into a wide smile. "Oh yes. The image of her. You're older than she was last time I saw her, though. Just a little. I mean, you're like Felipa would've been at, what is it, twenty-two years old?"

"Yes. She was younger when you…you last saw her?"

"Yes. I have very happy memories of Felipa, you know, Piper. She was the best sister, but she'd have hated me to the bone for what I did to you."

"Tell me something about her. I have no memories, you see."

His head wagged sadly but his eye flickered in a reflective stare. "I was her older brother and, well, I'd have laid down my life for her. Our mother died when Felipa was ten and I was sixteen. Nelson was devastated and, I thought, became too hard on the little girl, not letting her do this or that, or going to the sea which she wanted to. So I decided that I'd help her enjoy life."

Excitement bubbling inside now replaced Piper's dampened anger. "Tell me what you'd do to help her do that."

He sat back in the uncomfortable, hard chair and stretched his legs out. Passing people had to step over them, each giving him a look he ignored.

"We'd go up on the cliffs with a little Olympus camera and return with rocks, wild-flowers and pictures of butterflies and birds. She knew all the plants and insects: coriander, sorrel, poplars, oaks, sundews and grasshoppers. But she really loved the sea. That was the best. The fishermen used to let us use their boats, the little ones. Nelson never knew because, much as I knew he was our father, I didn't agree that she shouldn't be in the element she belonged, just because Nelson thought fishing was at that time *below* us. Ridiculous. The fishermen and villagers all loved her because she was so carefree, and she saw colors. In the sea. She'd tell the fishermen to go there and there and there, and they'd find exactly what she said they would." Gaspar's eye had become unfocused while he re-lived his memories, but it returned its scrutiny of Piper again, and he continued, "I hear you love the sea too. You see the colors like she did."

She didn't hesitate. No need for embarrassment about it now. "I do."

He twiddled his thumbs before clearing his throat. "My mother did too. Must be the girls in the line because I don't. The bay is now full of poison. Felipa would've been so sad about that."

"I saw it."

"Those damned drugs boats that Nelson got involved with came in a year or so ago and dumped it all on us. I told and told Nelson not to do it. I said we didn't need to live in that big house. But Lili was determined. She said if we didn't, I'd lose the animals we had. Stupid," he gave his harsh laugh again, "we lost them anyway."

"Would you like to work in the stables again, Uncle?"

"Oh I would. I really love the animals. Even the bulls. You wouldn't think it, but I do. That bull you saw. It didn't die, you know. It was back out in the fields later. Hurt... but...well..."

"I heard that the Royal Estates are going to get the Main House up and running again like it used to be. Maybe they'd be interested in your services. You took good care of the horses."

"I'd love to breed Lusitanos. Beautiful horses, they are." He pondered, his thumbs turning circles around each other. "You know, you could help the villagers clear the bay. I often thought that if Felipa was here then she'd be able to do it because she could tell where the parasites were, point them out, and we could get them one by one."

"I could do that. When I was here last time, I could see where the weed was and all those strange fish and mollusks."

"The fishermen say the best way to deal with it is to pull it up, catch the fish."

"It sounds good. We could dive down. I love diving."

"With proper equipment, I hope." He smiled. It transformed his face. For the first time, he looked human. He looked more than that; he looked vulnerable, scared and uncertain.

"It would be a good reason to stay in the village for a while," she said, moving closer to him. "Uncle." She put her hand on his arm.

"Niece," he said, his voice serious.

Tentatively, she reached out. He stiffened then relaxed into her arms as they embraced.

CHAPTER THIRTY-SEVEN

"She is not in good condition," the nurse told Leo as she led him to a side room. "Her lungs, kidneys and liver not in good shape. Like soup they are. And her brain. She has hallucinations. She will not be here long."

"You mean she'll be going home?" He wasn't sure where that was, but he had a horrible, sneaking feeling that it might lie with him.

"Oh no. Sorry, I no speak English well. I *quero dizer, Senhor* she will..." she searched for the word.

"Die?" he whispered.

"I look for better way to say, *Senhor*. But, *sim*. I am sorry." She opened the door.

Okay, he thought, let's take a look.

Leo thought the tiny figure in the bed was a bald doll at first. His mother.

Her mottled yellow skin had dark mauve bruise-like patches, interspersed with pus-filled sores. Under the paper-thin skin of her eyelids, her eyeballs moved constantly.

"She live in nightmare world," the nurse whispered, bustling around the bed, adjusting tubes and checking monitors. "She maybe wake a little in a moment. But maybe she already unconscious. This morning she wake with other man here, but I think she talk nonsense to him." With another twist of a switch, she said, "Now I leave you. I here if you need."

Leo took a claw-like hand in his and looked at it resting so small in his large palm. His mother. Should he feel something? Should he love her? Some small part of him wished that he could.

She moved and squeaked like a kitten. One eye opened half-way, but he wasn't sure she saw anything until she fixed on him. Her legs twitched and her lips moved. He put his ear closer to hear what she was trying to say.

"Bastard," she said with a force that made him start backwards. "Shit slinger."

He thought he'd be prepared for anything. But not this.

His mother's other eye opened and now she had both focused on him. A string of words issued from her, words that made no sense except he managed to pick out, "bitch told me you died."

"Mom." Mom? That didn't sound quite right. She didn't like it either.

"You shut up about Mom. You shit. You said you'd fix it. Take the cargo. Deliver and then Conceição would've been safe. But you pretend you're dead, you yellow...and I had to run."

He felt that if she had the strength, she would've spat.

"Conceição. I'm not Tom. I'm Leo."

Her lips moved silently and her eyes rolled back in their sockets, leaving just white showing. It gave him the heebies, but he leaned forward to try to hear what she was saying.

"Everyone lies. No Mom to little bastard. Only to my little boy. *Lavender's blue, dilly dilly.*"

She was singing? He tried to get a little closer, despite the fetid and festering odor she emitted.

"My jewel, my prince. My Leo," she sighed and shut her eyes. "Want to see Leo."

"I'm Leo, I'm here."

She shook her head weakly. "Leo. Want to see him. Not you."

****

Piper was holding Gaspar's hand as Leo walked back out the door. *Any more surprises you got in store for me, God?* Seeing her lovely face sent pleasure surging through him. She was turned away, listening to Gaspar. Leo paused to admire her. Just watching her went a good way to heal him, to relight his life.

Ever since he'd first seen her, she fascinated him, and now, as she turned to look at him with eyebrows raised, she made him feel like he'd hung the moon. He'd never felt like that with anyone before and knew he never would again. She smiled. He'd spend his life contentedly waiting for and provoking another of her radiant looks that, to him, were slow to come but worth the wait when they appeared.

"Any news?" Piper asked.

"It's not long now," he said. "Gaspar, do you want to see her?"

As the door closed behind Gaspar, Leo took his seat next to Piper. She kissed his forehead just like she had before he'd gone in with the nurse.

In companionable silence, they watched the people and wheelchairs pass by for several minutes before he found the courage to say in a low voice, "I don't love her."

Piper was as still as a statue, watching a porter carefully navigate a bed down the corridor. After what seemed like a lifetime, she asked, "Did anyone say you had to?"

His finger played circles on her outstretched palm while he thought. "I figure I don't even like her." He drew the circles again, counter-clockwise. "I feel sorry for her, though." He looked up when he felt her gaze linger on him, and he let a breath out he didn't realize he was holding. Her elfin-features and petite figure made him light-headed. "That's sad, isn't it?"

"It is. But it's not of your doing."

They waited in silence, expecting Gaspar or the nurse to come out any moment and say that it was all over. Leo wondered if there was something wrong with him because he couldn't feel more sorrow at his mother's passing. "Piper. Stay with me for a while."

She had rested her head against his shoulder but now she lifted it and flashed him the lovely radiant look. This time, it came quickly and she said, "A while ago. Nearly two months? I first met Etta and do you know what she said to me? She said, *from a mere nothing springs a mighty tale.* Well, Leo, I think our story has started, don't you?"

He dipped his head to kiss her, another one of those humdinger kisses full of promise of more to come. She entangled her hands in his hair at the back of his head and pulled, but not enough to hurt, in a way that was pure Piper. He was sure their story would be great because he would do everything in his power to make her happy.

ABOUT THE AUTHOR

Sue Roebuck was born and educated in the UK but she now lives in Portugal with her Portuguese husband. She has taught at various colleges and institutions in Portugal and her interest in dyslexia started with a discussion over lunch with a colleague and friend. Nowadays Sue's mostly occupied by e-learning courses which, when no cameras are used, are also known as "teaching in your pajamas". But, given a choice, writing would be her full-time occupation.

Working from home presents no problem for her since her office window overlooks the glittering point where the Tagus River meets the Atlantic Ocean. The huge container ships, tankers and cruise liners which are constantly on their way in or out of Lisbon harbor are a great source of inspiration (or distraction).

She has traveled widely through The States and believes that "being born American is like winning the lottery of life". If she could live anywhere, she'd live in the Catskills in Upstate New York.